BUNNY HAMMOND

# This Is Dismal

*Welcome Home*

*First published by Publish Drive 2025*



*First edition*

*ISBN: 9798991874540*

*This book was professionally typeset on Reedsy.*
*Find out more at reedsy.com*

*To my husband.*

*To my daughters.*
*And to my parents and to my in-laws.*
*With all my love.*

*To the great writers of the Nebraska prairie.*

*To the families in the Sandhills, past and present and future. To the ranching world. And to the modern American west.*

*To our ancestors and to the prehistoric world.*

*Thank you to my mom for reading so many early drafts. Thank you to my proofreaders.*

*Thank you to the readers of The Heartless Ranch Is Haunted. You have my heart.*

*This is Dismal. Welcome home.*

For God so loved the world that he gave his one and only Son, that whoever believes in him shall not perish but have eternal life.

–John 3:16 NIV

# Contents

# Preface

The railroad tracks came to Ogallala, Nebraska in 1867.

The Union Pacific called their steam engines the "General Sherman" and the "General Grant" and the "General McPherson."

The Ogallala and Brule Sioux were removed by military campaign in 1873.

By 1876 thousands of cattle had arrived from Texas to be put on the train to Chicago. On a knoll above the tracks a shallow grave cemetery was established. For ten years bodies in burlap sacks were laid to rest among prehistoric native remains.

This was the world of the Chisholm Trail destined for St. Louis and the Goodnight Loving Trail through New Mexico and Colorado. But Ogallala was one of the last places to be reached by barbed wire and settlers. So the Texas herds came to Ogallala and she earned the name the mother of all cowtowns.

In 1884 the state of Nebraska banned Texas cattle due to disease. And so the world of the cattle drovers shifted to the world of the cattle empires.

North of Ogallala the mighty Heart Seven ranch was an open sweeping land of high hills and low meadows wet with still murky water. This was the world of the antelope, the prairie wolf and the unbothered celestial bodies. And the wind.

There were no roads.

This was the world of Ashley's ancestors.

# I

# Part One

# 1

# Boot Hill

*Clyde the ghost sat his horse high on the ridge above the river. This was a dream landscape, an in between place where time and distance didn't matter anymore. From here he could see Ashley alone in her lab in Dallas.*

Clyde watched her carefully from his vantage point among the hilltop prairie graves. The wind rustled the tall grass around him and stirred his horse's dark mane. Beneath his hat his eyes were sharp and focused. *Ashley reminded him so much of Ivory when she had been young.*

Ashley's gun shook in her hand where it rested on a battered card table. She made homemade nuclear batteries for fun. So that part of the task at hand didn't scare her. Ashley was afraid of becoming a missing person. There would be no evidence trail, no trial, she would simply be gone. David was coming for her today.

"I have done everything wrong."

Ashley whispered her confession as she worked but in her heart she still wanted to watch David die. To see it happen slowly.

Ashley sat at a makeshift work desk, bobbed blonde hair and safety glasses. Like a cowboy in a wild west saloon, she watched the room behind her in a mirror with her pistol in her hand. The tactical team would have to take her in a rush. She had a classified meeting with David today about the technology she was developing. But she didn't trust him to wait that long to make his move. Either way she was running out of time.

Ashley's career was built on extracting data from phones that had been destroyed. She believed that nothing was ever really gone. She could force technology to cough up it's secrets. Not just the normal kind of data, but the echoes of everything the device had ever been present for or exposed to. Adrenaline raced through Ashley's heart. Nothing was ever really gone but the finding required a terrible amount of electricity.

The heat was getting to her. The radioactive exposure was a risk she chose to take and she tried not to be afraid of the burns. Ashley told herself she wasn't afraid of dying a hard death on her own terms. She was afraid of spending the rest of her life incarcerated in an underground military base away from the sky.

*Clyde the ghost cowboy watched her watching the mirror. He could tell she was experienced, she was probably a good shot. Clouds of dust rose on the southern horizon across the valley from him. The stockyards were waiting in the valley beneath him for the massive herd of cattle that would soon be cresting that southern ridge. This was a world from before he had lived. They were going to put all those cattle on the waiting train. Around him the wind swirled among graves that made his ghost skin crawl. This was a foreboding place for a meeting between souls.*

*Clyde watched Ashley as she stared at two computer monitors, in a small room surrounded by technology. He watched the gauges with her. He saw the sweat burning her eyes. He saw the desperation and the danger. Ivory would have been so proud, if she could see what he was seeing. Ivory had been a fighter. Ashley was a fighter too and they were going to have a chance. The ghost horse stirred restlessly beneath him. When the time came Ashley would not be alone. Clyde would be there to make sure of that.*

Ashley's data extraction was from an everyday object, a sticky note. This was one of the first intelligence gathering efforts of this kind. Ashley's stomach turned. David's handwriting made her sick. The words were just visible on the yellow piece of paper inside the clear pressure chamber.

"Develop your tech, I will be in touch in six weeks."

She had developed her tech all right. She smiled to herself in satisfaction. She intended to blackmail him with the data from this extraction. That was her way out.

# 2

# David's Plans

Ashley had been David's primary asset for years.

David's intelligence career was built on her abilities. Now he planned to use her to change the frontier of intelligence gathering. Ashley swore she would never ever perform an extraction on a human being, alive or dead. But deep down she knew that she would do it for her sister's safety. Or for her mom. She would give in.

She would have to be very brave for a while because she could not let herself come under David's custody.

Faux news print outs lay discarded next to the loaded handgun. A report about a vandalized art gallery, her mom's business and pride and joy. And her own missing person report conveniently drafted ahead of time. She had known this first round of blackmail from David would be coming. An obituary for a woman named Emmy that committed suicide. These people would not hesitate to murder her sister Emmy and frame it as a suicide. Ashley looked behind her at the rows of batteries. She had not expected this extraction to require so much power.

*Far away the prairie grass shuddered in the wind.*

A breaker popped as she applied more pressure with a rolling dial. The air was very close and still. Fear dominated as she applied more voltage.

*Clyde stood waiting for Ashley down by the tracks. He was anxious to meet her and to speak with her. He was nervous. His story was now her story.*

*She didn't know him or any of the people who had died. She didn't know about a vast cattle ranch called the Heart Seven. She couldn't know that their stories were part of how she had come to be in this position. She didn't know how very alike they were. He had made so many mistakes. He might have done everything wrong. Clyde pulled his hat down lower, he didn't believe in regret. His silver spurs were marked with the brand of the mighty Heart Seven.*

Another breaker popped behind Ashley. She looked down at the missing person report and her sister's obituary and gritted her teeth as she applied pressure again. And in that moment she finally lost control of it all. The gauges lay over left into the red and stayed there as a silent caution light whirred on and threw strange light all over the room. A compromised battery core spewed invisible waves of radiation into the converted bedroom space and Ashley's body succumbed to the shock of the exposure. Alone in her makeshift laboratory, she lost consciousness. In her mind's eye she thought it was all over.

Her body slumped over onto the table. She didn't know she was hallucinating. As her cheek fell next to her controllers her mind opened up, high and free. Finally free.

# 3

# A Good Horse Named Copper

*High noon tore over Ashley just as the sun broke through the windblown clouds. Leather reins and horse hair streamed back from her hands. She felt peace and exhilaration.*

*She was riding hard at a sprint across the high hilltops of the Nebraska prairie. This was the old west of American legend. She was riding a fast horse named Copper. He had a half life of 61.8 hours and a powerfully controlled long distance run. She had known she was a cowgirl. She had been better than Emmy at riding horses. She urged Copper on. This was the most beautiful place. Ashley wanted to ride high in these hills forever, to be free.*

*Ashley turned her head to look south and spurred in hard as Copper hesitated. They were racing down out of the hills. Towards the Boot Hill graveyard where the innocents and the gunslingers were buried in shallow graves in the sand. She would be there just before sunset. Copper was a good horse, the psychic kind that could run flat out forever. His nostrils flared as his hooves tore over the sand and grass and Ashley clung to his back skillfully.*

Back in her make shift tech lab Ashley lifted her face and checked her mirror. She had a battery leaking, but she might be able to finish this extraction before the radiation overwhelmed her. She set to work ferociously again.

Ashley had never needed to waste her time with common criminality. She had never needed to purchase controlled substances from terrorists with large sums of cash. She had never needed to illegally procure or steal uranium from government stashes to power her technology. Instead she made her own substances. It was too easy. She arranged for her materials to be exposed to her mom Barb, a strange and powerful woman. Barb's body emitted radioactive waves and functioned as a sort of reactor. Exposure to her mom was enough to create radioactive substances from innocent materials.

Ashley assumed that something terrible had happened to her mom. Some sort of radioactive exposure incident. Or prolonged incident. Ashley had been just a kid when she figured out that her mom emitted radiation. She still had her first Geiger counter and the notebooks containing her first observations here in the lab. Her mom had been her first science project. Ashley knew she was smart but honestly everything that she was and was able to do was because of her mom. Sadness eased in on Ashley's adrenaline.

Ashley missed her mom.

David was going to separate her from her family. Ashley felt the impending loss ache deep in her rib cage as more tears streamed. She focused on the work in front of her. Barb emitted strong radioactive frequencies. The molecules inside Ashley's samples would shift when placed in Barb's presence. The molecular structure would start to break down and become unstable. Then the sample far less innocent as it began to emit energy in an attempt to stabilize itself. This had all seemed so normal that Ashley had never felt guilty about it. Now Ashley felt the guilt wash over her with the radiation. She had gone way too far. People lived all around her, families lived in this building. She had not considered their safety. Given time the leakage would seep through the protective layers she had lined this room in. Silent sirens were whirring all around her again. She didn't hear the sounds that she knew must have been there. She could see in the mirror that she had a second battery leaking now. Her guilt shook her to the core.

The radiation levels in the apartment bedroom doubled and tears of regret fell down her face. In the prairie in her mind she slipped into hallucination again.

*The wind rang in her ears and swept her hair back. Copper raced through the grass along the hill tops. She was flying even as they faced the wind. She should have been much more cautious.*

*All the years of misdeeds were riding up hard behind her as fearsome horses without riders.*

*These strange horses were selenium, manganese, gold and silver, iron and bronze and tainted calcite and uranium adjacent pyrite and irradiated quartz and prehistoric ancient agate and many more odd choices from her experiments. Copper threw up his head in fear and ran faster. These were unstable horses with wild markings and bold colors, shrieking as they surrounded her. Copper reared beneath her to strike at the strange horses coming close and biting at them. As Copper struck out with his front hooves Ashley was jolted back into her body.*

Ashley's eyes fixed on the clear plastic packing tape that covered the card table beneath her face, it was discolored and fraying up in places. She had been right to bet on copper. Her mind started to clear as powerful relief mounted inside of her. She was well prepared for this.

Ashley had been dosing herself with unstable copper isotopes for weeks and the copper in her system was going to carry her through. Ingesting radioactive copper was a common medical procedure, but not commonly understood. Ashley thought the idea had adapted quite well to her specific problem. Copper was going to carry her through the radiation exposure. She would have time to finish.

# 4

# My Name Was Clyde

David would take her into government custody today.

Possibly they would take her mom and Emmy today too. Who knew what David would do? He was a cowardly piece of hidden bureaucracy shit. Very powerful, very smart, practical. She had known David for years. Take them all into custody Ashley admitted it to herself. That was what he would do. Probably to a top secret weapons development base underground. Claustrophobia caused Ashley's heart to shutter and panic started to rise. The sky, the air, she needed the air. She wanted out.

Another fierce wind razed the prairie grasses somewhere far away.

In Nebraska her sister Emmy rolled over restlessly in the spring night air. She mushed her face into the tight corner of a cramped love seat. Emmy had left Dallas to move to their grandfather's ranch in Nebraska and live in an abandoned ranch house reputed to be haunted. Now they both knew that it was indeed haunted. Emmy still thought that it would all probably work out. She usually thought like that.

This lab was built inside Emmy's old childhood bedroom. Still Emmy knew nothing about the extent of Ashley's work. If she would have, she would have told Ashley to give the intelligence agency her last fighting breath.

"Tell them to kiss your rear. You're ferocious. You might win."

"Yeah."

But Emmy didn't know.

Emmy would want to tell her about the ranch, the scenery, the treasures she had discovered and the questions she had about their family. Ashley wanted to hear it all. She wanted to go there. She hoped she lived long enough to see the ranch. She doubted she would remain a free citizen that long. She hoped she could visit with Emmy on the phone over coffee one more time. Emmy loved to talk on the phone.

Ashley's mom Barb slept on in her own bedroom across the apartment, hidden nearby behind her black out shades and sleeping tonics and dreams. Ashley wondered if she was okay, over there in her own little world. Ashley felt her presence like the steel holding the high rise apartment building up, come what may her mom would choose to be utterly unbothered.

Soon they would wake up. Both her mom here at home and her sister far away in Nebraska. Her mom would be driving to work. Barb lived for her routines. Ashley had to complete this extraction. She would blackmail David ruthlessly. She couldn't let Emmy be taken into David's custody. She couldn't let either of them disappear underground away from the sky. Emmy would suffer so much. She had to save Emmy from that. And so she applied increased voltage from her unstable batteries again.

*There was bad moonlight in her vision.*

Ashley felt peaceful as she struggled to stay alert. She bent over her controllers and the monitors in front of her. Sweat was rolling into her eyes. This time as she slumped into a pile her mind remained aware. She could feel her feet in her charge reducing house slippers. She could feel her charge neutralizing wrist bands. She knew she was hallucinating in free form and it felt strangely restful. She had been sitting here for far too long.

*Her dreams were full of cowboys in leather and felt. Their faces were covered and their forms painted by the shadows clinging to them. There would be no redemption for them.*

Ashley's eyelids fluttered in confusion and she moaned a quiet sleepy moan. Then everything inside her mind sharpened.

*She was sitting astride her beautiful horse Copper. They were high against the skyline, looking down into the valley. She could see the man but she could also feel the pull. There was someone waiting for her down south by the railroad tracks. They had something that she needed. Curiosity pulled her forward.*

*The ground was broken open by the hooves of thousands of cattle and the wind was swirling the sand high into the air. No one could inhale because of the dust. Ashley pulled her bandana from her throat up over her nose. The vast stockyard pens full of cattle stretched out into the evening sun. She felt a sense of wonder and awe as Copper carried her through this strange world. This was where the cattle were put on the trains. This was where the deals were made.*

*There was a man waiting for her in the shade of a six board fence. He had a medium build, square shoulders, purposeful and patient with a hat pulled low. He had been waiting there in the sun and the heat. He would wait for her there in the moonlight and shadows for as long as necessary.*

*She swung down from her tall yellow horse and approached the man boldly. She didn't have time to be given the run around. His face was lean and hard under the eyes. Copper tugged restlessly at the reins in her hand and she asked her question plainly.*

*"Who are you?"*

*Friend or enemy, Ashley couldn't tell from his face. He smiled from the shadows with reserved kindness. He seemed amused and very far away, even as he stood right in front of her. His shirt was light blue and his dark denim jacket a modern western style. Ashley didn't know what to make of him. She felt conflicted.*

*The cowboy asked her a sad but exact question in return.*

*"You don't know me Ashley?"*

*She shook her head no. She didn't know who he was.*

*After a pause the man replied stoically, his voice measured.*

*"I'm your family. Your story is my story."*

*Ashley didn't recognize the tense weathered face beneath the hat at all. She realized in a chilling moment that he wasn't a living person.*

*"You're dead, aren't you?"*

*The ghost smiled pensively before he continued.*

*"My name was Clyde."*

*Clyde could see that she still didn't know who he was. But he was glad to have seen her. She was much tougher than she knew and a thinker. They were going to have a chance. The cowboy started to turn away.*

*Copper shrieked and plunged sideways jerking the leather reins in her hand and bringing her back up to consciousness again.*

Her memories and dreams were full of gunshots, round after round. She lay on her desk and slipped in and out of consciousness. She needed angels to pray for her soul.

# 5

# David In Dallas

Ashley's picture, the one from her college ID card, was shown larger than life.

David was in Dallas because of Ashley. While Ashley lay unconscious on her desk the man named David, with the badge and security clearances, the watch and the phones, was wrapping up an intelligence briefing. The conference room smelled like new carpet and fresh coffee. Ashley's picture, the one from her college id card, was shown larger than life.

The men and women seated at the table were perusing her psychological assessment and history in manila folders. As they thought a few of them threw the occasional glance up at their boss.

Their most immediate conclusion was obvious. This kid knew more sensitive information than any one human being should be allowed to know. She had handled cell phone and laptop extractions involving multiple foreign intelligence agencies.

She could never be allowed to fall into the wrong hands.

They didn't know that she had also handled extractions concerning nuclear arms programs. And uprisings and civil wars. And weapons development. And domestic politicians. And technology billionaires. And every major criminal organization and gang affiliation. All for David's personal benefit. Only David and Ashley knew about that.

The agents continued working through her file. Clearly, she should never have been allowed so much access as a civilian asset. David spoke suddenly and interrupted their thoughts.

"This woman is the future of our nation's intelligence gathering abilities."

David was speaking from his position of authority and no one in the room doubted his power.

"Imagine we are handling a young Einstein here. Keep the long game in your mind at all times. Her work will determine the future of this country and this world. How she grows and what she will be able to do in ten years matters more to me than what happens right now."

The professional team in front of David listened carefully. A man in a tie spoke up with pen in hand and his eyebrows furloughed deep in thought. David could be intense but the program excelled under his efficiency. They trusted him.

"That's why she's still a public civilian?"

"That is why how we bring her into the base matters so much."

The men and women seated at the table went back to her psychological profile. The minutes stretched on as each expert made their private conclusions. This was a contrary individual with a high tolerance for pressure and an extreme track record for independent endeavors. She valued her freedom above all else. She was a good shot. It was easy to conclude that she would be almost impossible to take without drama, even more difficult to relocate without trauma. Sedation would probably be key.

The best case scenario could take place if she felt no pressure. It would be best if she had no early indication of what was coming. A solemn gray haired woman checking a reference in a separate file asked the next question.

"Has any initial effort been made?"

"No."

David lied solemnly. Ashley was his case. He was under no obligation to share the classified details. Honestly, she was his most interesting asset. She was the future. She was his future. Soon after that the meeting adjourned.

# 6

# Help From God

Ashley was almost done. The data was computing in hard drives and on screens across the room. Her phone buzzed aggressively as a text came in. Cold dread overwhelmed her soul. There were eight rounds in her handgun.

"Looking forward to seeing you today."

A printer buzzed to life on the opposite wall with the extracted information. Her heart lifted in the tiniest wave of optimism, the information that she needed was almost in hand. Hopefully the printer didn't jam. Another painful vibration shook the plastic table as the phone leapt again. Two texts.

"It's been too long."

Ashley felt her heart go cold a little as she shoved back from the desk. She would be blackmail ready. David could have a taste of his own medicine.

Behind Ashley another battery sprung a sweeping exposure leak and the radiation levels intensified beyond any human tolerance. Ashley's spinal cord collapsed as her nervous system shuttered and her face hit the sturdy card table hard.

Her future was all high water and angels singing in harmony. She missed Emmy and she missed her mom. She wanted them to hold her while she died. She could hear the printer but everything was all confused, equally sad and terrifying.

*She was riding a good fast horse named Copper. Her face was covered against the blowing sand. The sunlight gleamed as the heat rolled across her buckskin chaps.*

*They raced across the soaring hill tops. She leaned low over the saddle horn, one hand wrapped in the cream colored mane.*

*They were going to make it to the railroad tracks before the train. There was someone waiting there that could help her.*

*Someone that had something for her.*

*Copper's hooves slammed hard as they came down over the hilltop through the Boot Hill graves and the yuccas without breaking pace. The Nebraska sand shifted beneath their momentum. This was a land that didn't always keep secrets buried.*

*Ashley could see the train on the eastern horizon down in the valley flat. They had made it to the stockyards.*

*God was going to help her and Emmy and her mom were going to be okay. She could see the silhouette beside the corrals full of cattle and the waiting tracks.*

*There was someone waiting for her there. She had met him before.*

*His name was Clyde.*

# 7

# A Storm And An Explosion

Clyde remembered Dallas, the heat on the clean sidewalk and all the shining glass. He moved with much more confidence this time. Being dead had it's advantages.

An enormous thunderhead was brewing overhead and building quickly. Clyde didn't know that people were checking their weather apps and looking out windows and adjusting their plans for severe weather. Soon the storm would break over them. Clyde nudged his horse into a slightly faster walk down the sidewalk. Midnight wasn't shod against the concrete but it didn't matter because his hooves were ghost hooves. Clyde pulled his hat down stoically as the rain started. No one could see them in this vast city. A glimmering high rise apartment building came into view as they rounded a city block corner. The storm clouds darkened the sky ominously behind it's frame.

Midnight shied hard when lightning struck the top of the apartment building. Clyde followed his hard left duck fluidly.

They were taking on more form. The dark horse shook his head aggressively as they long walked faster. There was a white marking on the horse's face that looked a little like a bolt of lightning. Clyde had always thought that was a little funny.

The people in the lobby still couldn't see the cowboy on the dark horse as he rode up the front steps. Midnight nudged boldly through the door and Clyde ducked down under the door frame. They never broke stride. The power was out, they would have to take the stairs.

Ashley was afraid. She could hear the thunder and feel the thunder. Her blonde hair hung close over her face where her head had fallen onto her plastic card table desk. Paralyzed. Maybe she was paralyzed. She tried again to lift her head. Her lips were cracking. The red blood vessels were showing in the whites of her eyes and her sockets were starting to sink in. She was alone. A girl in a tightly lined bedroom laboratory in a luxury high rise apartment in a glimmering city full of people. She was going to die here alone.

Behind her Ashley heard the first of her safety breakers pop. Then with growing dread she listened carefully as every last one of them broke back. The technology in this room was powered within it's own circuit. Confusion gave way to panic. Then fear ran cold in her veins. Ashley couldn't see that she was part of a violent lightning storm but she did know what was going to happen next. She screamed the parched scream of a trapped wild animal when she heard the first battery explode like a gunshot. These were experimental batteries placed along the wall behind her and cased in sealed paint cans lined with lead. These were primitive forms of nuclear power, much more powerful and much more unpredictable. Ashley kept screaming. Like dominoes, all of the batteries were going to explode.

Behind her intense radiation was already leaking from the ruptured can into the sealed space. Ashley tried violently to make her body move. She was suffering some sort of nervous system failure. Panic raged inside of her. Too much copper? Not enough copper? The copper inside of her body was depleting quickly as it counteracted the increasing radioactive onslaught. Copper wasn't going to carry her through much longer. Another battery exploded viciously behind her as thunder roared around her in one long uninterrupted growl.

*Ashley's good horse Copper reared beneath her and spun to lash out like lightning with his hooves at the strange horses biting him. He was magnificent. The momentum of his strike carried them down hard as he stumbled and then fell forward. Ashley screamed for them both. Copper tucked his beautiful head and impacted the sand on his back. Ashley was thrown to the side and stumbled upward in adrenaline with the stupendous fall. Then she understood why. She watched in horror as her fast horse, her beautiful horse disappeared before her eyes. His shiny coat wavered into a mosaic and faded into the sand. The strangely colored and patterned horses screamed strange horse screams at the sand where the copper horse had been. As they rounded their hysteria on Ashley she screamed her own pitiful human scream. She never saw the blow coming as they circled her and she took a direct kick to the back of her skull.*

Part of a lead lined paint can struck Ashley in the back of the head in the explosion. Her brain began to swell sickeningly fast.

"Mom?"

She would never hear her mom's voice again. She fully expected the contents of her experimental batteries to eat away everything it touched. Someone would find her, the floor would give out after a while. This entire building would have to be condemned, there wasn't a hazmat crew on earth that could clean up what she had just done. There were families living in this building. Sadness and loneliness welled up inside her as her head started to swell. She was going to be consumed alive by her own illegal battery acid. Behind her she could feel the pressurized waves the acid gave off getting stronger as the radioactive byproduct spread closer. The first spiking neurons firing in her skin made her scream again but only a muffled sound came out.

"Mom! Help me?"

Behind her the last paint can exploded and peppered the room in one final round of sharp debris.

In a cement stairwell not far away the thud of a horse hoof rang out as it made contact. Clyde smiled in satisfaction as he spurred Midnight hard with glinting rowels and the horse leapt up the stairs. The storm outside escalated suddenly into a historic freak weather incident.

The foyer landing was jarringly silent and plush as Clyde swung down. He had expected debris. He could have moved through the apartment door but he broke it open with his boot heel instead. The beautiful home lay silent and dark all around him as he strolled through the eerie open space toward a discreet hallway opening. He could see the glow even though the seal on the residential door was suspiciously tight.

Clyde rested his hand gently on the door knob and listened to the silence for a long time. Then he used his shoulder to force the door in a casual gesture. He felt the impact of the fragmented wood as it shattered. He heard Midnight peel off a panicked neigh from the foyer. There she was. A mess of blonde hair collapsed in a heap. He could see the swelling at the back of the head even from the doorway.

Clyde assessed the swelling and the blood oozing from her scalp from a distance. She would live. He smiled ruefully at the irony, no one lived forever. This head trauma wouldn't kill her. He looked around him. The rest of this mess, he could take care of. He was not a scientist but he had already gone where the world couldn't hurt him anymore. They were going to be fine.

Ashley would not remember being carried out of her home-made laboratory in Emmy's old bedroom. She would not know when the storm died down or the lights came back on in the city. She would not know who had painstakingly contained and sealed the hazardous material in her workspace. But she would wake up on the sofa in the apartment living room to the sound of her mom saying her name. And she would unfurl her clenched fist to find a small rock that she had never seen before.

# 8

# There Should Be Another Rock Here Somewhere

"Ashley? Ashley sweetheart?"

Ashley could hear the pain in her mom's cracked voice. She felt so bad.

"Mom?"

Ashley's eyes were swollen and sticky and she struggled to bring her mom's face into focus. She felt strange. So very strange. Cold. After so much heat for so long.

Barb knew the moment her daughter opened her eyes that her baby was gone. The person she had been was gone, the light was gone. Loss worked it's way across her forehead in that moment. When had she lost her baby? Then she saw a familiar flicker in those black eyes. Maybe the fight wasn't lost after all, this was an incredible head injury.

"Ashley? What happened to you?"

Ashley could hear the bewilderment. She could only imagine what her mom was seeing. Barb wasn't actually touching her, sitting very close by with both hands clasped as if to restrain herself from reaching out to Ashley. To keep from touching her face. That's when Ashley realized that her mom was assessing her head trauma, trying to figure out what to do. Ashley felt afraid of how cold she felt. Even her voice sounded cold.

"I dreamed I was kicked by a horse."

Her own voice sounded like a stranger speaking. How extensive was her head trauma? She moved to stretch her fingers cautiously.

Barb crossed the room. She looked back over her shoulder at the prone figure stretched flat on the couch, pillows thrown down to the floor. She was working to move her hands and feet. It would be a little while before Ashley tried to turn her head. Barb looked at the swelling to the skull and wondered when the pain would kick in. Then Barb turned her attention to the quiet mini hallway that opened on to her daughter's childhood bedrooms. What had happened to Ashley? She moved her eyes carefully without turning her head. She could see the glow.

When Barb pushed the damaged door open she found the same lab she had expected. There had clearly been an explosion, an accident. Her eyes flitted over the shelves that used to contain rows of paint cans and across the room to the seat in front of the card table where Ashley normally worked. Barb saw everything she expected to see. Ashley was brilliant and reckless at times. She worked a high pressure job as an independent government contractor to intelligence agencies. In many ways Ashley went places no one else had gone. So there had been an explosion and she had survived but with a blow to the head. Still Barb felt there was more. Like blue horses standing in rippling water in a hayfield. She half expected to find dream horses in Ashley's lab. She even half expected to see a familiar silhouette in a felt cowboy hat. But this was very much just a miserable tech lab, cold and ruined. A mess.

Ashley was sitting up now and turning her head side to side carefully. She had two black eyes. Her light colored hair was sticky with blood and some unidentified gunk. The blood vessels in her eyeballs were over stretched and her lips were cracked and bleeding. The skin all across her face was stretching as it swelled and strange burn marks blistered across her cheeks and arms and the backs of her hands. Soon bizarre white markings that looked like tree branches or tree roots would start to show. She was truly frightening to see.

Ashley's eyes narrowed meanly as she found her backpack, propped neatly on the floor against the sofa she was lying on. Minimizing movement she unzipped it a little, aware that her mom was watching her from where she was filling a glass of water at the kitchen sink. There tucked inside the backpack were the pages of printer paper from the extraction and her gun. Who had helped her?

"Mom?"

Barb was already standing over her peering into the bag.

"Ashley?"

Her mom had been about to say something but she stopped mid beginning and changed directions.

"Ashley I don't think you can go to the emergency room."

"No."

Ashley felt very detached, very tired but her mind was moving more quickly than ever. She listened as her mom continued.

"I think they would detain you."

Ashley smiled widely as she started to laugh a cold new laugh. Oh, the laughter felt good. That was all the drug she needed. When she looked up she could see that she was scaring her mom so she stopped and moved to stand up.

"No! Just give yourself a little longer. Good grief. You'll be fine but that is one hell of a concussion. No. Just sit there."

"Mom I don't have all day."

Barb watched Ashley zip up her backpack while keeping her head level.

"Sure you do."

Barb's tone was brisk, no nonsense. But then it softened just a little before she continued to speak convincingly with a touch of warmth.

"What else do you have to do today? Your lab, you know your lab blew up right?"

Barb watched for Ashley's reaction unflinchingly as she dropped each syllable. And Ashley returned her gaze unflinchingly and asked her own question.

"Mom, why are you radioactive? What happened to you?"

In that moment Ashley looked down at her hand and Barb's eyes followed. The rock still clenched there had seemed to pulse just minutely. When Ashley looked up her mom was already looking in her eyes. Ashley saw calm quick resolve there.

"Where did you get that rock?"

Barb's tone was light and interested. She sat down on the coffee table again quickly and took the rock out of Ashley's waiting grasp with her thumb and pointer finger.

"I don't know."

Ashley's mind was already far away, her meeting with David, the print out's she needed to read, the blackmail she hoped she would be able to plan while her head continued to swell.

"I really don't. It was here, just in my hand."

Barb looked up deliberately and let her gaze wander all across the apartment. She had already seen the damaged front door. She already knew the company she would call to fix it. She didn't seem perturbed by that. Ashley could tell she was looking for something that she didn't expect to be able to see, just feel. But Barb didn't find anything. Ashley took the rock back from her mom. Her motions were abrupt, Barb could feel the increased aggression in her daughter's movements. This was a very severe concussion. Maybe the damage would be more than she wanted to admit. Maybe her baby was slipping away from her grasp.

Barb's voice was calm and resigned when she spoke again.

"There should be another one."

"Hmmm?"

Ashley looked up from trying to read a paper in her hand.

"Look in your backpack, there should be another rock here somewhere."

Ashley wanted to say, you look, I have to read this. Then she wanted to say, would you please read this to me? Because I can't see properly. But then she couldn't say that either. She really just needed to be alone so she could figure out what to do next. She needed her phone. Maybe her phone was in the backpack too, if it still worked. Ashley steeled herself in her mind to be calm and controlled with her mom.

"Would you please look through my backpack? See if my phone is in there somewhere?"

Barb nodded agreeably.

"I would. Would you like a sip of water now?"

Ashley nodded as a tiny tear streaked down her blistered face. The water burned like the acid Ashley had been expecting. That's when Barb held her for a long time.

# 9

# Cell 10

Clyde took his driver's license out of the front left pocket of his shirt. Since the day it had been issued to him he had kept it there. The ghost studied it carefully. He had been very old in that last DMV photo. How the world had changed around him.

All these people around here were showing their ID's and their badges at every entrance and exit. All of the bustle had got him thinking. These people all lived and died by their secrets.

He had seen enough. There wasn't a truthful identity among them. They were all agents in multiple agencies. These were the people that did the dirty work in espionage and interrogation so that no other bureaucracy would have to claim it. This was a festering cell of professionals that no one wanted to know too much about. Clyde would have spit if he would have been outdoors, disgusting.

Clyde had spent the morning shadowing David and listening.

David had spent his morning in a series of intelligence briefings. Ashley was not his only concern, far from it. But she was never far from his mind.

David spent much more time listening than he did talking. He listened for people's rhythms and their unique internal sense of logic. He listened for what they tended to include. He listened in order to know their motivations. And their weaknesses. He listened in order to build relationships and trust. David spent his days listening so that in the moments that counted he would be able to hear the sound of a lie.

Clyde sat in David's office and listened to David listening and lying. And what Clyde heard was that David sold secrets for profit with as much conscious as selling a crop. It was just a matter of price and timing. Clyde saw that David was an intelligent man with no morality. He was bored and competitively engaged in own interests. Ashley's college ID photo was displayed as a poster, taped to the painted cinder block wall. Unnerved Clyde tried not to look at it too much. Instead he looked at the three framed photographs on David's executive desk. A beautiful wife, David had a beautiful trophy wife with long soft brown hair, this photo was taken of the two of them together at a golf tournament. Clyde studied it closely. He wondered how much the wife knew. Clyde was unnerved to see that David also had two teenage daughters. This was a senior portrait of a bright young woman with a warm personality. And this was a school picture of a teenager just starting to find her take on the world. Sisters. Clyde looked away. Clearly David thought of himself as a successful family man. Clyde tried not to look at the poster taped to the wall. The truth was obvious to Clyde, David was obsessed with Ashley.

Clyde followed David down long gleaming hallways that echoed. He walked around the briefing rooms in David's footsteps. He stood along the wall in elevators. Midnight waited in the massive marble foyer and dreamed about the high mountains with one leg slack.

As David listened he heard a new set of footsteps on the shining floor. He felt a new presence watching him. And he knew he had picked up some sort of new visitor. An unknown entity that followed him from room to room and made echoing footsteps down the hallways. Something had attached to him. David wasn't overly perturbed.

"I understand your concerns."

David hung up from yet another phone call. Clyde sat still and listened as David picked up the phone again and dialed another number.

"Leslie, would you please bring me the files you've been working with? The ones from this morning?"

Clyde felt a cold sweat run down his ghostly back as he watched David hang up again. There wasn't anything to see. The lack of anything to prompt the fear worried Clyde even more. In the solitary silence David and Clyde waited.

Then the knock came and the door opened.

"You wanted these files sir?"

It was the psychiatrist lady with the glasses and the trim gray hair, Clyde recognized her from one of the briefings. She paused uneasily in the doorway. She didn't like what she saw in David's eyes.

"Sir?"

"I see you still carry your standard issue from forty years ago."

Leslie made to draw and turn at the same time and the gunshot reverberated in the cement office as David shot her down in the back. In the same fluid motion he fired again into a closet door and a third time into the front of her torso after he flipped the body hastily in the doorway where she fell. People were approaching in the outside hallway. Clyde heard calm unhurried voices.

"Self defense."

"She's been selling us out."

"She knew her time was up."

Clyde sat still in a very quiet ghostly world. He could see dust floating in the fluorescent light and hear the clock on the wall ticking next to Ashley's picture.

Two men carried Leslie away in a vinyl body bag between them and Clyde the ghost followed them forlornly down the hallways. They were going to cremate the body immediately. Clyde realized that there was no one to call. Leslie had ceased to exist a long time ago and he felt profoundly sad. He wondered what her real name had been.

When Clyde the ghost made his way back to the office he was surprised to find David cleaning the blood off the floor with paper towels. Somehow it made the scene worse to see that he was willing to do that himself. Clyde sat down and watched without emotion as David bagged up the blood stained papers. He didn't seem perturbed at all as he cleaned the floor with a series of spray bottles and more paper towels. On his hands and knees scrubbing he glanced up at the poster on the wall.

"Ashley Donahue, what are we going to do with you?"

For David the question of Ashley was really a question of optimum timing. She was unusually robust for a genius but he didn't want to stunt her creative growth too soon. She needed to pursue her curiosity and draw inspiration from the public world and the natural world in order to fully invent the way that he knew she could. Genius didn't invent in a box. Or in a void. These people needed inspiration and connection. The body of technological work she could produce in the next few decades would be astonishing. If her growth was not stunted. Still, she was getting out of hand. A little older, more mature, more desperate. He would need to act soon, probably very soon. He was looking forward to spending more time with her.

David looked up suddenly from his musing and floor polishing. There was a man in a cowboy hat and a denim jacket sitting behind his desk in his chair.

"Who are you?"

David's tone was rugged, competent. If David was surprised Clyde couldn't tell. He didn't seem angry or scared either. Clyde grasped the chair firmly. He was surprised. He grasped his own knee as he made to stand up, solid.

Perfectly solid and almost alive and just when he was getting confident as an invisible spirit. Clyde was really at a loss as he answered.

"Someone you used to know."

Both Clyde and David knew that was a lie. But David's unspoken thought connection spurred Clyde on to speak.

"Why did you kill her? That was a cowardly thing to do."

"Is that why you are here?"

David knew no one had come into his office while he was cleaning the floor in the doorway. David saw a fit man in his early forties but he also felt the spirit of a very old fighting man. If this was some sort of spiritual reckoning David was surprised. He had known Leslie for decades, she had no friends or family.

In the moment that their eyes met they both wondered what was going to happen when David shot him. Clyde fell as another gunshot tore through the belly of the bureaucratic maze.

When David pulled the trigger Clyde felt the pain rip through him. But there was no blood and no death. When he regained his footing like a winded middle aged cowboy he thought he understood what was ahead of him now. So he belted David across the smooth aristocratic jaw bone and followed up hard with another blow to the upper diaphragm. It was a close and compactly wound hit, like a boxer with a known advantage. They were both very surprised when David's defensive right hook landed Clyde's left eye so hard that he collapsed like a sack of feed.

Clyde felt the adrenaline building through the nausea. This was a wicked little son of a bitch, tightly wound beneath that loosely held charisma. That was at least twice the punch that Clyde would have expected. Clyde felt the fire building in his heart as he got up. Why the coward hadn't hit him again was making him nervous. David stood with his arms folded, watching Clyde get up. He was too busy observing for insight to bother. Clyde didn't scare him that much.

Clyde assessed him back. What was the point of being dead if you couldn't even win a fist fight? So Clyde rushed him to the ground in a stupendous hit to both shoulders. He could feel David's hands around his windpipe, trying to choke him out. There, that was the advantage. Clyde felt smug as he felt the pressure but no weakening. Why was he even here? He glanced around him. The gray haired woman shot down in the back. The body bag and the long corridors. The blood on this floor. The paper towels. The poster on the wall and the photos on the desk. He was here to extract payment. He was here to deliver just a little bit of justice. So he slammed David's head back into the concrete floor with his powerful ghost hand grasping his forehead one, two and three times before strong grips pulled him back up and away.

The security team had never seen Clyde before. Not in person and not in any of the building's security footage that day or in any briefing photos. They looked at the director on the floor, they could see the man was already too busy thinking to feel the pain yet. David waved dismissively.

"Put him in cell 10."

Clyde let the younger men drag him down the slick hallway. He could hear Midnight let out a frantic whinny far away. That horse had always been high strung. He tried not to feel nervous about this new sort of ghost existence. There was only a handful of reasons God would have sent him back. No need to get nervous. There was a lot more going on here than just him. Always had been.

When the doors were closed the cell block guard nodded that he was satisfied from behind his surveillance glass. So the young men in the body armor closed the last hallway door firmly behind them as they left. Not so far away David leaned over the security experts in front of the monitors with narrowed eyes. And that's when they all saw Clyde disappear. From the cell block guard to the men and women in the surveillance team, no one would contest that the man in the cowboy hat just faded away.

When the setting sun painted the Texas landscape, Clyde and Midnight were long walking north out of Dallas, past the city limits headed north to Nebraska. Headed home.

# 10

# My Sister's Story

My sister's story started, really, when she was in college. Ashley was gifted, brilliant and surprisingly down to earth. Good at pragmatic problem solving. She caught the eye of an agency scout working as a professor and they developed a mentor relationship. Ashley trusted her.

"I can extract data from hard drives that have been erased."

"That's interesting, will you show me?"

The scout took her time to earn Ashley's trust. She waited to make her reports until she was sure Ashley could execute in several scenarios. She wanted to really understand Ashley.

"And that girl can deliver. There's something extra there."

"You are overstating it. Set up some interviews, bring her in."

David didn't believed the reports. He put his faith less in art and more in predictable things, like human nature.

"This is not something you want to go through the usual people. I am not overstating it. I am 90% sure this is one of the most consequential things we will see in our lifetime."

She was a persistent scout. She believed her agency needed Ashley and everything she could do and everything she would grow to be able to do. So she stood her ground.

"This girl is going to change the very nature of defensive intelligence."

They had squared off across the desk. David had other things on his mind.

"And if you are wrong?"

"No harm done, we can proceed to offering an interview."

Later on David would pride himself on deciding to listen. He took an old phone from a stash in his desk drawer, a throw away piece of tech as dead as his lab assured him it could be. He had used it for one phone call, something that had mattered at the time and didn't matter anymore. He handed the phone to his subordinate.

"Here's your project, bring it back with a full report."

He said it with the kind of assurance that would put this potential new world changing asset back where she belonged, in standard intake process. Like a hawk he could see the world below him.

Looking for the residues made Ashley feel like a duck in water. As capable as if seeing the invisible was more natural to her than her own heartbeat. Being excellent at something is it's own kind of high. Pieces of technology were the easiest, not just everything they had ever transmitted or received, but everything they had ever been exposed to was written in the plastic and metal as clear as day. Seeing what wanted to be seen was exhilarating. Everyday objects were more difficult because the materials weren't as malleable but extractions were still possible.

Ashley remembered her professor leaning over her shoulder. She was a very smart woman. It was nice to have someone appreciate the wonder of what was going on beneath her own capable hands. That was the last happy moment of Ashley's life, before the data started to come across the monitors.

The older woman, who had believed in Ashley's abilities, should have known what was going to happen. The phone from the metal desk drawer contained imprinted audio waves from every word that had been spoken in David's office and memories from every other piece of tech it had ever shared that desk with. As recently as yesterday. David had killed a man yesterday.

The professor tapped the corner of the screen with a flick of her finger as her eyes roved across the monitors at the transcripts of hundreds of top secret, incriminating conversations. Astonishing.

Ashley knew in that moment that it was too late for her. She didn't look up. Didn't make eye contact. She knew she had been very, very stupid and it was going to cost. She knew in that moment that she was going to pay for her stupidity for the rest of her life. Not a word was spoken. She lifted her hands off of her controls and slid back from the desk.

The older woman lifted the phone out of the extraction chamber. Then she started to disconnect the many cables.

She was very smart, she understood Ashley's entire setup. She also understood that the setup was nothing, just tools in the hands of a master. It took Ashley to make it work. She had set at that desk with her hands on her controllers like a medium with wet hands to spinning glass. Ashley was what they would need to understand, not her tech.

Ashley helped her mentor put the homemade controllers, the holding chamber and power units, and all the rest of her tech into a bag and cardboard filing boxes. She helped her carry the boxes down the long academic hallway. Ashley stood alone in the parking lot after her professor drove away.

Ashley would have liked to believe that her mentor would have protected her if she could have. She would cling to that belief in the years to come.

# 11

# The Funeral

Ashley wept, sitting in a pew near the front, at her mentor's funeral. The casket was open and then closed and covered with flowers. She cried like a little girl. Terrible fountains of grief and the fear and rage and confusion of an adolescent wild animal. Ashley had been very young then. She didn't care who was watching her. But she could feel the assessing gazes. She attended that funeral alone. Not many people were there.

Later on she would wish that she would have taken her sister or her mom with her to the burial of a professor she had been close to who had passed away unexpectedly of a seizure in her home. But even then her instinct had been to try to protect them. They were all that mattered to her. Maybe if they would have been there from the very beginning things would have shook out differently.

Later that day she opened the apartment door to the very first courier delivery from a intelligence director named David and her career had begun.

If her professor had been alive, or been there, Ashley was never completely sure about that funeral, she would have invited Ashley to a series of formal interviews on a highly secure military base. Then she would have been hired and gone away for training. From there she would have emerged a loyal public servant, putting herself and her skills between her country and her enemies everyday. Her talents would have been highly valued. She would have known many people in many bureaucracies and been known to many, even the Presidents of the United States. She would have served, grown, learned, taught and mentored and eventually been recognized as a hero after a distinguished career of service.

All of that disappeared from Ashley's future when David made the decision to keep her a secret. Just one of thousands of contacts, informants, assets, and independent contractors connected to him and the agencies he worked with.

She would answer to him and him alone, living and operating in his shadow. Her abilities were too good to pass up. And due to the unfortunate incident with the first phone, he couldn't allow her to be interviewed or brought on board. So Ashley became David's own personal asset. Well paid and motivated by credible threats to her loved ones, she was his ever present ace in the hole.

For David that was the true beginning of the height of his career, with the information Ashley could provide for him there was virtually nothing he couldn't maneuver. For Ashley that was the end of her ever having a chance. She would never have a healthy life, a happy life. Instead she lived under constant surveillance and pressure, growing into a ferocious survivalist. Then beyond that, into a gifted woman dabbling in dangerous nuclear substances to pass the time.

Her sister and her mom never really glimpsed the extent of it.

Now, for Ashley, a new sort of story was beginning. One born of head trauma and nervous system damage. As she sat on the sofa and her head continued to swell she sifted through the extracted data that had cost her so much. Then she began to follow leads and put pieces of David's life together.

When her mom left for the gallery that afternoon Ashley ordered a ride to the firing range. She was going to need to see Frank.

# 12

# The Gun Range

"Good morning Frank."

The difficult part of love was that the cost to Emmy and her mom would likely be everything up to and including their lives. Ashley had no one else. She had no friends, no boyfriends, no lovers and she was grateful even as she felt the loneliness and the anger. There were only the three of them in her world.

Three lives was what it would cost, probably in the end. Three lives and a story that no one would ever know. That was a great plenty.

Frank tried not to stare at Ashley's two black eyes and the massive swelling. He tried not to notice the sunglasses and the cap and the long pants and the long sleeved shirt and the band-aids on her hands. He tried not to look at the white patterns and the burns on her face. He had known Ashley for years. He had wondered about Ashley's profession for years.

Ashley was holding something in her pocket, between her

thumb and fingers. She moved differently, Frank noticed. Something in her body language had changed since he had last seen her. The way she carried herself was like a different person.

As she watched him watching her Ashley felt how far outside the law she operated. She had not noticed before. Her backpack was full of cash and uranium and highly sought after uranium equivalents. She smiled at the agents that had shadowed her every move for years as they watched her from across the street. It was all so funny.

They didn't know that she was just a girl. Doing the best she could.

"Is this all of it?"

Frank was referring to a stack of cash that Ashley had slid across the counter at the gun range in exchange for newspaper wrapped packages that had slid smoothly into her backpack. Ammunition. Her heart was breaking that he would ask her that. She spent more time at Frank's gun range than anyplace except her lab. He knew her as well as anyone. She would never have stiffed him on ammo.

Ashley met the old man's eyes as if she herself had been David. She felt the change in her reaction to her own anger and made note of it. Maybe she was turning into David a little bit. Why not? He was one of the best and so was she. Lord knows she knew him better than anybody. She had had a front row seat so to speak.

Frank was used to people dabbling in substances that fundamentally changed them. But Ashley was dabbling not in drugs but in half lives and isotopes and unstable atomic weights. Ashley sounded like her mother when she spoke.

"Never ask again."

He was afraid of the change in her and she could see that he was afraid. And something shifted for Ashley in that moment, something that felt good, that felt so very good. She wouldn't be anyone's doormat anymore. She wouldn't be anyone's behind the scenes worker or anyone's victim. From now on, the world would know the moment they laid eyes on her, that this woman paused for no man. She smiled condescendingly.

"Have a good day Frank."

# 13

# The Phone Call

Ashley shook back her fears. She was as free now as a rowboat out to sea, they would never catch her. There had been no meeting today. There was only one step left to complete before she could quit for the day and go to sleep in her own bed. She dabbed at her eyes with a scrap of paper towel and she checked a few parameters on the laptop in front of her. She took a tiny sip of water. Then Ashley reached for a weapon unfamiliar to her and slowed and softened her voice into what she hoped was a suggestive purr.

"Hello, would you please tell your husband that Ashley is calling. He will know what it is about."

Ashley's hand that held the phone shook violently as the silence lingered, game on. She had never heard her own voice sound like that before. She had performed the line better than she had expected. Confidence building she concentrated her thoughts through the phone connection.

Your husband betrays you and this nation every single day.

And on some level, you know it, don't you? The woman on the other end of the line made a decision.

"One moment."

Pens and scrap paper lay all over the coffee table in front of her. His many identities, his given name, lists of phone numbers, addresses, bank accounts, ID numbers, birth certificates and every document concerning his family were hers now. Ashley smiled in satisfaction. Finally the power dynamics between them were starting to even out a little. To think this had been within her reach the entire time. He had been busily dealing people dirty for decades. She would have plenty of material to work with. Inside her deepest consciousness, she sat her horse alone in the desert, waiting for the sun to come up.

The laptop in front of her was filled with snippets of conversation, family psychology dynamics, passwords, impressions and memories, colors and the kinds of maps the mind holds inside. To learn how to analyze it all would take time. But there it was. The kind of deep mind data that David and his agencies would kill to have access to. Everything about this man, made into electronic data on a flash drive. He was in a very vulnerable position indeed. That was his own fault, these deep data points were from his handwriting.

That hand writing sample was from one of her own sticky notes. An agent had lifted them from her workspace to let her know that someone had been there. Then David had sent her own sticky note back to her with his own writing on it because he had a playful side. He was about to find out that she did too.

"So you found me."

He sounded like Christmas had come early.

"Turns out all I needed was hateful motivation."

Her voice sounded different. He let her feel that he had received her sarcasm and when he spoke he sounded sage and respectable.

"You should be proud of your work. This break through will change the world."

"I thought you knew me better than that."

"What do you want Ashley? What is it going to take for you to actually enjoy life?"

He sounded pensive, considerate even. He waited patiently for her to speak again. Ashley felt what was left of her stomach take leave on permanent vacation in that moment before she took the dive into a terrible territory.

"I want to get to know YOU better."

She put the emphasis on the word you. She knew she was his deepest obsession.

David intended to weaponize her ability to extract secrets from people. She intended to make him go first. There was a pause before he replied.

"Ah. Very interesting."

The man known as David took a seat in a leather chair in his private den, in the basement of a sweeping home in a gated community. He took out a pair of reading glasses and put them on in the dim light. The darkness felt soothing. He needed to listen. This would be some of the most important listening to a young person that would be done in this century.

"Are you in love with your wife, David?"

"I think you could safely say that."

"What about your daughters? Do they think you are a good person?"

The man who had kept Ashley away from his profession had been serving in high stakes intelligence for decades, he was still listening for the things around what Ashley was going to say as she continued.

"Well you should know that I think you are."

"That's very generous of you."

His voice betrayed nothing. He waited patiently like a sign reader watching the clouds in the mountains. He would play this game all night with Ashley if need me. She was worth it. He could feel that she was starting to calm down, starting to feel a little more comfortable in her first bold grab for power. Even starting to enjoy herself. Oh yes, he certainly had all night. That was quite some concussion she had sustained. He had expected that Ashley would require some time as she regrouped. He was thrilled that she had completed an everyday object extraction. Thrilled that she had found his phone numbers. Ashley at work was astounding to see. Now that she was trying her wings a little, who knew what could become possible?

"Have you ever wondered if what I do is an innate ability or a teachable skill?"

David opened his eyes, interest peeked against his will. He waited for her to speak again but she didn't. Just when he thought he might have called it wrong she spoke again.

"To answer YOUR question, there are a lot of things I am going to want."

Ashley had nothing she could describe as experience in seduction and that was why she knew it was going to work. When you aren't bluffing you can pretend to bluff until the sun goes down and the crowd won't be able to look away.

She hung up the phone. Would a front eventually become your soul if there was honestly nothing but deadness behind it? At which point is the front no longer, technically, a front anymore? Her fingertips and mouth were dry. The stars burned overhead in the Dallas sky.

She swayed side to side a little like a cat. This was the most dangerous game she could imagine.

She could not afford anything except a genius level of strategy. And the only way to consistently achieve that was to let your subconscious play. Not to play at playing but to put your soul on the casino table and smile obnoxiously as you slowly lose it all on whim after whim. That was what she had to do.

Multiple strikes were scrawled out as available options. He was a complex man with a lot to lose professionally, personally, monetarily and legally. So she had materials ready to be sent to his wife, his colleagues, his enemies, his superiors. With the stroke of a key his life would start to see schismatic changes, one thing leading to another.

She smiled again as she looked over her work. She had known there would be a lot to work with and there was. This was his arena of genius. Still she knew that, on some level, the more she ruined his life the happier he would be. She had never terrorized or blackmailed anyone before. Once again the dynamics between them were woefully uneven, this was a man that spoke coercion in his dreams instead of English. She had data in front of her to prove it.

She didn't have anything to work on except instinct and this didn't feel like the moment for a strike.

Now was a time to sleep, as the adrenaline fell off great convulsing tremors were rising. She would have to get warmed up, maybe have some soup. She was thinking like a professional athlete about how to convalesce before the next match. There was only so much of her body left, she would have to make it last.

As she tucked herself into bed she felt that she had been very brave. She could sleep deeply tonight. There was no way David would make a move immediately after this exciting development. So as she drifted off into surreal scenery she knew that she had accomplished everything that she needed to for now. This wild world would go on without her. After all, she didn't have to win. She just had to make sure he kept playing.

# 14

# Emmy In Nebraska

Emmy looked back at the path she was walking. This would be a good place to call her home. She hummed happily.

In the spring, there is magic from the old country in the fog. Emmy strolled disembodied through the wet, touching each fence post she came to along the fence line. Water droplets, cobwebs, rich saturation even in the brilliant white light. This was a giant photography light box. She didn't even take any pictures. She needed this stuff in her soul, not her phone.

If her mom would have been there she would have told her the names of the birds she was hearing. She pursed her lips together in a whispered effort at imitation. She put a stem of grass between her teeth and rolled it gently before releasing it in fingertips to the breeze. Another fence post, another view lying secretive, waiting for her in the misty shroud.

Looking down, the dirt showed in patches of wet sand and sharp plants of all kinds, how up close it could all be so harsh and then looking out, be the very picture of lush bounty spoke to the opposites that the natural world usually deals in. Dismal was uncanny, sort of weird.

The ground beneath her feet was roiling in electrical charge, how deep she couldn't say. This land was mist laden; peaceful on the surface but tense enough beneath that to just combust.

She brushed her fingertip gently along the wet barbed wire, the surface was unusual. Emmy smiled to herself, as she thought that she couldn't quite put her finger on it. And then she did. Heat. This metal had been very hot and then cooled again. She wanted to ask Mr. Hammond and Beth about that, maybe they would be able to explain. Her feet and her jacket were soaked, her hair was rich and fluffy in the air born moisture. She was the only soul in blue heaven and golden earth at that moment, alone in her color bound Eden.

Then she heard a knicker, a horse sound. She saw the horse picking it's way slowly toward her on the other side of the fence line. He looked shaggy and lazy and so friendly that she could have snorted out loud. He was probably a very light gray but his winter coat was still shedding in big poufs of white clinging fluff. His mane and tail were long and wild with light and dark shades and his eyes were as resigned as his belly was round. Emmy patted his nose from across the barbed wire. He seemed taller up close.

"What's your name?"

She rubbed his face under his eye a little.

"Who do you belong to?"

She rubbed the forehead under the fetlock and the big horse

seemed to sigh gratefully as more white hair came off.

"Oh you really are a character. I would feed you a snack if I had anything."

The horse's big liquid eyes shone warm and reflective, it really was a beautiful morning. He would have eaten the snack if she would have had one.

She followed the overgrown path back to the yard to tell Phoebe.

# 15

# Phoebe Paints

The most fantastic light filtered through the dirty windows onto Phoebe's canvas, she could see the dust particles in the light beams. She felt the silence was so thick she could have poked it with the blunt end of her paint brush and it would have squeaked like bubble wrap. A silence so far deeper than death that you are smushing your face up against heaven she mused. She was working an energetic directional abstract in dark burgundy reds and tan, brown and yellow.

The ghost of a young cowboy named Don stood behind her and to her right in the art critic's pose. The globs of acrylic smeared and careened into the rough gesso in gestural energy. She was looking for something. She was fantastic. Ivory would have adored her. Don leaned forward to ask her a question.

"You're very good but what are you looking for?"

Phoebe paused with her paintbrush in hand. She thought she heard somebody. Her eyes moved about as she held her head still to the side and listened carefully. Then she shrugged, if they wanted to be heard they would have to do better than that. Don pushed his hat further back and reached for the cigarettes, his pocket was empty. Then he realized something that made him smile and shake back his posture.

"You are looking for me."

Phoebe painted along intuitively. Art wasn't about answers. Art was about finding the questions. Today's work wouldn't matter but one of these today's, suddenly it would. Her eyes fell on the piano and the empty piano bench, something about the light. There was something shifting the shadows and the light, so she started to paint faster.

Don kept the good side of his face toward her, so that the light would fall over it and tried not to move too much. He wanted to dash around to the front of the easel and see what she had painted but he knew portraits took time and he tried to hold still. Finally, Phoebe dropped her paintbrush in a bucket, tired and exasperated she went to find a glass of water and a granola bar. Don stood up in faux indifference and followed her to the wide doorway into the kitchen, then turned to lean on the trim and get a casual look at the work. The breeze and the light shifted outside the two windows when he smiled. She couldn't see him, these were the barest abstracts but they were certainly of him. Art wasn't about the outward appearance of things but instead about their inward meaning, Ivory had told him. That's how he knew a picture could be of someone and look like anything under the moon.

The smile broke into a grin, she would get there. She was using the wrong colors but she would find him eventually. Phoebe would keep looking until she found him. She had joined him in the doorway to look at what he was looking at, the way new friends do.

"You're not using the right colors."

"Maybe I'm not using the right colors."

The screen door slammed behind them and Emmy slid in on wet shoes, her hair askew and eyes alight. Phoebe was glad to see her. Don retired happily to the love seat to gaze languidly at the pictures uninterrupted.

# 16

## What You Are Looking For

Emmy set a foam cup of coffee down on the grimy kitchen table for herself and Phoebe joined her by asking a question.

"Did you find what you were looking for?"

"I don't know, maybe, I feel like I did. But I don't know anything more than I did yesterday. What have you been working on?"

Phoebe gestured into the living room while taking a careful steaming sip and Emmy leaned over in her chair to look. Phoebe spoke again before she could comment.

"I'm pleased with the motion but I decided I need a different color palette."

"Ah. I understand that one. Oh! Oh, have you ever tried this?"

Emmy brandished her phone.

"It's an app that captures the colors in your image, see you can drag the little points around to identify the color you have your eye on. Then it gives you the codes and you can save it and export it into your work flow."

Emmy was so enthusiastic she didn't mind that Phoebe

seemed lost in thought when she replied.

"Cool, I think I've seen that."

"Well I'm not surprised you don't rely on it because it certainly has it's limits. Just like everything, tech doesn't usually see what I see. But, I'm addicted. Look, it has this feature where you can prism it and then turn and keep turning it."

"Like a kaleidoscope?"

"Exactly. And it looks like heck at first. Or maybe always."

Emmy navigated carefully to a specific image and handed her phone to Phoebe before jumping up to cross the kitchen.

"That is taken off of this little piece of curtain here. Go ahead and swipe, look at how this developed. There's dozens of them there. I've been turning it over and over again since we got here."

Phoebe had aspired to be clairvoyant. But she didn't need to be to see what was going on here. Emmy was like a bulldog when she latched onto an idea. Phoebe suddenly remembered Emmy's beautiful mermaid house with the cottage garden. Her friend had designed the most exquisite interior and landscape. Then she had put years of remodeling labor into a house that she didn't own only to see her boyfriend sell it out from under her for top dollar. Phoebe reminisced pensively that this series of events was actually what had led them to be living in this abandoned house in Nebraska.

"You found it didn't you?"

"I did, it's like I'm trying to bring something into focus. There's something here that I need to understand. Keep swiping."

Phoebe knew immediately when she had hit the right image because her heart moved in peacefulness, she looked up at her friend. Emmy smiled and kept talking.

"And there it is. This is what it looks like when it's been brought, into focus, so to speak. It's so beautiful I could cry. But I still don't what it means."

"It is very beautiful."

Phoebe handed the phone back to Emmy. She hoped that whatever idea Emmy was latching onto it would serve her better than the last several had.

"Thank you."

Then Phoebe reached over and took the phone back. She needed to see that picture again. She expanded the image on the phone screen. Emmy was right, this was eye candy for the sophisticated. She wanted to keep looking and looking. Maybe her friend was onto something after all. Phoebe was a veteran artist, they needed to keep this project moving along. She didn't want Emmy to park in this early stage so she spoke again.

"We should get this printed, what are you thinking?"

Emmy smiled happily and caressed her thumb across her fingers.

"Fabric."

Phoebe was surprised and surprisingly exhilarated by the idea.

"Oh!"

The print on the phone in Phoebe's hand included muted soft shades of green on a background with dozens of shades of warm grays. She knew what it reminded her of.

"This reminds me of the old cabbage leaf dishes."

"Exactly! Cool, huh?"

"And it came from that curtain? Can I see the original image?"

"Sure, swipe back until you find it."

Phoebe nodded as she confirmed her suspicion, the image included many striking features but Emmy had locked in on one square half inch of it.

Emmy was still leaning into how the ridges of her fingerprint felt against the ridges of the skin on her pointer finger as she caressed imaginary fabric.

"Waffle knit. I want to feel this pattern in a thermal, with little textured squares and boxes. That would feel so good."

Don had wandered in to see what all the fuss was about and then wandered back to the living room. Now he was shifting through Phoebe's loose piles of sketches that she had done that morning before starting to paint. Emmy was a talented nut for sure but Phoebe had skill and poetry. He held some of the drawings up to the light.

# 17

# Someone Knows The Answers

Don sorted the sketches he liked to the left and let the others fall to the right. He held them up to the light from the grimy window. These were all non-objective and full of strong motion and a deliberate point of view. He smiled, he wanted so badly to be found.

The girls stopped talking. They could hear someone in the next room, paper brushing against paper. Emmy's heart beat in her chest. There was no one in this house but the two of them. What was moving around in there? The skin on her arms rose into goosebumps painfully. She could hear the papers moving around in the eerie silence. She didn't dare move in that moment. Was this it, were they going to see the ghost? She wasn't sure she was ready. In that moment, she didn't want to.

Phoebe listened carefully while watching Emmy absentmindedly. Their spirit was going through her papers. Making artwork in the living room was going to do it then. They wouldn't be able to resist. This is how they would make contact. Phoebe wondered who they had been. Had they lived here? Were they some of Emmy's family? Where were they laid to rest? And what unfinished business did they have in this house?

Phoebe jumped when she heard the piano bench in the living room creak long and loud like a door on stubborn hinges. Don's ghostly fingertips rested ever so lightly on the old fashioned keys. The moment swelled with possibility for the three of them. Phoebe could feel it, their ghost wanted to play that piano. More than that they wanted to play piano for them. Maybe that was how they would make initial contact. Phoebe met her friend Emmy's eyes. This was all too much for Emmy. For all her bravado about this house, the supernatural scared her easily. Phoebe reached across the table and gripped her hand reassuringly.

On the front step the spring air was bracing. Emmy hadn't realized that the house was close and tight. Full of a strange sort of energetic charge, well, obviously.

"Thank you."

She mouthed the words to her friend quietly and Phoebe grinned broadly.

"Don't mention it. We don't have to make this journey in one day."

Emmy's stomach somersaulted. Phoebe was that sure then, the thought jolted her into motion.

"You think, we can," Emmy waved her hand vaguely behind her as she walked down the sidewalk "do something with this then?"

Phoebe rolled down the windows in her car before settling in to chill in the driver's seat for a while.

"I would sure think so yes. Why not?"

Emmy pulled on a sweater from her own car and came to sit in the passenger seat next to Phoebe and look at the house they were parked in front of.

"Well, for starters, this place is haunted as hell."

They both laughed for a moment, laughing felt good.

Phoebe coughed and cleared her throat first.

"Seriously, your mom never gave any clues about why the place she grew up in was haunted?"

Emmy shrugged.

"At this point I think you know as much as I do."

"Well let's talk through it again. This ghost wants to be found and resolved."

"You think so?"

"I know so. It could not be more obvious."

"And that's a good thing?"

"Yes!"

Phoebe insisted again with a laugh.

"Yes! You were born for this place Emmy. You belong here. You need a house, this house needs you to fix it up. If it wasn't haunted anymore this would all be perfect. And I don't think this is a mean ghost or evil, I think they just need to be acknowledged."

Emmy looked a little sick.

The two women looked around them at the brilliant light in the fog still lingering around the yard. One would have thought it would have burned off by now. This was a strange feeling place. Emmy began again thoughtfully.

"My mom grew up in a haunted house. This house. So it was haunted during her childhood. Her parents were Clyde Donahue and Gladys Donahue. They passed away when I was in school, so they were alive that whole time. So the ghost isn't either of them."

"Who lived here before them?"

"I don't know."

They were both thinking it before Phoebe put words to it.

"I'm sure Mr. Hammond knows. Maybe he would tell you. Or maybe Nora or Beth could find out and tell us."

Mr. James Hammond leased the ranch property that Emmy had inherited from her grandfather Clyde Donahue. James' wife Nora had said that their families had been friends for a long time. Their daughter Beth was a freshman in college this spring. Beth and Emmy got along like two peas in a pod.

"Someone around here knows the answers."

Phoebe spoke confidently and Emmy replied cheerfully.

"You're right, this is all going to work out."

# 18

# A Bigger Loveseat

A painfully abrupt buzz jerked both of them back to the here and now. Emmy's phone was vibrating aggressively.

"It's Ashley, I wonder why she's calling."

Emmy picked up the phone and Ashley's voice burst into the car with them.

"Emmy! It's so hot, everything is melting down-"

Ashley sounded like a sleepwalker or a child dreaming a night terror, Emmy could only catch a few of her words as she ranted on. Emmy motioned to Phoebe.

"I don't think she's even awake."

Phoebe looked concerned.

Emmy spoke loudly into the phone and when it didn't work she raised her voice again.

"Honey! Sweetie! Wake up sweetie. It's okay, you need to wake up."

"I can't do this. I was worried I would be able to do it. But now that I can, it can't be done. I can't do this."

Ashley's words were slowing and becoming more coherent as she continued.

"The cost to the body is just too high."

Phoebe looked at Emmy curiously as they listened.

Emmy's voice was soft and kind when she spoke again.

"Hey, hey sweetie, are you awake now?

"Hi. Hi, I think so."

Ashley was looking around her bed and her bedroom.

"I'm sorry I called you, I must have been asleep. I'll let you go now."

"Honey, sweetie. What can't you do?"

Ashley felt the grip of it all coming over her again as she hugged a heavy fluffy pillow against her and made to roll over and go back to sleep.

"Just something for work."

"Are you home alone? Maybe you need a drink of water? Try to calm down sweetie, we will figure this out."

The phone was loud but Phoebe had inclined her head close by to make sure she didn't miss anything. Her beautiful face looked pained with concern and Emmy felt tears coursing down her own face. Emmy cried easily.

"You know, why don't you leave them? Tell them you quit. Come live out here with us for a while?"

Ashley smiled sleepily as she pulled the duvet higher over her shoulders.

"Sure. Where could I fly into?"

After she hung up the phone Emmy turned to Phoebe with a question.

"When were you planning on going back to Dallas?"

Phoebe was having the same thought.

"Well my friend Jeremy is staying in my apartment, that's saving me some money, he might even take over the lease for me this summer. I guess I could go back anytime and get the rest of my stuff."

"Maybe we should go get Ashley."

"I know-"

Phoebe stared blankly at the haunted little house in front of them with the broken screen door and the wide cement front step.

"We might have to get a bigger love seat."

# 19

# Someone Somewhere

From the gun range window Frank watched Ashley cross the street and exchange angry words with the agents that were following her. He had never seen her approach them before. She was dressed differently. She moved recklessly and aggressively. She was moving like she wanted to get shot. Frank continued to watch discreetly through the tinted front window. Her handlers were a little at a loss, he could tell by their body language. So that was it, she was testing the relationship, finding out who was really in charge. Frank concluded at the same time Ashley did that Ashley was in charge. She stopped yelling. They didn't dare touch her without prior authorization. Someone somewhere was highly invested in Ashley existing in a certain way.

Frank didn't know how to tell Ashley he didn't want her coming here anymore.

"Good morning, Frank."

The old man wished she wouldn't use his name anymore as he slid three packages across the counter top and they disappeared into the backpack. She set a wad of cash, folded double and tied with a rubber band down in front of him. She looked out the window at the agents across the street so that he could take the money without her watching him. He had been her closest thing to a friend or acquaintance. This had been her spot for years.

"Thank you Frank."

He took a phone out of the cash drawer, the phone numbers she had asked for were entered into the contacts. She wouldn't need to make small purchases through him anymore. She could form her own network. She smiled brightly before she stepped out into the glare and pulled her sunglasses down. She was getting tired but she would be back home before her mom even woke up. She waved goodbye to Frank with a smile and her mind on her next task.

"Bye. See you later."

# 20

# Evolve Without Selling Out

The gallery assistant handed Ashley a cup of coffee. Ashley sipped it as she trailed along behind her mom at the gallery. There were far more agents trailing her now than there had been at the gun range earlier.

She probably shouldn't have confronted them directly. They hated that, it insulted their professional ego. She had made them feel powerless, like the babysitters they were.

"This is an artist named Caroline, she has been showing work with us for a little more than a year now. What do you think?"

"I think she is one of your best sellers."

"Is it obvious?"

Ashley laughed.

"No, not at all, I just hear more than you realize."

Barb grimaced a tight smile.

"Well do you think she can evolve? This world is always changing. If she can adjust her aesthetic just a little for the upcoming season I will be able to sell more than ever before."

"And if she can't? At least not on command?"

Ashley stood with her feet and shoulders squared up with one of Caroline's pieces. Barb shrugged.

"Who knows? Sales might hold steady regardless."

Ashley considered it all a little blankly.

"So she has to sell out to remain relevant?"

"No. Quite the opposite. She has to evolve without selling out. A much more difficult task."

Ashley could hear birds chirping outside, people were walking on the sidewalk. The sales ladies were conversing softly and paper rustled, one of them was answering the phone at the front desk. Barb looked at her daughter. Ashley wasn't getting any better. Even when Barb looked beyond the black eyes and the burns and the new skin markings and the lingering temperament changes due to concussion. There was still something very bad around the eyes.

If Barb had ever sought medical help, she would have done so that day. But she thought she knew what they would find. Barb called it heat. There was just too much heat, too much residual electrical charge which meant too much strain on the nervous system and too much inflammation on the brain. Barb gave her daughter another worried assessing glance. Ashley had a constitution similar to her own. For Barb the heat would eventually pass on it's own. Barb turned back to the day's work in front of her.

"So how do you bet? I should be seeing some work from Caroline in the next couple weeks. Will she have evolved?"

Ashley looked at the artwork again.

"I don't think so. This looks like she would like for things to remain the same."

"I know."

Barb strolled confidently, making some notes to herself as she went. Ashley trailed along behind comfortably. Barb eyed the sweatpants and hoodie Ashley had wrapped herself in, the girl was holding her arms across her torso as if she was cold. Their eyes met for a moment. Ashley knew her mom was very worried. Otherwise she would never have let her follow her around while she worked like this. Ashley smiled a little wryly. Barb smiled in spite of herself.

"So the next question I have to ask myself, is who will be the next top seller within my business?"

The front desk lady handed Barb a sticky note with a soft murmur. Barb looked back at Ashley questioningly and she answered.

"It's going to be Phoebe isn't it?"

"I usually put my money on myself, Phoebe understands how to do that."

Ashley wished the enormous front gallery windows were tinted. The way they were standing here, this was a good way to get shot. The agent across the street smiled back at her without moving his face as he correctly interpreted her body language. She was uncomfortable, like a deer in an open meadow.

Barb's phone pinged.

"Just a sec sweetie, I'm going to tell Allan I'm going to the

Santa Fe gallery."

"How are you two getting along?"

Her mom had dated Allan all through Ashley's teenage years. Ashley liked him and thought the two of them made a good couple. They suited each other. Right now, she would have liked for her mom to start living with Allan, that would be safer than living alone.

"Well he's ready for something more and I'm not, so there you go."

Ashley sighed aloud, they were going to Today's Cup next. She gestured with her head as she spoke. So much for that idea.

"There you go."

# 21

# Today's Cup

Simone was happy to see Barb and Ashley but surprised to see them together. The coffee shop was all the comfort that Ashley had counted on. The smells, the sounds, Simone had a gift for ambiance and welcoming people and her business thrived. Simone was one of Barb's oldest and dearest friends. In fact Ashley had been born in Simone's car in the emergency room parking lot. Ashley let her head rest on Simone's shoulder while she hugged her tenderly.

"What happened to you?"

Simone stroked Ashley's head for just a moment. Then Simone was back to the professional version of her caring self. Simone was Barb's visual opposite in every way. Barb was pale, thin and borderline severe though terribly chic. Simone was cocoa, curves and motherly gentleness wrapped in a generous dose of fun. Barb and Simone had been best friends for decades and Ashley loved her dearly.

Simone eyed her friend carefully from back behind the coffee counter. Barb was a solitary cat, you just didn't see her out in public with her daughters. Barb didn't realize what treasures her daughters were. Simone had only had sons, but now she had daughters-in-law and amazing grandbabies. At any rate, Barb was not simply stopping by for coffee with her daughter, she needed help. Barb had texted her about Ashley's accidental lab explosion but Simone was still shocked by Ashley's appearance.

Ashley looked withdrawn and shadowed under the eyes, terminally ill even. Simone found herself wondering about her blood pressure or blood sugar levels or even if the young woman had a serious health condition they weren't aware of. Simone took Barb's order without hearing a word of it. Barb avoided the medical establishment but did Ashley need to see a doctor? Simone met Ashley's eyes across the counter.

"How about a water with some lemon? And an apple."

Ashley knew Simone would hug her again, would hold her as long as she needed, if she would have asked. Simone had always been there for them, all through her childhood.

"That sounds good, thank you."

Mother and daughter stopped to admire the merchandise display and smell the bags of coffee beans. Simone took an order from a smart looking woman she had never seen before while watching the two of them thoughtfully.

Then time slowed for Simone as the woman who had just ordered grabbed Ashley forcefully by the elbow and Ashley produced a handgun from nowhere and put it in the woman's shoulder.

"David's waiting for you outside, come with me, he wants to

talk to you."

Ashley had seen the black SUV park on the curb in the no parking zone moments before.

"Like hell he is."

That's when the agent had grabbed Ashley's elbow.

Ashley spoke with a pleasant smile in her voice.

"Give me any reason. I will never stand trial."

The woman's eyes widened just perceptibly as Ashley kept talking.

"Actually this could be good for me, bring me into the public eye. So many witnesses."

The agent's pulse changed just a little and Ashley smiled.

"You really screwed up this time didn't you."

Then Ashley shoved her hard with her palms in both shoulders.

"Get out of here. Don't bother me again."

The agent's face was unreadable. She even paused to collect her hot drink from the counter as if nothing had happened. Ashley called out sarcastically after her as the agent pushed on the coffee shop door.

"Say hi to David for me."

Simone could feel Barb looking at her and she met her gaze on her own terms. Their tiny baby girl, their genius in a little backpack, they had lost her. This woman in front of them, this was someone they didn't know at all.

# 22

# A Difficult Time

Emmy's old bedroom was dark and full of shadows, even brilliantly lit with work lights. Agents had been in while she was away. She hoped they were prepared for radiation sickness. She had told her mom she would be going away on a personal and work trip.

"I have a government client that is setting up a new tech lab, I'm on contract to help with the design and installation."

Her mom hadn't seemed surprised. Ashley had barely looked at her while she said it.

"I'll be in touch. I might hit a beach somewhere before I come home."

Barb appreciated Ashley trying to make all this seem normal. Ashley had traveled for work frequently for years. And she often lingered for a short nature vacation. Barb knew Ashley would never be coming home.

"When do you think you will come home?"

"I don't know, it's a big project."

She hadn't been able to read her mom's expression.

Ashley was rearranging and packing and she moved slowly among the piles of gear chaos, lost in thought. She ignored the twisted remains of the card table and pressure chambers and power units that had oozed out into the middle of the floor and hardened like a carcass that was no longer relevant. She needed to concentrate.

People had been touching things while was gone. She hated that. She was so sick of David and his hive of professionals doing his bidding. She laid her hands on item after item, imploring muscle memory to take over. She just wasn't sure what she would be needing next, what she would be needing when. She tried to feel her way into the future and touch the hand of the woman that existed there. She felt so deeply disconnected.

A phone vibrated across the plastic of a work table.

"I'm glad to see you're packing. Don't forget your good luck charms. Your own sheets, things that remind you of home."

Ashley typed out a sentiment involving a four word obscenity. Her phone buzzed again in reply almost immediately.

"Manners. I know this is a difficult time for you."

Ashley strolled across the room to where she had left a variety of strike options ready at hand. Then she pushed the space bar on an ordinary keyboard and spoke aloud.

"It's about to be a difficult time for you too."

# 23

# David's Money

David checked his pulse for the third time. This office was cold.

"Just handle it."

He waved at the other man to get out of his office. He didn't have the concentration for inconsequential matters today. Ashley had stolen his money. Emptied some of his bank accounts. Specifically the most deeply hidden ones. His lip turned upward sightly in contempt.

Ashley was struggling and she was going to take it out on him. The damage to his finances was inconvenient but nothing he couldn't withstand or recover from. She knew that. Like an adolescent she was trying the boundaries. Sitting down at his desk he picked up a ringing phone.

"Interesting. Let them know that our interests will keep up there for the foreseeable future."

He listened with the phone in the crook of his neck while he checked the pulse in his wrist and stared at the poster on the wall. He had only one matter truly on his mind today. He would have to establish some consequences. Ashley would realize that this was a game that he could easily win. He was in a much better position.

"Sounds good, I will want a full report when you get back."

David coached himself to maintain his patience with her. She was an asset not a professional he reminded himself as he looked at another of his phones in irritation. Assets eventually get caught or destroy themselves. He couldn't have that. Ashley was going to need more structure in order to keep working. Eventually she would quit throwing a tantrum and get back to work. Then the important work could begin. She loved to work. In the meantime he was going to have to let her feel the boundaries she was testing. He picked up another phone to make some arrangements.

Growing pains, he thought to himself, what a waste of effort and time. Kind of a shame. In the end he would probably just take all three of them into custody.

But Ashley didn't need to know that. He had all sorts of perception options. His stomach turned over again as he looked at the financial withdrawal notifications. Actually that money had mattered to him. Her school picture loomed larger than life over him where he sat at his desk. She would be much easier to work with in a professional setting.

# 24

# Matt's Orchids

*In which we revisit Emmy's long time boyfriend and find that he misses her. Matt has never met a ghost and he has no idea how far away Dismal really is.*

The boxes were properly stored in the storage unit. The furniture wrapped and waiting there too, until the new duplex was move in ready. The orchids were all that was left from Emmy's beloved cottage bungalow. She had built that backyard flower farm from scratch and they had put in some good years there together. He wondered if she would ever forgive him.

"Thank you! These are beautiful."

Emmy's ex-boyfriend Matt handed the dumpy sloppy woman the last orchid and she nestled it carefully in the front passenger seat. Two small children and a baby were screaming in the back. He doubted the orchids would live for two weeks.

"You are welcome."

He watched from the curb for a moment. He had sold Emmy's dream to finance his own.

"Actually, I'm sorry, could I take one back from you?"

The mom in the stained t-shirt smiled. She was about to drive away looking like a florist's van.

"Of course."

Matt stood in the street holding one blooming orchid in a pot and watched the woman with the children drive away with Emmy's orchid collection. That was that, he would take this one to the office tomorrow.

"Good morning Mr. Carter."

The new girl at the front desk had long dark hair and a nice smile. She seemed very normal, competent. So very different from Emmy. They already had great chemistry.

"Good morning, these are for you."

She wondered if he meant for the front desk or for her personally. He smiled and she knew he meant for her personally. She looked from him to the orchids and back again.

"Thank you."

She set them beside her computer.

The retirement party went off without a hitch. The office was crowded with a lifetime's worth of friends, family and business connections. Tomorrow would be a new beginning of sorts but tonight was all about the old man. Matt handed him another drink.

"Well you have done it, congratulations."

"I've done it all right, it's all yours now. A shipwreck forty years in the making."

The older man had been his boss and then his business partner and now Matt had been able to buy him out. The business, the duplex, Matt had almost achieved everything he had planned to. Matt watched him drink deeply and listened for him to speak again.

"It's been a good life for me."

The retiree looked around, as if he couldn't find someone he had been looking forward to seeing. He always enjoyed visiting with Matt's girlfriend Emmy. She had a great sense of humor.

"You will do better with it than I did, you and Emmy. You know I haven't gotten a wedding invitation yet, did you two set a date?"

Matt didn't tell his mentor that Emmy had left him to move to Nebraska or that there would be no wedding invitation on the way because she had called it off. His pride still hurt too much.

"She's gone to Nebraska to take care of some family property. I think she is going to like the new duplex when she sees it. It has a nice backyard."

# 25

# Insurance Reports

The red and blue lights from the sirens threw strange shadows over Barb's face as she spoke with the officers. They were wrapping up their report. Most of the fire department would be leaving soon. Barb had never seen anything like it and she had thought that she had seen everything.

"I just don't know anything else, why someone would do this."

"Thank you ma'am. Please don't hesitate to call if you think of anything."

Barb shook the young man's hand.

An artist working late in a studio across the street had called in the blaze. He had been badly shaken, the building was already almost gone. Everyone was in shock. This place was packed with priceless historic architecture in close quarters. State of the art fire control systems were everywhere. They had not been enough.

Barb was rattled. She was a prominent member of this

community. If the fire had spread, the churches here were some of the oldest in the country. Her building had been compliant. She steadied herself deliberately. Priorities. No one had been in the building. No one had been hurt. The fire had not spread. All this amounted to was a deliberate scare tactic.

The young officers in front of her were still busy with paper-work on clipboards. The acrid smoke was still thick in the air. This had all come to a close so quickly.

"Sign here please."

Barb felt sad about the artwork that had been lost, they had been originals, such beautiful pieces. Barb thought about her dad as she signed her name.

So this was what decades of her work could all came down to, smoke and insurance reports. Everyone knows they can lose it all in an instant. Barb's mind sharpened, time to move on from the pity party. She could recover from this loss. There was so much more going on here. She privately agreed with the police. No casual vandal could have done this. The security systems in place in this area guarded millions of dollars in heirloom jewelry. And for the building to go up as fast and hot as it did, Barb's eyes drifted over the smoldering ruin, this was a master arsonist. Motive remained as the major question.

Barb wondered where Ashley was, if she had left for that so called work trip yet and if she was safe. Barb remembered the woman at the coffee shop. Then paused as she remembered how brutally confident Ashley had been. Barb wondered who her daughter was, professionally. As she stood alone in the desert night Barb probed the air around her with her mind as if she could easily find that out if she had a mind to. She wondered who her daughter was involved with, who was David? Who were they really? And against her own will she wondered and wandered into that most painful territory. Had Ashley already left? Would she ever see her younger daughter again? Barb reached for her phone.

# 26

# Too Easy

The high rise apartment was dark and very, very silent when Ashley was finally organized and packed. Her mom was in Santa Fe. Emmy was in Nebraska and she was here in Dallas. Ashley would be heading to the airport soon. Her mind was on her mom when her mom called her.

"Ashley, how are you?"

"I'm okay mom, what's up?"

Ashley thought she knew why her mom was calling. Barb knew that Ashley knew. This thing between them was about to break like thunder overhead.

"Well, I'm here in Santa Fe and, the gallery has burned down."

"WHAT?"

Ashley had not expected the news to feel the way it did, like her own soul rotting in the secrets of her sins and own inadequacy.

"Now don't be upset, they've got it put out and the police have been here."

"What happened? What do you mean it burned down?"

Ashley knew the building, with it's security and sprinkler systems, new construction components like steel, glass and cement, it would not have been an easy target. David usually worked with the best, she started wheeling a suitcase toward the apartment door. She herself was a case in point. Her mom's voice held her to the phone.

"Evidently arson, it lit up pretty quickly and got very hot too. The girls had all gone home long before that. No one was hurt."

Ashley felt the pangs of the shame she had been expecting. Her loved ones were going to suffer because of her. She had been dreading this part of it all for years.

"Oh mom I'm so sorry."

The sadness in her voice rang with more than just empathy. Barb didn't miss what she was hearing and she moved on the offense.

"It's just stuff. Just things. No one was hurt."

Barb felt that her daughter was so very distant from her and she didn't know what to say. Ashley needed to know that she was on her side. Barb had never wondered if she knew that before now.

"The cops said they might want to talk to me again in the morning. I'm going back to the hotel, going to have something to eat."

Ashley was on her way to the airport when a text from David lit up her phone.

"That was some very fine artwork, such a waste."

She wanted to say, David you are wasting your time. I will

sacrifice my family and myself before I develop that tech. If they knew the whole story, they would tell me that's what I should do. My mom would have said to let it burn. In her own way, she already did.

Instead Ashley could have said, I will make sure there is nothing left of either of us. Possibly she should have wondered, will Emmy be safe in Nebraska? But she knew David better than that. She had been the object of his ambition for too many years. She knew she was very, very dear to him. He would not willingly damage her beyond repair. So instead of slowing down she accelerated.

In the dark in the back of the car she wiggled her shoulders and cracked her neck sideways. He was missing his money or he never would have made such a bold move. She needed to give him more to think about. In her mind's eye Ashley saw the arson of the sturdy stucco gallery, it must have been quite the incendiary setup. Then she replied to his text.

"Well I hope you at least brought some marshmallows."

Then Ashley keyed in a code on a different phone to put into action a strike on his personal life. She closed her eyes to rest as she enjoyed this moment. David was about to lose his trophy wife and his status as a successful married man.

Ashley had taken the time to understand this woman and the life that she had led so that she could plan this strike for maximum impact. The public drama this jilted woman would create would be insane. Ashley smiled knowingly. David deserved all that and more, it had really been too easy. His wife would be calling him shortly.

# 27

# Angel Made Of Wire

Smoke and flames encircled an angel made of wire. The barbed wire shape was just visible after the explosion, hanging from the scorched rear view mirror. Swaying gently.

*Barb felt so very alone. The memories were making her cry. Her Dad was handing her the crudely made piece through the car window. She had just gotten her driver's license.*

He had made that for her because he understood her and he loved her. He had known how much it would mean to her. Barb had kept her barbed wire angel hanging up in whatever she was driving ever since, her angel.

The sun was coming up on Ashley sprawled in a chair in an airport lounge when Barb called Ashley again.

"Hey, it's mom. I'm here at the police station in Santa Fe."

"Are you okay? Mom, what happened?"

Her mom was an old battle ax but Ashley could hear her voice intone just a little as she admitted why she had called, saying it out loud made it just a little worse.

"Someone torched my car while I was at the hotel."

Ashley shifted her lower jaw in a calculating motion. Her mom loved that SUV. To her mom, a car was an extension of a person. Barb was feeling the violence of the attack much more than she had felt the loss of her gallery. In her mind's eye Ashley could see what was left of the eternally sparkling car. Like the mess she had left behind in the bedroom turned lab, it was all a little sick. Barb continued speaking.

"The police here they want to know what might be behind a personal attack. They seem to think I should be taking this seriously. Can you think of anything?"

"Oh my gosh Mom. What are you going to do?"

Ashley's eyes roved across the security cameras absent-mindedly and looked for the surveillance agents she knew were around somewhere. She was very sorry to have caused her mom uncertainty or even fear.

"Well I called Allan. He's on his way down."

"Oh that's good. Maybe you two should just hang out for a while."

Barb heard her daughter's advice but didn't comment either way, she was still at the police station but she needed to touch base with Ashley right away.

"Honey, I know you don't know anything about who would do this to me. But are you still going on that work trip?"

"Actually, no. Plans have changed. I'm going to stay with Emmy for a while."

# 28

# Emmy And Phoebe

*In which Emmy finds a sewing machine and Phoebe meets the package delivery man and they decide to get out of the house for a while.*

Emmy found her first buried treasure hiding out in one of the back bedrooms. Now she had recruited Phoebe to help her carry it out into the sunlight in the living room. Phoebe groaned for dramatic effect as they maneuvered the doorway. It was a green sewing machine, complete with it's own table. Phoebe exclaimed aloud as she did most of the lifting.

"Oh my gosh this thing is heavy! What is it made of?"

"I don't know, steel. Lead?"

"Why? Just why?"

They set it down in the middle of the room in front of the love seat. One of the table legs was threatening to fall off so Phoebe took a moment to make sure it was propped and wedged semi securely. She didn't want it to fall on Emmy.

"Thank you!"

Emmy was already happily flipping through the little vintage pamphlet manual. Phoebe smiled. This would occupy her friend for hours upon hours. Different strokes for different folks, she had her own excitement planned for the day.

"You are welcome."

"I think this was probably my grandmother's, and it looks like it's been used a lot. Maybe she liked to sew?"

"Maybe."

Phoebe was reminded of her own grandmother in the textile industry and the missed video chat notifications piling up on her phone. She wouldn't be able to ignore them forever.

They heard the package delivery truck not long after that. Phoebe went out onto the front step in her bird slippers. She had received an email so she was expecting the package today and she was glad to see the carriers had been able to use the address. The delivery man in uniform smiled at her.

"You are new out here, huh?"

She smiled at him, he must spend most of his days alone.

"Yeah, just staying with a friend for a while."

"We've never delivered to this address before."

He looked around curiously, the tree branches were dead and dark against the sky and a coven of crows broke out crying together. Phoebe tucked a strand of dark hair behind her ear. He was still thinking about that when he bumped back down the overgrown driveway and onto the highway.

"What'd you get?"

"Art supplies."

Don and Emmy watched Phoebe unpack heavy weight

mixed media paper, a few small tubes of some very fine watercolor and lots of large tubes of some not very fine acrylic in lots of colors, a white colored pencil and pad of black paper.

"Did you sort these sketches?"

Phoebe was looking at her artwork in two piles. They had heard the paper moving but she had not guessed that she was getting collaborative feedback. The ones the ghost liked were set neatly in a tidy pile next to her brushes. The rest had fallen haphazardly further back, some had drifted to the floor.

"No, I wouldn't touch your work."

Phoebe wished she would have thought before she spoke, everything earlier had freaked Emmy out.

Emmy got up to come look. Phoebe decided to downplay the incident.

"Say, I need to go walk around and make a jar of found objects, do you want to go?"

Emmy was all for ignoring the unexplained.

"Of course, I could have picked up some things this morning."

Then Emmy continued thoughtfully.

"You know I was planning to get together with Beth this weekend, she is home from school, this might be a fun thing to invite her to do with us. Does that work for you?"

Phoebe nodded and smiled.

"I think she would really like that. Yeah that would be great, she has a good eye."

And she knows a lot of interesting things Phoebe thought to herself.

Emmy sat down to send the text and Phoebe went back to

looking at the sketches in the keep pile. She had planned to mail some work to Barb in Dallas today. Given the current forces at play she wanted Barb to touch the physical work. Now she knew that this pile would be the ones that she would send.

# 29

# Welcome Home

Phoebe's dreams were from her artwork and her artwork was full of her dreams. Horses. Square little paper horses, like paper doll horses. Black rabbits. Crows. Cattle under the starry sky. Unseen presences. Untold stories.

She would have been ashamed to tell her grandparents that she had decided to dream her bosses dreams for her. That's how Phoebe knew for sure that she was doing something wrong. Probably Barb should be dreaming her own dreams, that's how issues got resolved. Not by putting them onto someone else, even a willing recipient.

So Phoebe was avoiding her grandmother until she had something more positive to report. Her mom was working on the west coast now. Her last design collaboration had been a sold out success. Phoebe's mom worked in fashion and generally succeeded in everything she did, despite being very American. Phoebe not so much. She was even more American and she was her own woman. She didn't have many conversations with her mom. Thank God.

They had moved around for work and lived in many cities when Phoebe was growing up. Dallas had been her favorite. Until coming here Phoebe hadn't thought that she needed a home.

In retrospect she had made Dallas a home of sorts. Now she found herself wondering if while Emmy made her home here, Phoebe could make her home nearby. Dismal was a cozy little town with a relatively low cost of living and surprisingly good cell phone towers. She could do much worse. So it turned out that she wanted a home.

She had known how badly she had wanted Barb's mentorship and the shiny success that would mean. She still very much wanted to have her mom and her grandparents see her that way. She was still willing to do what it would take. But as she watched Emmy face her family's dysfunctional past one lead sewing machine at a time she was inspired. Nora might not understand why Emmy wanted to move slowly. Barb might not understand why Emmy wouldn't listen. The world might not understand what they were trying to do here but Phoebe did. Emmy was taking the story she had inherited and making her own story. Phoebe decided that, one stupid step at a time, she would try to do the same.

Ignoring her grandparents, becoming a stranger to her mom, Phoebe thought of Barb letting her dad pass away in a nursing home without her. Phoebe didn't want her life to turn out like that. Emmy didn't really look like a brave or self aware woman. That table leg was going to fall off and that sewing machine was going to fall on her. Phoebe watched while deep in thought. This sort of thing probably looked different in each individual.

"You know what I have noticed?"

Emmy began vaguely. Phoebe replied gamely.

"What?"

"This place is called Dismal. It's such a miserable word. I looked it up, not very many things are called Dismal."

"Hmm?"

"And when you walk out in the grass and the weather, it is a beautiful kind of super sad prairie place. Melancholy. Like all those difficult emotions made into a physical landscape you can live in. I can see why someone named it Dismal. With me so far?"

Phoebe nodded from where she was packaging up her sketches.

"But underneath the ground, it feels, exuberant. Have you noticed how the energy field feels under the ground? And I know it's spring but everything feels so alive. Like there is so much life packed into every square foot of this place. Almost maximalist. Like if this place was an interior design scheme it is a full on pattern on pattern color clashing maximal party. No holding back, exuberant and bold. Masculine. But wild."

"Okay."

Phoebe was listening intently.

"And I know it was the sixties and the seventies but have you noticed how much color and motif my grandma was into? It's a riot in here."

Phoebe agreed gamely with a slight sideways head nod, the

owls on the canisters and the wall hanging certainly stood out.

"Anyway what I am getting at is that Dismal is colorful. Dismal is expressive. Dismal is color clashing pattern maximal irreverent. And at the same time it is still prairie and mist and these cottonwood trees and all the miserable sad emotions too. It's both. At the same time."

"With you so far. I see all of that."

"And it feels like looking at myself. You know how you can be so incredibly deeply sad for years and years and then enjoy the sun and coffee so intensely much in the morning? Like, you are both at the same time. This place and that way that a person can be. They are the same."

Phoebe smiled.

"That's beautiful. I really like that."

Spot the kitten chirped in agreement from his patch of sunshine on the carpet.

From the arched doorway Don thought about family and Ivory. Emmy was just like Ivory, she understood this place. Emmy wasn't ready to hear it from him so Don the ghost just whispered the words he wanted to say to her.

"This Is Dismal. Welcome home."

Phoebe heard him.

# 30

# Beth And Trains

"Knock knock?"

Beth held the screen door open and opened the dirty interior door with the crackled white paint slightly to yell out the greeting.

"Come on in, we're in here. Do you want some coffee?"

"No thanks I've had enough for now. And how have you been?"

Beth picked up Spot the kitten off the end of the love seat and flipped him over on his back to snuggle him like a baby and pet his belly. The kitten looked at her adoringly and purred loudly.

Emmy went first, she walked enthusiastically with big steps like a man. She detoured left and right as her determined focus ebbed and waned.

"I saw a horse over there this morning, a big light colored one, he seemed really friendly."

"Oh yeah, you two would get along really well actually. Have you ridden before?"

Beth asked without thinking too far in advance then wished she would have used a different tone of voice.

"I'm sorry, that came out a little tactless."

"Actually I rode at summer camp growing up, no worries, I really liked it. Ashley liked it okay but I really liked it."

"That makes sense. Anyway that's Pokey and that's our pasture there and he belongs to us. You could probably have him to ride if you wanted, he's more of a kid's horse."

Beth felt she had opened her mouth and inserted foot again. Emmy was a very important person for her family's business. The land they leased from her had made their expansion into feeding yearlings over at the Heart Seven possible. She wanted to be Emmy's friend and Phoebe's friend and she normally excelled at making friends but today she felt hyper aware of the business relationship.

Emmy had interrupted her anyway.

"That sounds like it would be a good match. I think I'm okay just petting him for now."

Phoebe listened bemusedly as Beth and Emmy visited.

"Is it okay if I feed him treats?"

Beth laughed.

"Of course, if that makes you happy. He will love you for it for sure."

"Do you have a horse?"

"Beth what is this?"

Phoebe nudged a big piece of timber with her outstretched foot.

"A railroad tie. A very old railroad tie."

Phoebe looked at Emmy, Beth was a wealth of information,

and Emmy asked the next question.

"What do you mean?"

"Well they are what's under the railroad tracks. Big pieces of wood that have been soaked in oil, creosote maybe, don't quote me on that. Then of course all the weight of the trains, makes them very dense, very hard. They were probably very dense lumber to start with now that I think about it. Anyway, they're wonderful for building with."

Phoebe worked a piece of the rotting timber loose with her foot as she asked the next question. She wanted to keep Beth talking.

"Why is this one just laying out here in the grass?"

Beth nudged it with her foot, mimicking Phoebe's body language.

"Well it's so old it's almost gone, see how rotted and crumbly it is."

"Why is there just the one?"

"Well there are not a lot of them around because they are not very legal to build with, to have. They belong to the railroad. I mean there's some around that people came to have through respectable means but the railroad doesn't let them go very easily. If people had had their way through the years," Beth smiled with humor and swept her hand out around her broadly.

"Everything would be built out of these suckers."

"Is there a train track near here?"

Beth pointed over her shoulder towards the hills beyond the rows of trees.

"North. Up there. Not really close but close enough that they used to put the cattle on the train right up there at Lena.

Like a piece of the old west."

Phoebe and Emmy looked at her blankly and the three of them strolled on, breaking off little pieces of grass and other plants for their collection as they went. Phoebe had collected a piece of the rotting railroad tie.

"Why did they put cattle on trains?"

Phoebe asked the question. She had seen a lot more of the world than Emmy, she knew that every industry is a world unto itself that outsiders have to work to gain even a basic understanding of. And she knew that Emmy wanted to understand the cattle industry a bit more so Phoebe kept the questions coming. While Beth was here with them school was in session.

"Oh to take them to the slaughter houses. You know in the wild west they had the big cattle drives coming up from Texas and they would put those cattle on the trains in places like Nebraska and take them back East to feed people. You know the major railroad line runs east to west right through Nebraska."

Phoebe and Emmy were still contemplating the journey from Texas to Nebraska but Beth continued on.

"So even after that was over, locally here they kept putting cattle on the trains. Even as late as in the 1950's I think. Now we use trucks, semi's. My brother August has one, a cattle pot you know, it's a certain body style of truck with a big aluminum cattle trailer. You've seen them right? I'm sure that's a Texas thing too."

Emmy had been sidetracked.

"Are there trains on this train track?"

She pointed the way that Beth had pointed. She was envisioning abandoned and deserted rails and decaying wooden bridges similar to the piece of timber they had just been looking at.

"Oh yeah, all the time. I don't know like every nine minutes or something."

Emmy and Phoebe stared. The meadow around them was as pristine and silent as it could be. Beth could hear their thoughts.

"Sometimes at night you can sort of hear it. We are far enough away here. Dismal was not one of the track towns."

Now Phoebe was intrigued.

"What is going through here on a train ever nine minutes?"

"Coal from Wyoming."

"Oh."

Phoebe had stopped to pick up what looked like a small shard of bone. There just wasn't much for found objects around besides plant life. The conversation lagged as they walked.

"It's a good thing to be a little farther from the tracks. You know in the Great Depression and after that people would ride the rails, you know crawl up on the boxcars. And they would get off in the track towns around here."

Her voice had taken on the tone of someone repeating a story that had been told to them as a child. Phoebe and Emmy could tell something was being communicated but neither of their wildly disparate guesses were remotely correct.

"That doesn't happen so much anymore or really at all.

Sometimes further south in the major rail yards it does. But even in the 80's and the 90's there were some escaped convicts and like that that ended up out here because of the train."

Beth paused to see if she still had an audience, she did.

"There was an old couple my dad talks about that lived a little further east," Beth paused to gesture north and right into the towering hills again.

"And one night a man they didn't know came walking up their driveway in the dark. Knocked on their door. And I guess the old man ended up shooting him. And it turned out to be a good thing, he was wanted for murder. Bad, scary murders. So it was a good thing, but anyway he got off the train and saw their lights and walked into their place. There's a few stories that go like that."

Phoebe looked at Emmy but Emmy was lost in thought.

# 31

# Beth And Lightning

They were walking along the fence line when Emmy remembered her question from the morning in the mist.

"Beth do you know what's up with this wire?"

Beth didn't know what Emmy was talking about.

"See guys, it's all funny. Like metal that's been too hot."

The three women leaned in to look closely at the wire that Emmy was showing them.

Beth wondered how in the heck anyone could be that observant. Phoebe watched Beth wonder and felt a little proud of her friend. Emmy asked again.

"What do you think happened?"

Beth looked a little sheepish. Emmy was reminded of Nora, Beth's mother, when she had come over to meet them after her car had been stolen.

"Lightning."

Phoebe was thinking very quickly and she replied quickly.

"Lightning?"

"This, particular piece of ground, has a very high incident of lightning strikes. I guess you two should probably know that anyway. I just didn't think of it until now. As I think about it you two should definitely know, since you live here."

Emmy was having trouble keeping up, not with the conversation but with the implications.

"Like lightning strikes the ground during storms? Trees and power lines and such? And this fence line?" Beth looked even more guilty.

"Ummm, yes. It also strikes just kind of, out of the blue, without a storm. That's what they call dry lightning."

Emmy and Phoebe stared at Beth, then Phoebe turned her footsteps back toward the house while keeping the conversation light and nonchalant.

"So it just strikes the highest points? The metal wire here on the fence. No people have ever been hit have they?"

"Well no one has ever been killed. There have been grass fires started. I got to help with a major one back when I was a freshman."

Emmy thought Beth was evading the question so she followed up a little breathlessly. They were both having trouble keeping up with Phoebe.

"No one has ever been killed, but people have been hit?"

"Well, yeah. My dad has been hit here twice. He was horseback both times."

Phoebe was wondering what in the hell they had signed themselves up for. Emmy was wondering why her mom had never made the communication jump from, that place is dangerous to people get hit by lightning there. That was the sort of specific example that could have helped her understand.

"Killed the horse both times, but he was okay."

Phoebe rolled her eyes to herself. People were weird wherever you went. But really, no one that got hit by lightning was going to be okay. That was an either or scenario.

# 32

# Don At The Fuel Station

"Do you want to come back over to my mom's to eat?"

Beth was getting back into her pickup and Emmy was sorry to see her leave and Beth could tell. Her mom would love the chance to visit with the two of them more but Emmy had other plans.

"Oh thank you, I think we were planning to go into the grocery store. Phoebe needs to mail some things before the post office closes."

"Gotcha, maybe next weekend, I'll be home again. I know my folks would like to have you."

Emmy was quiet in the passenger seat of the Mustang as they soared across the deserted highway. She wondered exactly how excruciating being hit by lightening was. Phoebe turned up the music as she cruised down the straight stretch of highway between towering hills and a standing water lake. She was wondering what her grandparents would say if she asked them for advice on how to avoid being the most attractive charge connection point for a bolt of lightening.

She needed to start using her grounding mat again, couldn't hurt anything. She had a question for Emmy.

"Do you think your mom was ever hit by lightening?"

"You know, you know she is really weird. Like electrically weird. Maybe that kind of fits!"

"I think she probably could have been. We should find out."

Neither of them really thought that Barb had been hit by lightning.

The grocery store was quiet after the noon rush. The lunch special was gone but Kathy made them ham sandwiches. The post office was even quieter.

"Do you need any stamps?"

The woman behind the counter didn't have to ask who they were or how they were getting along or if they liked their new community. She was a voracious gossip and she knew all of those answers. She felt a little intimidated, they were very beautiful city women. Phoebe wasn't in the mood for small talk anyway.

"No, thank you."

"Hey Phoebe, we should check out this greenhouse nursery next time we come to town, I bet they have all sorts of cool stuff coming on. I miss my plants."

Emmy was reading the notices and fliers pinned on the community bulletin board.

Phoebe's hair fell like a curtain as she leaned out to make sure no one was coming around the bend in the highway.

"I'm going to get some gas."

They pulled up to the historic looking station Emmy had seen on her very first trip to Dismal. She hadn't taken the time to look at it more closely again. The pumps were analog with pieces of tape adding a dollar placement to the price of a gallon of gas in front of two rattling spinning dials that marked the cents. A middle aged man in a gray felt cowboy hat emerged from the door when the white Mustang parked.

"Can I help you?"

Phoebe stepped out of the car and Emmy followed suit, her mind far away.

"Do you take cards?"

"Yes we do. Just go ahead and get your gas, you can see this one here is gas and that one is diesel. Then go inside and tell them your numbers here-"

He tapped the dials on the pump in a friendly sort of gesture.

"And they will ring it up for you."

Phoebe reached for the nozzle but the man beat her to it.

"Here I can do it for you this time, next time you'll know what to do."

He seemed a little awkward, he had given away that he already knew who they were.

Emmy thought he seemed very nice, he probably had a wife and teenagers at home.

"I'm Emmy Donahue."

She stepped forward to shake his hand and resolve the awkwardness.

"And this is my friend Phoebe."

Phoebe shook his hand too.

"Phoebe Laurent."

Emmy could feel people watching the exchange from behind the tinted windows and soon a woman came out to say hello and make introductions. Emmy thought she seemed really nice. She had only been a little bit wrong, he had a wife and teenagers here at the gas station. The gas station man in the cowboy hat was talking to Phoebe but then he turned back to her.

"I did business with your granddad for oh probably twenty years or more. He was a good cattleman, one of the best..."

As they visited with the couple Emmy felt the conversation layer and merge until only snippets were standing out to her.

"I heard you had come home, we're all so happy you decided to come back..."

Emmy smiled and nodded.

"Old Clyde had fuel barrels out there, do you think you will want bulk fuel?"

Emmy didn't know what that was. Luckily they didn't expect an answer.

"Well before fall gets here I'll make sure you're full up on propane..."

"I heard Nora went over to help you clean up a bit, you know I knew your grandma a very long time ago, back when she still went to church..."

"I delivered propane out there, you know, well probably for thirty years..."

The middle aged man pumping the gas for Phoebe didn't follow that up with, that place is so haunted it always scared the living hell out of me. How's that going for you? He just tried not to stare too much.

The woman was legitimately just as nice as they came, Emmy could tell.

"If you need anything, you just call here. We don't do a

lot for repairs, but we do tires and oil and that sort of thing but we'd try to help you with about anything and you can stop in anytime, we have the pop machines. Oh and there's bathrooms in there, you just stop in and say hi next time you come through..."

The pump made a satisfying click.

"Well that oughta just about do it for you. Your granddad told me a war story once that I never forgot..."

Phoebe was reminded of some place in the Australian outback or any desperate backwater place much farther off the grid than they actually were. Emmy was reminded of the Andy Griffith show.

Neither of them could make heads or tails of the story that Emmy's granddad had told the middle aged man back in the day. Things were just starting to get awkward again when the woman exclaimed with a puzzled look.

"I think I smell cigarette smoke, do you smell that?"

She looked at the two younger women and then at her husband. Emmy met Phoebe's gaze with a blank and worried look. They hadn't talked about the persistent cigarette smoke. They probably should have. Don smiled carelessly from the backseat of the Mustang. No one could see him. He was having the time of his life. Dismal never changed that much.

# 33

# Still Here

They were speeding down the highway when Emmy answered her phone, mouthing to Phoebe that it was Ashley. Phoebe kept her eye on the road as she nodded. The cell service was surprisingly good in this region.

Ashley had dialed the phone with dread.

"Hey, it's me."

Emmy had never heard Ashley sound quite the way she did now, like a scared Ashley and like a totally different woman underneath that, cold and detached. Reckless, even. That was the part that scared Emmy the most. Ashley's work had hardened and changed her personality through the years but Emmy noted the sudden severity of this change.

"What's wrong?"

"Someone burned down mom's gallery in Santa Fe."

"Oh my gosh. Oh my goodness. Is everyone okay?"

"Yeah, there was no one there."

"Phoebe someone burned down the Santa Fe gallery!"

Ashley could hear Emmy telling Phoebe. She imagined the two of them, they were millennial through and through.

"Ashley I'm going to put you on speaker phone, Phoebe is here with me. What do you mean burned it down? Surely they got it put out before it was totally gone? How do they know it wasn't an accident?"

Don leaned forward from the bench seat in the back of the Mustang to listen closely.

"I guess it burned up hot and fast. Listen Emmy, Phoebe, that happened first and then someone burned up mom's car."

Ashley felt constricted as she forced herself to say it. Before they were done galleries and cars would be the least of it. Emmy felt the tears. Phoebe wondered who was competent enough to complete either task in an upscale security setting like that without getting caught.

"She's been talking to the police. She called Allan to come get her. So she should be fine."

Ashley didn't believe much of what she was saying and Phoebe could tell. Don listened and then tilted his head back in a motion of conceited defense. No one would ever hurt his family while he was hanging around with time to spare. His face lit up with imagination at the challenge. The windmill tail spun in the stillness back at the ranch, clanking violently. No more being lost in the past. Interesting times were coming again for this ranch and for this family. That was why he was still here.

"I'm flying into a place called East River, can you come get me?"

Jolted back to the moment by the girls talking Don fought with the regret and frustration inside. From the sounds of the conversation someone had already come too close to hurting his family. Barb deserved better. That was the trouble with being a spirit, he was still just a man. What could he do about what was going on in Santa Fe? How could he protect Barb from here? What was she even needing protection from?

He felt saddened by how little he knew about Barb right now. They just weren't close anymore. Who would destroy her building and her car? Don bet that it had been a beautiful one too. She had good taste. What were they trying to prove? They must think they were pretty tough. He turned his head to look out the window reflectively as the scenery flew by and for him other scenes flickered in and out of the light playing on the glass.

# II

# Part Two

# 34

# Don Donahue

Dismal, Nebraska
April of 1951

"I'll have Don take a look at it. He has an edge on this sort of thing."

There were cars parked at the pumps in front of the gleaming filling station in Dismal and a uniformed young man pumping gas. Gregory, the owner was behind the counter inside. The side garage with the glass plated overhead doors was a world of tires and hoses, belts and oil. Out back of the filling station, working in the shade was Don.

Gregory counted on him. Customers knew him by name now and it wasn't just because of his family in Lena. Or just because of his rodeo fame. Or because of the scandal him and Ivory getting married had been. They knew him these days because he could work on almost anything. Modern, military or one of a kind it didn't matter, he had a valuable gift. That was what he would have chosen to be known for. Out of the public eye suited Don Donahue just fine.

Don felt his skin prickle as his stomach turned over in the wind. He wondered how many more days like this there were going to be for him. The world was changing again. He might be called overseas.

Don turned his head to listen to the hushing sound of the leaves. They sounded like God and a thousand little voices saying his name. They had cottonwood trees like this over on the south place where they were living. He felt that wherever Ivory was right now, she was listening to the cottonwood leaves too. She was thinking of him too. He wondered how her day was going, if she was happy. She had been headed over to the main place and then on a long water checking excursion in the spring wind.

He thought she was probably having the time of her life. She loved these sorts of days. He turned his attention back to the wire brush in front of him as the cool breeze brushed his shoulders. He was too.

# 35

# Ivory's World

The Heart Seven Ranch, Nebraska
April of 1951

Ivory was busy shooting glass pop bottles. They felt cool and smooth in her hands as she lined them up in the sand. Fragments and shards lay sharp and pressed into the sand under her boots. Virgil had designated this blow out high in the hills for target practice. He was the one that bought the ammunition and let her help herself to the gun safe in the downstairs hall at the main house. No one knew she had come here today but Virgil would have guessed.

The isolated trail called her back through the tall grass. The rain had been good this spring and the snow had been good before that and the grass was high and swaying. The pairs hadn't been turned out into this pasture very long. Ivory thought that this must be what Eden had been like. Hereford cows and red calves with brilliant white faces and liquid eyes peered at her. She drove slowly to look at them carefully, everyone was doing well. A gang of calves raced alongside her jeep as she drove on, playful at first and then stretched out running hard with tails high in the air, racing their friends. One by one they dropped off and turned back to find their moms.

Mothers and babies were on her mind. She had been visiting the spare bedroom lately, moving things around, placing one graceful hand on the antique cradle. Sitting in the matching rocking chair, she remembered her mother and soaked in the sunshine. Ivory didn't know what she wanted. She needed to make up her mind soon.

Ivory sped up as she bumped past yuccas, soap weeds, building their blooms. It was early yet. The wild roses hadn't come on. Next time she came this way there would be wildflowers galore. The far windmill was pumping fine. She made notes in a little book with a pencil. Virgil trusted her. He could have come himself, or sent Joe or Fred or any of the hired hands. He let her feel that she was a business partner in this vast enterprise, the way he had treated his mother. Ivory remembered her seated on a big palomino horse, wearing gloves and a hat with a stampede string. Grandma Kate had ridden these hills like a queen. Ivory hoped she could be half the cattle woman her grandma had been. Katherine Hart had built stability out of pure chaos and then established elegance to boot. Ivory swore to herself that it wouldn't fall apart in her care. At any rate, Virgil trusted her to do this task today. Ivory stowed her little book away, the roses hadn't even come on yet. When the time was right, when early spring shifted to early summer, they would drive the herds to the end of the ranch where her house was, to summer range.

High in the hills and then deep in the grass filled valleys Ivory drove on. A cool breeze buffeted her hair this way and that. She had started with a scarf and driving gloves but that hadn't lasted long. Enormous clouds sped by in the winds overhead. Their shadows came up fast behind her, then passed over causing the air temperature to drop and then they sped on ahead of her and the light was brilliant again. This was a wild and desolate place. This was her home.

That evening found Ivory tired but exhilarated, finishing up some stitching in her sewing room, putting together some supper over the stove, sitting in the bathtub filled with soap bubbles. Scrubbing her cuticles with a little brush she spoke softly.

"Thank you God."

Her life certainly didn't feel easy. But she was well aware of the many things she enjoyed that other women did not.

This had been her mother's house on the south end of the vast Heart Seven ranch and now it was her house. Every surface burnished to gleaming, every square foot in perpetual improvement. Her own home. Don would be home soon.

# 36

# Beneath A Cottonwood Tree

The Heart Seven Ranch - South Place
April of 1951

When Don got home from the filling station Ivory was wearing the newly stitched house coat and setting out plates on the table. He took it all in while he pulled off his boots, his feet were swollen and his socks stained with sweat and dirt. Then he rushed around the table and swept her up over his shoulder like a sack of potatoes. She laughed raucously and beat his back with her fists until he put her down. Ivory was a petite straight up and down sort of woman with an unexpectedly crude sense of humor.

Don wanted to take the red silky fabric between his fingers before he asked her about it but he kept his hands to himself, he had probably already gotten it dirty.

"You look like an Arabian spirit or a geisha girl or something."

Ivory was amused that Don couldn't narrow it down to even

a continent.

"It's incredible. How do you think of these things?"

She had pieced panels of floral embroidery and red lace into a narrow, floor length silhouette with a wide belt and a generous off the shoulder collar. There was even a matching hair ribbon. The sewing room was piled high with books. She could have told him how she thought of these things.

"Hmmmm. I don't know."

That first kiss was everything she hoped for. She entwined her long narrow fingers in his. The cracks in his hands were filled with black residue, mechanic's hands. He twirled the hair around her ear and when she started to talk pressed one finger to her lips. Don was skilled in romance and love.

Later that evening Ivory sat up in bed, the lamp on her side was the only light in the dark house. The bedroom was a corner room with one window facing south and one window facing east. Ivory kept the windows without shades or curtains so that the room felt a part of the wilderness outside of it. There was a large cottonwood tree rooted in the ground outside this corner so that the roots held the house from underneath and the branches held the house from above. When the wind moved in the leaves shimmers ran all through the studs and lathe and plaster of the house.

In the daytime this room was filled with light, but tonight it was very dark. There was no moon tonight. This room had been her parents' room. Ivory's thoughts flitted to another bedroom, the nursery. She remembered her mom as an eternal vision in cream crotchet and bisque lace. She had worn the most incredible house coat. Ivory tried to change her line of thinking. The crotchet coat was a fantastic piece of workmanship, silky and light. Ivory kept it draped over the carved rocking chair in the sunlit room with the door shut.

Don was sleeping the deep sleep of a happy young man that works hard. Ivory admired his chest falling up and down and the curve of his biceps and forearms. She pulled her knees up under her chin in contentment. Then she pulled out her nail polish and started work on her manicure for tomorrow. This was the most perfect shade of red, tomorrow was church. She had some ladies to scandalize.

# 37

# The New Church

Dismal, Nebraska
April of 1951

When Ivory shut off the car in front of the church she looked over her left shoulder and made eye contact with Doris. Doris grimaced a tight smile. Doris hated her guts. Ivory tried not to laugh at her situation, this was going to be one of those Sundays. She hadn't even gotten out of the car yet. Today was going to be a long one too, the service, Bible study and the potluck. Her obligatory apple crisp waited on the backseat. Ivory's red leather handbag coordinated perfectly with her red manicure and her buckled leather shoes. She wore pearl stud earrings and a hat with a tiny lace veil piece around the forehead. The handbag swung as she marched up the steep cement church steps, it was a brutal climb but Ivory never broke stride as she smiled and nodded to everyone in sight. Straight up the center of the pews to the very front pew on the left. This was in theory the family pew. This had been Grandma Kate's honorary place and Ivory's place on her right and now Ivory sat there alone.

Ivory had been in church every Sunday of her life. With her mom and her grandma they had made a happy threesome. After they lost her mom it had been just the two of them, somber at first but then companionable.

Ivory kept her eyes on the sparkling stained glass behind the alter, there were doves rising to the heavens above green hills. Her Grandma Kate had designed, and paid for, almost every aspect of this new church. Ivory remembered the years of thought and meticulous planning, the sketches Grandma Kate and Uncle Virgil had poured over on the kitchen table as they tried to envision the needs of a community far in the future. These were all the things the community didn't see. Still, Ivory thought it had all turned out rather well, from the dark blue velvet seat cushions in the pews to the lilac bushes outside. Her grandma was known for her lilac bushes.

The two of them had sat together in this new pew, after the church was finished, only a few times before Grandma Kate had passed away and Ivory was left alone. Hers had been the first funeral held in the new church. Every Sunday since that funeral Ivory had sat in the front pew alone. Coming to church was difficult. Still, she believed her grandma was right, a community needed a church and that required people putting in the effort. This work was their privilege and their responsibility. Now it was Ivory's responsibility. It had all made sense when Grandma Kate explained it. Ivory was not Katherine, no matter how much she wished that she could be.

Ivory could hear people chatting openly and people speaking in hushed voices behind her as she opened her hymnal ahead of time. She loved the new book smell and the blue linen texture of the covers, they even had gold embossed titles. She remembered unpacking these brand new hymnals.

The congregation had never felt the need to hide how they really felt about her. They had loved her mom and respected her grandma but in Ivory they finally found a target.

"Her Grandma never would have tolerated such behavior."

"I heard her husband was drinking in the bar again last Saturday."

"Her mother was so beautiful, always so elegantly dressed."

Unchallenged the momentum had grown until these days they barely bothered to lower their voices. Ivory sat ramrod straight and let her gaze soften over the large altar and rest on the handmade lace altar scarf. It was an even finer piece of workmanship than the house coat she kept in the nursery. Grandma Kate had said that church would be an easy place except for that it was made of people and people were difficult.

She let her warm feelings for her grandma and her mom well up in her heart and she offered them up to God. She had decided a long time ago that Sundays were for celebrating their lives, not missing them. Whatever happened, she never acknowledged the graveyard outside.

"The Heart Seven might be cutting off their financial support, we are going to discuss it at the board meeting."

"I suppose we could all look like that if we had that much money and free time."

Snippets floated up to Ivory in the front pew.

"Mom, where does she buy those shoes?"

That last one made Ivory snort and smile. She would have to tell Don about that. He would tease her for leading the young ladies of the congregation astray with colorful shoes. Ivory's face turned sad as the imaginary conversation played out in her head. Next she would feel bad because maybe her grandma would be disappointed in her wardrobe choices. Maybe her grandma would have thought she could have been a better example. Ivory sat extra straight and decided not to tell Don about it after all.

"It's all bravado. Underneath the spectacle she's not that pretty. She just wants attention."

"She's been like that since she was a little girl."

Ivory felt a little sting. She was no blonde beauty like her mom had been. Her hair was brown and her eyes were brown and she regularly took too much sun. Still, her outfits, her things, they were so much more to her than that. Color helped her to survive this dismal world.

Thank goodness the pastor was finally getting this service underway. Ivory fixed her imagination on her afternoon plans. Joe was coming over to help her with her new picket fence. She smiled and the tension in her shoulders relaxed a little. And of course Don would be home tonight, she wiggled a little in the pew to adjust her posture. Actually there was a lot to be thankful for in her life.

"So I heard Don was at the bar in Lena last Saturday night."

The sheriff was a tall square man. Ivory put a spoonful of beans onto his plate.

"Thank you sheriff. Don is home with me, every night."

The sheriff was a man of large stature. He was a nervous type, insecure that he could never stand up to her uncles or her grandfather the way that he felt that he should. Ivory sighed. So here they were.

He lowered his voice but Ivory felt the entire church basement listening.

"I won't have trash like Don bringing those problems here."

Ivory's armor started to crack as she sat the bean ladle down on a little holder so it wouldn't drip onto the tablecloth. Then the bean juice dripped onto the tablecloth anyway and she moved the ladle and made the pool of drippings worse. Then she moved the holder. She was just making a bigger mess of everything.

Deep in concentration, her own concern about the doomed tablecloth made her snort and then she started to nervous laugh, at herself, at the entire situation. At the stupid beans and the stupid tablecloth that she would try to get the stains out of and at the sheriff standing in front of her. She had been wrong to try to carry on without her grandma. They would all be better off if she stayed at the ranch. Her stressed laughter rang through the church and Doris watched everyone stare. That was the problem with Ivory, even laughing at the sheriff, she made condescension look easy. The minister prodded the sheriff on and Ivory ladled some beans onto his plate.

# 38

# Joe Hart

Dismal, Nebraska
April of 1951

Joe was waiting for Ivory when she left the church after all the dishes were washed in the new, modern kitchen in the large church basement. Most of the congregation had gone home from the potluck dinner.

He was twirling a showy white rope and jumping in and out of it, side to side in a beautifully fluid motion. Joe's trick roping was slow and mesmerizing. Kids were crowded around him.

Her grandparents had had three children. Virgil had been their oldest son, and then her mom Rose and then years later, Joe had been their youngest. He was a very athletic man in his twenties with a light heart and a youthful spirit. The age gap between them was more that of siblings than generations.

The kids dispersed ahead of Ivory and Joe hopped in the

passenger seat. As they pulled out of the church yard and turned down the lane with the new fence along the old prairie cemetery Joe offered her a stick of gum. Peppermint. She ignored him.

"Ah, come on. I know how much you love Sundays."

Ivory ignored him a little longer.

"It could make you feel better."

She took the gum between two fingers of her driving gloves with an exasperated look.

"You think it's that easy."

She was in a very bad mood. Joe was thinking about his horse. Joe slumped down enjoying the ride, staring out the passenger window at the grass and the sky. He had a bad feeling lately.

"It isn't?"

Ivory sighed as she chewed and drove, occasionally checking her lipstick in the mirror. Joe was the youngest son of the Heart Seven, situated somewhere far below his dad and older brother and far above the hired hands. He understood what she was trying to do, that's why he was there. He tried to do the right thing too. Even when there wasn't much hope for the situation. They drove on in companionable silence.

Joe and Ivory had driven together through some of the most difficult times of their lives. When Ivory had come to live with Fred and Kate and her uncles Virgil and Joe she had been just a kid. Joe had still been at the high school. So he had dropped her off at school in the mornings and driven them back home to the ranch in the afternoons.

Even after she had gotten her school driving permit he had still driven her sometimes, just because. Now that she was married and out of the house they didn't spend much time together. Joe looked out the window morosely. The world was about to change all over again. Ivory was starting to feel a little better, it had been really nice of Joe to come meet her.

"Thank you."

"Ah, don't mention it. For old times' sake if you will."

"How is Biscuit?"

Biscuit was Joe's horse.

"You'll have to ride him a little this spring and see for yourself. Smooth, very smooth."

Ivory started to talk animatedly about a picket fence gate at the end of the cement sidewalk and how far she wanted the fence to extend on either side and how it would look with the roses. Joe tried to shake the bad omens coming over him like a dark spring cloud.

"Do you wish you had this?"

Ivory gestured to the yard and house around her with her eyes and her arms, shovel in one hand. Don knew she meant more than the physical things around them. He shrugged and smiled with open hands held low.

"Maybe someday I will."

Ivory was intrigued and her voice rushed ahead of her harshly.

"Do you have a girlfriend?"

Joe laughed.

"I wouldn't tell you if I did."

He paused kindly before he corrected himself. He had spoken without thinking.

"No. Actually you'd probably be the first to know."

Ivory was contented.

"Good."

"Where do you think you would live?"

Joe shook his head at her.

"I haven't the slightest clue."

They finished the picket fence and the gate that afternoon.

They were sitting on the front step in the evening light when Don got home. He worked at the garage every day.

Joe hopped up and shook his hand with a spring in his step.

"Well I'll let you two get to your supper. Good to see you."

He grabbed Don's upper arm in a farewell gesture and bounded down the sidewalk humming a tune. He would have been at home in a variety show or song and dance chorus. Those that knew him best would have said that the happiest people are usually the saddest on the inside.

Don took Joe's place on the cement step and lit a cigarette. He was tired but glad to be home. When Joe had driven Grandma Kate's church car around the bend and out of sight Don lit a second cigarette for Ivory. She accepted it gratefully without looking at him.

"How was your Sunday, my wicked lady in red?"

His voice was dripping with drama. She smacked him playfully with her leather gloves and he grabbed her wrist and pulled her close.

"And I have a more important question for you, do you want me to play the piano tonight?"

"Yes. And I want to play poker too."

# 39

# The Last Happy Night

The Heart Seven Ranch, Nebraska
April of 1951

Don was as good as his word. He had learned to play from Ivory but these days he played far more often than she did. This was her mother's piano, a very old family heirloom complete with keys made from elephant tusk ivory. He thought that must have been where Rose got the idea for Ivory's name. Ivory had suffered through formal piano lessons as a child and played for the church on occasion. Don played dance hall tunes and simple classical pieces from Rose's sheet music stash. He managed to make it all sound languid and seductive.

Ivory sat cross legged on top of the piano lid, graceful as a cat and smoked her cares away. She imagined this was a saloon in Paris and that in this whole world there was just the two of them. She imagined this was Singapore and a fleet of ships and their contraband were the stakes in this poker game. Don made fun of the congregation until her laughter was broken with gasps for air and cries for him to stop. Overhead the cottonwood trees quivered in the dark.

Don's voice broke the contented silence between them.

"Sweetheart, do you want to have kids?"

Don had stopped with the horseplay and was stretched out on the floor, his eyes fixed on the closed bedroom door with the rocking chair behind it. Ivory thought she was lucky to be with someone who knew her so well.

"I have been thinking about it."

She admitted it reluctantly.

"I think I do want to be a mom. Maybe just not yet. Maybe in a year or two."

Don nodded and smiled before rolling over to grab her in a roar of laughter and giggles.

Ivory's playing cards from the 1920's were spread across the quilt and scattered on the bedroom floor where they had fallen. Don was asleep in a heap where he had fallen. Ivory was looking at the plaster ceiling and the trim work, wide awake. Over at the main place calving was in full swing and calves were bellering for their mothers. Some old cowboy would get up in the night and check the herd with a flash light under all of God's stars. There at the south end of the ranch on the summer range Ivory's world was silent.

What a day, how could she go to sleep now?

In May they would brand and sort and move the herds by early morning light. Ivory looked forward to the coming weeks, she would ride her horse Blue almost every day. Blue was not a blue roan. Her grandfather Fred and her uncle Virgil had carefully chosen a well mannered gelding for Ivory after shopping for over a year. Then before the deal was done Grandma Kate had changed their minds. She had been peeling potatoes in the kitchen with her back to them.

"You know that would be a fine horse for Ivory. But you two need to think about what Ivory would actually want. What would make her happy? Not just make you two happy."

When Virgil brought home the golden yellow and white pinto with the eyes like a bandit and the exaggerated mane and tail, Fred thought he was the ugliest horse that had ever been on the place. He said as much too. Both men were still thinking about the little blue roan gelding with the conformation and the smooth gate.

"We'll call him Blue."

Virgil said it without a touch of humor. Fred never gave the sorry excuse for a horse another thought. Ivory was ecstatic and Grandma Kate was proud.

When she drifted off to sleep in her mind's eye she was horseback high in the hills with the wind to her back and the sun coming up in front of her. She didn't know that this would be their last happy night together in the little house under the cottonwood tree on the south place of the Heart Seven ranch.

# III

# Part Three

# 40

# Nowhere To Run

The Heart Seven Ranch - South Place
April of 1951

Don saw her hands shaking and Ivory saw him notice.

"I haven't been feeling good, the last couple days. Nothing to worry about."

"It's been a long time since you've seen a doctor."

Don tried to keep the panic out of his voice. Ivory had never seen a doctor.

Ivory chewed her words before speaking.

"I think I will go to Denver, just once."

The Hart family had gone as far as New York and even San Francisco to see doctors before Rose had passed away. For Don that morning was the beginning of the end.

"Virgil could take me. So you don't have to ask Gregory."

That afternoon Ivory talked to Virgil and called a doctor she remembered taking her dying grandma to. The one that she had liked.

Standing alone out in the horse pasture Ivory looked to the hills rising around her home. The horses stood close around her. The Sandhills were a home like a forgetful mother. Robust and brimming with wealth but a person could certainly starve or freeze to death here. Without the man made landmarks, there was no way to keep your way.

Ivory knew she was in for the fight of her life. She was afraid of pain and a long drawn out demise. She was afraid of losing courage.

Would she be brave enough to do a good job of dying when it came to that? She had been set the best examples by her mother and grandmother. In so many ways she was still standing by their graves. The horses around her stirred uneasily. The graveyard in Dismal called out to her and fright shivered down her back. Crows circled above the little piece of hard ground.

# 41

# Into The Dark

The Heart Seven Ranch, Nebraska
April of 1951

That night at the supper table Virgil told his younger brother Joe and his aging father that Ivory was sick. The three men ate every meal together in the kitchen of the big house. Virgil cooked and the fare did not vary. The once glorious kitchen had been reduced to a stark and empty place without Katherine and Ivory there.

Fred could tell by the feeling in the air that tonight was different. Tonight felt like an oil lamp night from a long time ago. Even though the house had been wired for electricity Fred kept the lamps where they had always been. This felt like an oil lamp night, once the light went out, there would be nothing but the deepest darkness until morning. Virgil was clearing the dishes when he gave the terrible news in the best way that he knew how.

"I will be taking Ivory to Denver in a few days. Shouldn't be gone long."

The house was so quiet Joe could hear the moon moving in the sky and his own heartbeat stopping. Virgil continued on in his measured tone.

"She has not been feeling well. The pairs in the east pasture..."

Joe walked out of the kitchen. Outside in the meadow Joe looked up at the stars. He could not listen to the monotony. He could not pretend the pain away. The stars cocooned in around him, so close and so full of life. God was right there in these stars. Joe could see God all around him in the starlight as plain as day.

How could he feel alone? He held out his hand as if to an unseen angel. How could any of us ever feel alone?

Joe bowed his head, holding the stars humming light all around him in his mind's eye. Then he lifted his head and spoke plainly to the stars.

"God, I can't bear this. Please don't let her die. She has so much life to live. I would rather go. If that is your will, please let it be so."

Back in the main house Fred was left to wander the empty rooms. Virgil had gone to bed and Joe had left for a walk. Fred Hart was an old man now. He had inherited this ranch from his father and he had strengthened it into the empire called the Heart Seven. He had raised two sons and lost one daughter. Downstairs in the library off the hall Fred stared out the long narrow windows into the dark. He missed Katherine. He had lost the love of his life.

Katherine had kept a chess board for him. She kept it set out on a side table near the fireplace. A master of strategy and memory, he had never touched the thing. He didn't need to. He stared at it when they tried to save Rose. He stared at it when they tried to save Katherine. Now he just stared out the windows into the dark with the chessboard forgotten behind him. Ivory would be with her mom and her grandma soon. Long before he would be.

Upstairs Virgil glanced out a bedroom window into the darkness on the other side of the house. In a little book he scrawled with a pencil the miles to Denver, the time of the appointment, he looked at the name of the doctor. Older little books sat neatly in tidy stacked piles nearby, waiting for him. Daily journals from when his mother Katherine had fought this disease, medications names and dosages, addresses of the experts, his own observations. Against his will his mind flitted briefly to the death certificates where he kept them in the downstairs safe. That was all he had been left with in the end.

The valleys and meadows nestled all around the three of them, the moon pulled the tides in the aquifer beneath their feet. Bonnie the collie dog yapped at the coyotes from her secure position on the front porch. The scrappy little scavengers cackled like witches goading each other on, closing in around them.

# 42

# A Girl Alone In The Wind

The Hammond Ranch, Nebraska
August of 1951

From the hill behind her house Doris Hammond could see the trees behind Ivory's barn. They had been neighbors and to some extent friends. Doris both despised and stood in awe of the enterprise that was the Heart Seven. She was milking cows to make ends meet. They were filling entire trains of cattle cars with yearlings bound for the hungry cities. Her parents had come here after the first war. The Harts had been here before the pioneers. To see anything at the scale that they operated in captured the imagination. Doris hated herself for even looking.

Then there was her neighbor Ivory. Their lives were very different despite being very much the same. Doris had four children that ruled her days and nights. Ivory had no babies. Doris was often tired, strict and cross. Doris felt the lack of money and security. She was aging quickly. She felt that Ivory put on too many airs. The way Ivory always showed up well rested, perfectly groomed and alone, with no one to attend to, grated on Doris' nerves. Of course Ivory was able to help with this project and that committee, do the dishes and sweep the floors and tend the flowers. She didn't have anything else to do.

Ivory had the time and she certainly had the resources, why couldn't she find some shoes and handbags and coats in nice shades of tan or blue or even yellow like the rest of us? Who wore a red hat to church of all places? She was just looking down on women like Doris. Complaining about Ivory to her husband was one of Doris' favorite distractions and he tolerated it. He was often the focus of her unhappiness and he welcomed the relief.

Now Doris had a memory she couldn't shake. Ivory had missed church and there had been rumors that she wasn't feeling well. Doris had been telling her husband all about it during the evening milking.

"There isn't a thing wrong with that girl! She is just so very self centered. If she would stop feeling sorry for herself and thinking about her mom and her grandma all the time and worrying she would be just fine."

Doris spoke with the bitterness that was welled up inside her.

"You wait and see, she is going to make herself sick just by thinking about it. She is going to get what she deserves."

Her long suffering husband stopped to set down the milk pail and stare at her and it occurred to Doris for the first time that maybe she had crossed a line. She carried on so much that she didn't realize she was doing it anymore. Her husband hadn't said a word because he hadn't needed to.

Doris remembered the incident when she and the kids got the milk cows in off the high hills behind the house every night and she saw the trees over at Ivory's place. That poor girl was probably over there right now.

Ivory tried to attend church but it had become impossible. The congregation was privately relieved and then internally horrified at their relief. It had been disturbing to see just how much her condition had deteriorated from one Sunday to the next. Doris had heard a rumor that Ivory had chosen to die at home. So she was certainly over there right now. Probably alone, dying alone. Doris shuddered. Her kids were singing loudly, rough housing and picking on each other. Doris hadn't been alone in years. In that moment she was thankful for her children.

Doris was milking her second cow and watching the barn cat kittens play. There was an all white one with two black front feet that was especially cute. They had never a cat with markings like that. No one had. Then in a moment of inspiration Doris knew what to do. She needed to make a trip into town to the fuel station.

Doris Hammond might spend the rest of her days living in the shadow of an empire that didn't care but Ivory was just a girl in the wind and the grass. Before all the babies she had been just a girl too. Just a girl alone in the wind and the grass. Well Ivory would not be alone. Doris would make sure of that, one way or the other.

# 43

# Mittens The Kitten

The Heart Seven Ranch- South Place
August of 1951

Don carried a worn out wicker basket carefully into the hot and silent kitchen of their home. The kitten let out a questioning meow and he shushed it.

Ivory's eyes were open when Don eased the bedroom door open. The corner bedroom was filled with golden afternoon sun that shifted as the leaves moved outside the windows. A glance at the nightstand told him she hadn't eaten anything since he had been gone. He sat down beside her on the bed and opened the lid of the basket.

Don didn't know what Ivory would think, how she would react. Ivory loved fun above all things. She just wanted to have a good time and forget the world. Don knew that better than anyone. Now he was at a loss. Now she was angry and taciturn. He couldn't blame her.

She tried not to acknowledge Don and the basket. She tried not to lean over and look inside. The kitten was peering out at them shyly from the shadows, he didn't know what to expect either. Then Ivory wrapped her long pale hands into that white fur and lifted him out of the basket and into the air. The kitten looked around inquiringly. Then he locked eyes with Ivory in a sort of understanding way. They were two of a kind.

Don swore that in that moment that that kitten understood the situation completely. Ivory was looking at his white face and his black front feet, holding one and then the other playfully. She looked up at Don.

"So unusual."

"Doris Hammond dropped him off at the garage today."

"Doris?"

Ivory sounded surprised but she didn't stop petting the whiskers on the little snow white face in front of her.

"She said that she thought you would like him."

"Well she was right. I've never seen anything like you."

Ivory shrugged before holding the kitten out in front of her again.

"What are you going to call him?"

"I think I'll go with the obvious choice, Mittens."

Ivory nuzzled the fur on top of his head with her nose and the kitten started licking her hand. They were the only two in the world right now.

"I think Mr. Mittens needs some cream, don't you?"

Her eyes flashed up to his in adoration, just like they used to.

Don barely made it to the kitchen before the grief in his throat started to choke him. He loved her so much. He wanted the old Ivory back. He missed her so much already.

The next day Mittens sat in bewilderment and then hid slyly under the bed but he never took his eyes off his new mistress. She slid down onto the braided rug beside her bed and started ripping pieces of paper out of a book and then ripping the pages angrily into tiny little pieces. She wanted to throw the book but she was too weak for that to make much of an impact. Oh how she wished she had some scissors. The quilt on the bed would have been next. The complete destruction of the book took a long time, it had been a new one left on her night stand.

Then Ivory dozed off sitting up and she struggled for each inhale. Her skin was turning a shade of oatmeal. The bed sheets slid off the bed with her and now her chin nodded on her bony collarbone. Don wasn't keeping up with the laundry and her nightgown was stained. Ivory's hair was dirty and thinning. Don tried to keep it braided back off her face so she wouldn't notice but she pulled out the braid and let it hang despairingly around her face.

"I hate you God."

She whispered vehemently as she ripped the pages into ever smaller pieces. She couldn't find the words for the truth raging inside of her. The truth was the pain of betrayal.

"You hurt me God. Why can't I live?"

Mittens crawled up on her leg and snuggled himself near those thin hands for a very long nap until Don came home.

Ages passed as Don walked up the front walk. All day he had thought about the desert. Strange visions like heat mirages flitted across his imagination and in the corners of his eyes. Everything had gone to hell. Now he was home. He remembered how much Ivory loved vulgarity and wild behavior. He smiled because he was one of the few people who knew the extent of it. She loved to smoke cigarettes and play poker in their living room. She loved to go dancing and she loved to dance at home. She loved to drive too fast, he frowned. She had loved him. She was proud to be with him.

Don loved being the only one that could give her what she truly wanted. Most of the time that was freedom. She wanted to be herself or whoever or whatever she thought she wanted to be at the time. She loved to cuss, my God how she loved vulgar language. His dainty little wife would cuss up a storm and then pause to look at him and then they would laugh. She had been his best friend. He was thinking of her in the past tense. He was thinking of all the things only he knew. Of all the things he loved about her that he would not get to say at her funeral.

There was a certain burden and loneliness in being the only one that knew Ivory in that way. She loved him for it though. Don stood a little straighter. He knew in the depth of his soul how much Ivory adored him. Just him, for who he really was. He missed her so much.

Don had been angry all day and then pensive and now his hand shook a little on the front door knob. All the emotions were making him so tired. He slept in an old rocking chair he had brought into their room. He couldn't abandon her but he couldn't bring himself to sleep in the bed next to her anymore.

Dishes and laundry piled up and remained and he was too tired to care. The church ladies had deserted the cause and he didn't blame them. It was better for Ivory this way. More protected from the relentless gossip. He didn't intend to stay after the funeral, the entire congregation could come close up the house for all he cared. For a moment he wondered if there was anything he wanted to take with him when he left. His shoulders jerked hard. He just wanted to take her with him.

Don finally stepped through the front door and it all hit him exactly the way he knew it would. Only his dedication kept him from going right back outside. What was it like to be Ivory right now? How could God bring her any lower? Bring them any lower? Don choked on his own suppressed tears as anger burned inside him all over again. He was getting so tired. The August heat was making him think about the desert.

# 44

# Joe Is Going To New Mexico

The Heart Seven Ranch- South Place
August of 1951

Joe remembered his sister dying. He remembered the sunshine in these lace curtains. He remembered the finality of it all, the separation and the emptiness. He would never be able to speak to her again. They had all been right here in this room.

Joe spoke from the kitchen chair he had brought in next to the bed. He twirled his straw hat between his hands.

"So, I wanted to tell you first."

Ivory leaned forward in anticipation, a sort of ghost of her old self.

"What? Did you meet someone?"

"No."

Joe snorted a little laugh, Ivory was nothing if not persistent. She thought he needed an epic romance and a family of his own. Likely she was right. Joe measured his breathing, this smell reminded him of when his mother had died.

"I've decided to go to New Mexico."

Ivory looked at him for a moment in surprise, lost in thought. Then she grinned.

"You are going in search of wild cowboy adventures."

Joe smiled back cautiously.

"I guess I am."

His heart was breaking.

"Why New Mexico? Why not Arizona? Or Montana? Montana would be prettier. Cooler."

Ivory was clearly taken with Montana. Joe had been worried that she would ask why now but Ivory was smarter than that. Joe hesitated to answer her question only a moment.

"I wouldn't tell everybody this but I'm having these, moments of vision, if you will. Of the heat in the desert. There's something in New Mexico that we need."

That you need. Joe kept that last part in his heart.

Ivory looked happily scandalized at this news.

"How exciting! I bet you will fall in love down there too!"

Ivory wanted Joe to bring home the most beautiful and interesting woman. She couldn't wait to meet her. Joe could see the entire progression of thoughts on Ivory's face. Maybe they would be friends? Maybe that would be too much too ask. No, actually that wouldn't do at all. Still she couldn't wait to meet this wonderful new person in their lives. Maybe Joe would make it home before she died and Ivory could meet her. This way she would have something to look forward to. They would have beautiful little children. She could see their little faces already. A tear slid down Ivory's face.

"Oh stop that."

Joe's voice was gentle and he grabbed her hand bracingly like he was offering a man on the ground a hand up. Ivory smiled and dabbed her face, a little embarrassed. He very much doubted he was being called to New Mexico to fall in love so he continued on.

"I don't think that's it at all."

Ivory smiled pragmatically as if she knew better. Joe was never going to fall in love if he lived his whole life being afraid of losing family. She had never let being afraid of death hold her back from living a full life. She looked around her, she had made a pretty good run of it all. Joe would too when the time was right.

Ivory was so glad Joe had come to tell her in person. She hadn't known that she missed him.

"I'm so glad you told me first."

She snuggled down like a reassured child, at peace for the first time since her fate had overtaken her. She wanted to ride Blue one more time before she died. But now she knew, after she died Joe would keep going.

He would have the family that she had wanted. Maybe they would even live here. This was a handy little place. And maybe God would let her be an angel auntie. Maybe Joe would have daughters that rode their horses too fast and loved target shooting. Maybe it all wouldn't be so bad after all.

For once Joe had absolutely no idea what she was thinking but he could see that whatever it was, she had found her peace.

# 45

# An Uncanny End

Heart Seven Ranch Headquarters, Nebraska
August of 1951

Saying goodbye to the hills was harder than Joe thought it should be. He knew deep down that he would never be coming back. He would never be coming home. His soul wanted to desert him. To leap from his body and stay here, a wild thing in the deep meadows. While his body went on to an uncanny end.

If he was called to service he could travel to where they wanted him from New Mexico just as well as he could from here. Joe thought that anyone that knew him at all would know that. He was not the sort to run away from anything. Why shouldn't he see a little more of the country while he waited? What was a few weeks here or there? What he needed in New Mexico was no one's business but his own.

Fred felt that his youngest son was deserting this land, their family and his duty to them. Without Kate there to correct him, he had said as much. Joe felt that his father had reacted as expected. Virgil thought that his dad and his little brother felt things too strongly.

Joe spent the early morning walking in the August fog. He felt that there were angels walking all around him. He said goodbye to Biscuit.

"If you leave us now, don't ever come back."

Joe let his eyes fall to the side. He couldn't explain why he thought so but he knew for sure that he would never be coming home again. He hated to leave his dad upset like this. He hated for it all to end with so much misunderstanding and hurt feelings. Maybe his dad would understand later on.

"I won't."

Joe stepped down into the car. His friend Roger was driving. Virgil shook his hand.

"Take care of yourself now."

Roger put the car in gear.

"Take care of Biscuit for me. And I'll miss you both."

# 46

# Virgil Hart

Heart Seven Ranch Headquarters, Nebraska
August of 1951

Today Virgil was going to mail a letter to Joe, he didn't expect it to do any good but he had sealed the envelope all the same. Almost enough time had gone by. Maybe Joe was almost ready to come home.

The sun was just starting to come up and Virgil's reading glasses lay discarded on top of a pile of ledgers. His bedroom window faced east. The man at the desk had a purposeful build and creases were starting in the corners of his eyes. This had been his childhood bedroom. Now it was sparse and tidy. A place where a forty year old man slept hard on a hard cot and spent hours on the books and day to day finances of a mighty cattle operation at a small desk in front of a window facing the rising sun.

He thought about cattle prices. They were up but would the

increase be enough after he adjusted for the coming inflation. He thought about water for the cattle. He thought about weather patterns and drought levels. He thought about the hay crop and the hay that had been put up. He thought about replacement heifers and bull purchases. He thought about the quality of the cattle herd. He thought about the political environment and the railroad.

Taxes were high, shipping costs were higher. He thought about the bank accounts of the Heart Seven and the interest rates. They would be wise to expand with another land purchase rather than hold too many assets in the bank. He thought about possible acquisitions.

He thought about repairs and supplies and purchases and bills to be paid. He thought about the seasons, what needed to be done, what had to be done, this week, next week, last week and this week next year. He thought about the day unfolding in front of him. He thought about the day's work, he thought about the horses, the machinery, the hired men. He thought about the community and the Heart Seven's place in it. He thought about the future of Dismal.

He thought about his dad, presumably asleep downstairs. His dad was wasting away without his mom. Virgil supposed that was to be expected. He thought about his brother Joe's future and where he was this morning. He thought about his sister Rose in heaven and the memory of them as children. He smiled. He thought about his mom in heaven and how this ranch had run when she had been here. He looked forward to her lilac bushes blooming next spring. He thought about

Rose's daughter Ivory, over on the south place. These days he thought about Ivory more than anything else.

He pinched the bridge of his nose with his left hand in concentration. He was a man that knew there was a right way in front of him somewhere and that he must have the self discipline to find it. Rose had died, his mom had died, Ivory was laying over there right now dying.

Virgil was a natural pessimist. Still, he would never hang his head in defeat and yet he was fatigued. The sun was up now and he strode down the stairs to the front door of the ranch house quietly, stamped and addressed letter in his hand. He would get this outfit rolling and then he would drive to town to mail this letter to Joe. He needed Joe to come home. Joe ought to come home. Joe probably wouldn't come home.

# 47

# Fred Without Katherine

Heart Seven Ranch Headquarters, Nebraska
August of 1951

While Virgil had been at his desk on the east side of the house, Fred had been at his desk in his study on the west side of the house on the main floor. He had no letters to write or ledgers at hand, that was all behind him now. He didn't have anything more to prove. Sock footed he tilted back in his fine wooden swivel chair and stared at the ceiling in the dawning light. Handsome double doors opened to the left at the foot of the dark carved staircase. The house was enormous and silent.

His parents had built this house about the time he and Katherine had gotten married. For them it had been a monument that said the wealth in Dismal was as fine as the wealth on the east coast. His mom had lived a little longer than his dad, not a lot longer. They had enjoyed this home very much. They had both been born in dugouts. For them this house was a symbol of something very important. Kate had taken excellent care of every aspect of this place, everything had smelled new an extra long time. Now the mansion was empty and quiet.

Fred missed his wife Kate so much that he was withering away. He thought a little about his daughter Rose passing away and he thought about his granddaughter Ivory's illness but his thoughts always came back to Kate. He was becoming a useless old man and he knew it but he was too sad to care. He reached for his boots, he could hear Virgil starting down the stairs.

# 48

# Virgil Mails A Letter

Heart Seven Ranch Headquarters, Nebraska
August of 1951

Virgil's faithful rough collie dog met him on the last front porch step, the dog's name was Bonnie. Ivory had given him Bonnie the puppy at Christmas, a few years ago now. Virgil scratched her ear briefly in greeting. She was a big long haired thing but quiet and wise. Letter and checkbook in his left hand he had other things on his mind.

When he slid the letter across the post office counter he fought the urge to snatch it back and rip it up but he allowed a reserved smile for the post mistress instead. She saw Virgil often but had never seen him express any emotion whatsoever. The smile struck her as odd.

"Nice morning."

He offered in a polite even measured tone.

She didn't reply with anything more than a cautious look. The letter disappeared and the deed was done now. She handed him the ranch's mail but his mind was already far away.

Virgil took the time to visit a little at the bank. He withdrew cash to pay the hands and transferred a donation to the church account. He had continued on with the tithe his mother had offered. It was an arrangement he preferred be kept between himself and the church treasurer and the church board and the bank, which ended up meaning everyone and their dog. Virgil dropped his shoulders to relax a little, there were just some things he could not control.

He needed to get back to the ranch but he took the time for one more stop, likely no one was missing him anyway. Virgil put flour, coffee beans and ammunition on the counter by the cash register. Then his sad imagination finally ran away with him. For many years now he had bought ammunition and set it next to his ammunition on top of the gun safe in the downstairs hallway. Ivory would take what she needed from there for her target practice and Fred and Kate wouldn't need to know. She probably did spend too much time target shooting. Virgil bought the shells and set them there for her anyway. He wouldn't need to restock that supply. The mercantile manager was speaking to him but Virgil couldn't hear what the man was saying.

Virgil bent over the long mahogany counter writing the check to cover the charge accounts when he remembered something else. He needed to order in a new hat. The store lady brought out a catalog and he stowed away his aviator sunglasses and brought out his horn rimmed reading glasses. His hand started to shake imperceptibly as he tried to turn the catalog page. The store lady took the catalog back.

"Something formal, something gray."

She said she would let him know when it came in. She didn't say that if she ordered it today Virgil's new hat might be here in time for the funeral. She would do her best.

He was about to turn the Sunday car out of town when he stopped in the road, backed up and turned around. There was no getting around it. He parked at the pump in front of the filling station but Don was not there. Virgil had not expected him to be. He proceeded inside and tipped his hat when old Gregory spoke.

"He's out back patching a tube."

Virgil strode and picked his way politely through the auto garage and out the back door into the shade by a hydrant and stock tank. Don looked terrible. His eyes were sunk in, his shop uniform wasn't sharp the way Ivory did it. Don shook his hand. He was glad to see Virgil but there wasn't anything to say.

"Does, does Ivory need anything? I could take a package over to her. On my way home."

Don grimaced in a kind of warm emptiness. The only thing Ivory needed at this point was a faster ride to heaven but the doctor wasn't administering morphine yet. What could you bring a dying woman who deserved the world? Virgil stumbled on.

"Could I bring her something to eat? Is she eating?"

"No. She drinks a little water sometimes."

The world was quiet around them, even the garage was silent.

"Any problems with the doctor?"

Don's stomach flipped over and over.

"He won't give her the heavy drugs yet. But she wants them."

Don hung his head slightly.

"She still has a long road before this is all done."

Virgil wanted to turn away, walk out through the garage and to his car.

"She must need a lot of care. Can we get one of the ladies from the church?"

Don cut him off.

"She would hate that."

Virgil privately agreed.

"Would you stay at home with her, if..."

Virgil trailed off as he looked around the garage. There was a time when the suggestion would have gotten an angry response out of Don but there was a sort of peace in total emotional exhaustion.

"I don't think either one of us would like that very much."

Virgil had a brief image of Ivory and Don sitting in the silence, waiting for death to come along, one of these days. He gagged a little in the back of his throat and started to leave.

"Should I stop and see her today?"

Don shrugged with that same warm emptiness, he didn't have any more answers. Or any answers at all. There was nothing you could do with fate but slowly find out just how much pain your soul can survive.

# 49

# Virgil Visits Ivory

The Heart Seven Ranch- South Place
August of 1951

Virgil drove so slowly that a horse at a walking trot could have kept up with his car. He turned down the gravel road toward the south end of the ranch. This was the part used as summer range and his day to day business did not bring him to Ivory's yard. The car puttered and eased to the gentlest of stops in the dust outside the picket fence. Would she know he was here? Hat down, sunglasses in place he strode up the cement walk and knocked softly. He opened the door a crack and called aloud.

"Ivory?"

The smell hit him the way that he had known it would. Virgil had been through all of this before. The house was quiet, would he find her passed away? Would today have been the day? No, they probably wouldn't get that lucky.

He crept into Don and Ivory's house, a house Fred owned on the south place of the Heart Seven. He set his boot heels down gently on the linoleum and leaned in to peer into the bedroom off the kitchen as politely as possible. She was sleeping. Her hair was stringy and matted. The white pillowcase and sheets were stained. Virgil felt no judgment. Her skin was a bad color and texture, her hands were looking thin.

Virgil had to agree with the doctor, they weren't there yet. He could hear a fly somewhere in the empty house. Sunlight was pouring through the rustling leaves outside the window making beautiful light patterns cascade over the room. Virgil thought it was like a sacred sanctuary in one of the magnificent churches of Europe.

When his sister died, it had been right here. Virgil had picked up the little girl Ivory and carried her out of there. In their grief he built a new family. His mom and his dad, his younger brother and their little niece Ivory, together they had forged ahead for years. Now he could not pick her up and carry her out and build her something happy and safe. He had to let God do that. He stayed there and watched her sleep until the sun had moved on from the window but she did not stir. Virgil felt helpless and alone.

# 50

# Bring Joe Home

Heart Seven Ranch Headquarters, Nebraska
August of 1951

Evening found Virgil and Fred at the supper table in the ranch house kitchen. Virgil put beans, bacon and beef on two plates while Fred read the local newspaper with his ankles crossed.

"I want you to bring Joe home."

Fred spoke into the silence, he had an articulate exacting voice.

Virgil arranged the lids on the stove.

"Joe will come home when he is ready, not any sooner."

His dad knew that.

Fred appeared not to have heard him.

"He belongs here. He has responsibilities."

Virgil didn't reply but started eating instead. His dad continued.

"You could go down there. You could bring him home."

Virgil raised his eyebrows over his evening coffee cup, he was aging. Short of kidnapping his younger brother and hauling him home in the back of the car there wasn't anything he could do to make his younger brother come home. He didn't say that to his dad or tell him about the letter he had mailed that morning.

"I know you can get him to come home, somehow."

Virgil waited to see if his dad was going to ask about Ivory, or Don, but the meal stretched on and not another word was said.

# IV

# Part Four

# 51

# MFTR

MFTR, New Mexico
August of 1951

Coyotes slipped along the ground in the dark. The sky stretched enormous from ridge to butte and beneath that all the deep inky blues reflected and were gently held in the shadows.

Before eminent domain this piece of desert had been the McAllister ranch. Now the McAllister family was gone from this place. Going forward this forsaken piece of ground would be called the McAllister Federal Testing Range.

The secret military base beneath the ground was much larger than even the locals guessed at. Actually it was so big that the human mind had trouble conceiving of the size of that complex beneath the butte. Nuclear reactors required a lot of space in that day.

A man in a bunkhouse over on the neighboring Landin ranch tossed and turned as bad dreams racked his body and dark memories stalked his mind.

# 52

# Reno's

New Mexico
August of 1951

Part sandwich counter and part mercantile, Reno's was the picture of dirt covered patriotism in motion. The aqua painted windows weren't tight. Chloe kept the mahogany bar, a relic from more than a century ago, and all the shelves behind it sparkling. The rest she let go to hell. Reno's saw a surprising amount of traffic and Chloe was a one woman show. God knew what it was actually called, to Otto, it was Reno's.

Otto planned to stop by to visit with Chloe for a while, if she wasn't too busy. She knew everyone and everything that went on. She was a bright kid, fun. As Otto stepped in from the heat the quiet angle of Joe's hat caught his eye. Joe reminded him of the Montana cowboys he had known back in the day. The way he handled a rope was softer, slower. Like time moved more slowly for him. Otto knew from the gossip that Joe had been running with the kid Roger that Callahan's hired sometimes.

The two of them were leaned against the counter, talking to Chloe, much as Otto usually did.

Joe looked like a scholar next to Roger but Roger had never won any smarts contests. Chloe looked like a flower. Her pink lipstick complimented the bright blues and soft muted greens in the painted wood behind her. Her earrings glittered against her dark hair as she moved this way and that, still working at top speed. She was laying it on thick, pursing her mouth in the shadow of a pretend pout. Otto laughed to himself.

Joe first met Otto at Reno's. Roger had been chatting with the waitress behind the counter at the soda shop, her name was Chloe. The girls down here were something else, a different world of beauty. They matched the brutal landscape, awe inspiring and demanding all of your attention. Reno's was pure magic to Joe, from the cobalt blue front door with the chili pepper riastras on either side to the smell of brewing coffee, tobacco, hard candy and peppermint. Everything was extra down here.

If only Ivory could have seen this place. The way Chloe dressed, those two would have been friends. Ivory would have taken it all home with her in her eyes. Then she would have made new dresses. She could have shown those Dismal women what wild really looked like. Ivory would have loved New Mexico. Joe was waiting for news of her death.

Joe heard Otto's spurs first. Then he saw the subtle leather boots. Silver from the spurs flashed in the sunlight behind a glass display case, the dark leather highlighted against the red and cream linoleum. Otto walked softly like a cat but absentmindedly in a good natured sort of way. He was an ageless cowboy, one that had seen too much in the war. He looked like he knew everything that went on in the desert and was pleased with himself about it. Otto shook his hand warmly.

"Knew a kid that roped like you once, from northern Montana. He never hurried."

"Never been up there. Good to meet you."

Chloe brought Otto a cup of coffee and he settled into his usual spot. The gleaming cash register shattered behind them as Chloe took cash from a man in uniform.

"Saw you last week, I'm Otto, over with Landin's-"

Otto had known what and who Joe was from the moment he had seen him.

"Joe Hart, from Nebraska."

Chloe let the conversation fade behind her. There was something about Joe. He was a soft touch sure, transparent to a fault. He was in some kind of trouble, some kind of pain. He was smart, educated and she liked the way he spoke and the kinds of words he used. He was a thoughtful man. She wanted to touch his face.

Just then a group of active military men came down the steps into the sun filled canteen. No one in either group wanted to make eye contact and the newcomers found stools further down the bar. Chloe got a pencil from the cash register and jerked her head at Otto to get out. She had things she wanted to find out.

"Roger I want to see this kid throw a loop again. They know a different kind of poetry up north than we do here."

Roger put some coins on the counter. He would have to come back and buy cigarettes later that Saturday night. Otto was right to give the soldiers from the base a wide berth, top secret was nothing to get too close to. Roger didn't need any trouble. The bell on the door rang brightly as the three cowboys stepped out and up into the adobe lined street. The light was starting to drift toward evening. Chloe leaned her neck to see them out the window. Joe was stepping through his own loop like he had all the time in the world. That man could practically stop for coffee between flicks of his wrist. She hoped to see quite a lot more of him.

Joe couldn't know that evening twirling a rope in the street that everything beneath the ground in this new magical place was about to change but on some level, he did sense it.

Soon Roger would move on. Then Joe would take work at the Landin ranch with Otto and stay in the desert. He hadn't seen enough of the colors of New Mexico. Otto was a curious character, good to be around. Joe believed that working down here he might be able to lose his grief in the purple haze. If he was lucky maybe he could lose himself down here forever. It wouldn't be a bad life.

# 53

# The Last Shipment

MFTR, New Mexico
August of 1951

A pup coyote wailed to his siblings where they scurried through the sage. The sound was jarring, the deeply disturbing kind of haunting. Little coyotes are like that.

The buttes outlined against the stars watched like long deceased ancestors as three trucks rumbled across the flat.

They were cleared at the security gate as they followed the road to the old McAllister ranch. The trucks were cleared again before they took the ramp hidden inside the large warehouse that led them down into the desert ground.

Deep in an underground corridor men in unmarked rugged uniforms unloaded a series of crates marked MFTR-7 with the utmost care. This was the final shipment but this was not their first deadly cargo. The men didn't wonder about the contents of the crates or the future here at the base because they already knew. The testing of bomb type seven would soon be underway.

They continued on without hesitation because they were the best in their field. Deep underground they worked on, oblivious to the layers of rock between them and the clouds far above and the passage of time as they focused. They would soon be building the most deadly bomb to date. There was no room to think about anything else.

In a bunkhouse not far enough away a veteran named Otto tossed and turned in his sleep. He dreamed of antelope. In the recesses of his mind he could hear the ground beneath him shifting, humming. The next morning he would set his eyes on the testing range headquarters, something over there had changed in the night. Something beneath the ground was changing.

# 54

# Agent X

MFTR, New Mexico
August of 1951

"Everything is in order?"

"Yes the shipment came in fine. We are ready when you are ready."

A colonel spoke into a phone from his office underground. He had taken the call from the intelligence agent, he didn't know where the other man was calling from. Agent X spoke without any hint of emotion.

"You can expect me on Thursday."

Agent X hung up the phone. He was not a nuclear scientist but he was an academic by nature and an unnervingly intelligent man. The colonel respected and feared him.

They would be testing a new kind of bomb soon. MFTR was the ideal location. This achievement would set them ahead in the arms race, if no foreign entity knew about it. The 7 bomb was Agent X's pet project. No one was going to know about it.

The colonel hung up the phone. The less he saw of Agent X the better he could do his job. He dealt with the physical; the materials, the men, the equipment and the timeline. Agent X dealt with the most unexplained and uncanny souls in espionage the world over. Together they would make this weapons advancement happen. They had to. Lord knew what was going on underground across the world right now. They couldn't afford to fall behind.

Agent X didn't think instead he oozed in the air. Even his physical appearance was hard to lock down, hard to focus your eyes on. A tall man on the verge of middle aged, he usually wore large glasses and a hat. Beyond that the colonel couldn't say because when he tried to look at the younger man he became distracted by invisible insects around his shoulders, neck and collarbone. Some sort of a hypnosis trick the colonel decided, very effective. The younger man was considered to be the best. Agent X was a patriot and a very strange sort of individual indeed.

The building and testing of the 7 bomb was going to be successful. And not a soul outside of this team within this base was going to know about it.

# 55

# One Strange Cattle Drive

The Landin Ranch, NM
August of 1951

The horses didn't like it here. They side stepped and showed the whites in their eyes and sweated a lathered foam in their coat and blew snot out their noses. The cattle didn't like it here. The cows tried to take off and run. The calves tried to turn back and run for home. They all bellered in a panic, looking for their baby or their mama. And Otto, hell he hated it here. The pressure around his ears and in his neck made it hard for him to think. All the hairs on his arms were stood up. He just wanted to turn tail and give his horse his head.

Hell. Otto pronounced the word "hell" aloud as he rode hard back and forth across the herd in a cloud of dust. They did this cattle drive this time of year, every year. The herd would come out the other side across this flat. He was riding with several good cowboys today, it would take everything they had but they would hold the herd. Back and forth, Otto spurred his horse harder. The gelding started to rear, thinking about crow hopping and Otto hit him hard with the reins in a movement that jolted them forward as one. He knew the other hands were yelling, their cattle calls were as much for themselves and each other as for impressing momentum on the herd. This was a terrifying and solitary place.

Through it all Otto felt someone watching him. There was a car on the road in the distance, on the government property side of the barbed wire, headed toward the testing facility headquarters. After the feds had seized the ranch in eminent domain they had tested nukes on the great empty flats. Then they had set up testing underground. There was a labyrinth under dirt over there on that side of the fence. God only knew what was going on over there but it made the animals go crazy with fear. Now the car was sitting still in the road. The driver must be watching them try to force the herd across this flat. Otto could feel their eyes on him.

They knew that he knew that they were new to the area. They were watching him instead of the others because they knew he was watching them. There was something very specific about the car that made Otto extra nervous. He wondered what was in the backseat or maybe the cargo in the trunk. He was sure they were new the area, coming to the government facility for the first time. He didn't have any reason to think that, he just knew. The new car, a new person, some sort of cargo that he didn't like. It all made him think of some kind of new activity over there. Otto didn't like it at all.

Otto was a service man that had returned to the desert. He

loved to tell stories about tracking cats. He loved to track wild cats and they knew he could easily track people. They guessed at what he had done for our nation during the war. His skin was desert skin and his mannerisms made it impossible to pin down where he had come from. They knew he spent time on the reservations and over the border. He cut a pretty wide path. People everywhere knew Otto. From his silver spurs to his saddle blankets to the symbols on his bridle, Otto sought out the best artisans and the wisest medicine men. There were things like that about Otto that people could plainly see.

He had a quick smile and a focused strength of will that radiated on the air around him. He could be a little nervous and high strung. They knew Otto was a good roper and a trusted man in his outfit, loyal. They guessed that Otto loved people and was, perhaps, a little lonely. They knew Otto best by his smile and his ability to turn small talk into conversation. Otto knew everything about everyone. But very few facts were actually known about Otto. No one knew who his family was or where he had come from.

Otto may have just appeared in the desert one day, the improbable outcome of an unlucky congress between some sagebrush and the sunset. That was what his face looked like. Or maybe a rock and a cacti. Perhaps a coyote and a strange summer breeze. Joe abandoned the metaphors and turned back to the work at hand. This was a land that felt unlike anything else, the land of purple haze. Everything was different here. The people, the customs, the horses and the cattle themselves. He may as well have gone to a foreign country.

The cattle drives he knew were further north, where there was so much more grass and the cattle were positively fat. Hot, bleak, weird and unnerving, this was the cattle drive he was on now. They were passing close by what used to be someone's ranch before the government took it over for a top secret testing range. Otto had spent the last week telling Joe all about how hard it was to drive cattle along that flat. He had been right, the cattle had totally lost their minds over it. And the horses too. Joe thought about it, Otto had talked and then Otto had talked some more. Surely anyone who hated a place as much as that wouldn't still willingly go there, regardless of the circumstances. Joe thought that Otto held a dark fascination with the place that he wasn't admitting.

Joe thought about how he had left his home. He thought in desperation about how he had left his dad and his brother and the hills and meadows of the Heart Seven. He had never before in his life thought of leaving the ranch. He spurred the horse beneath him. He missed Biscuit.

His dad and his brother were continuing on stoically, waiting for Ivory to die. Just like Rose had died. Just like his mom had died. They were mentally preparing for the funeral. They were already standing out there in the cemetery, hats in their hands. Just waiting for the body to show up. It turned Joe's stomach. Everyone was just waiting for Ivory to become just Ivory's body. Joe didn't know what to do but he was sure it wasn't that. He was younger than they were.

Otto stretched in a lazy and stiff sort of way. Every year was harder than the last. The herd was resting and milling and stirring up the dust. Otto stepped off his horse and stretched again. Joe was still horseback on the other side of the herd, everything here was new for him. Otto watched as Joe got off his horse and walked a few steps, bent down and picked something up of the ground. Otto looked at the sky, the clouds, the ground and the cattle but he never stopped watching Joe. The younger man was looking at something small in the palm of his hand. Then he tucked it away in his left front shirt pocket and got back on his horse. He felt Otto watching him and met his gaze with a smile and a casual shrug of embarrassment.

Joe wasn't sure what he was supposed to be doing on this outfit. He was nervous. But he was a good hand and a good soul, Otto had been glad to have him by his side that day. The outfit was glad to have him. Otto wondered what he was running from. He was from a good family with a high quality upbringing. He was tough enough and a humble worker. Honest. The usual running away scenarios didn't fit Joe.

# 56

# Joe Receives A Letter

The Landin Ranch, NM
August of 1951

Joe rolled over and stretched. What a night, everything seemed to hurt, too much lying awake and too many dreams. Otto banged a pan loudly in the bunkhouse kitchen, the sun was starting to come up. Halfway through buttoning his shirt Joe remembered the rock in his shirt pocket and walked over to the windowsill. He had spent some time inspecting it closely last night and then set it there in the windowsill for the night. There was a line in the the dirt on the ledge. It looked like someone had set their finger on the rock and pushed it through the dust and moved it about six inches to the left, leaving a line behind it. Joe grimaced thoughtfully.

Otto crossed the room in a few purposeful steps to look at what Joe was looking at.

"And how's your rock this morning?"

Otto held a frying pan as he joined Joe in looking at the

windowsill. He wore the frilly yellow floral apron his sister had made him for Christmas over his clothes with his boots and hat already on. Otto made a giant mess when he cooked and he liked to cook.

"I didn't do that."

Otto was holding out one thick brown finger in the air over the rock, visualizing what Joe had just imagined.

"You didn't do that either, I fell asleep after you and got up before you. You lazy hound dog. Maybe you did it in your sleep, you were up a lot last night."

Otto shrugged before he continued.

"You better get in here and eat and do these dishes."

Joe usually did the dishes and cleaned up the table, and the stove and the floor. The food was good and he didn't mind. He was just thankful he wasn't being asked to cook.

"I wonder if..."

Joe stopped listening as Otto launched into his ritualistic debate about what the day would entail. Joe knew he hadn't done that but he still questioned himself. Looking to see if Otto was watching him, he tucked the rock back in his left shirt pocket deliberately.

Joe saddled his horse slowly in the morning light. Mrs. Landin thought he seemed tired. She handed him a letter that had come for him, a letter from home. She hesitated a moment. They understood that Joe might be called away to service and that he would go. She exchanged glances with Otto, they hadn't known him long but they would miss him. Joe knew they were nervous about that so he forced himself to rip the letter open and glance through it.

"Just family news, nothing to worry about."

He put the letter in his pocket and tried to give Mrs. Landin a reassuring smile. Then he just pulled his hat down and got on his horse, she would understand. Mrs. Landin struck him as a very tough lady.

From there the day took several unexpected turns. They rode one long trail after another. Joe was taciturn and Otto wished the mood would lighten, making his companion laugh made his days go faster. Finally in the late afternoon sun they sat on quiet horses, waiting for the cattle to settle down. Joe took the letter out to read Virgil's writing more thoroughly.

Joe's face tightened and tightened more as his eyes moved along the rows of writing. Worry creases were coming in around his eyes and on his forehead. Joe had the kind of innocent face that women pegged immediately as an emotional or sensitive type and Otto had to agree with them. The recent aging was helping though, ruggedness was starting to disguise the intuitive soul that he wore on his face instead of his sleeve. Otto's voice broke a silence so deep it physically hurt them both and startled the herd.

"What's the news?"

Joe choked and coughed and folded up his letter. Staring at the herd as if thinking about the day's work he started to talk. Otto would understand this sort of story.

# 57

# Otto Learns About Ivory

The Landin Ranch, NM

August of 1951

"My niece Ivory, she's dying. She has decided to die at home."

Otto listened kindly.

"This is from my brother Virgil, he says there is still time for me to come home," Joe inhaled sharply, "before she passes away."

"I'm sorry."

Otto meant it. Losing family was a very hard thing. Otto waited, he could tell Joe wanted to talk.

"Ivory came to live with us, when her mom passed away from this sickness. My dad and my brother, they didn't handle the loss very well."

Joe spoke carefully as he tried to find the right words.

"My mom, she turned her sadness sort of inside. She said things like how Rose had always been an angel. So it seemed kind of just Ivory and me having to move through it. I used to drive her to school."

Otto had sisters and nieces, he could imagine the love and connection of a family. This was a deeply sad story.

*Virgil worked as though they he could undo the death in the family if he only worked hard enough. Fred and Kate had lost their grown daughter after doing everything they could to save her. Now they had their granddaughter and their two sons. Rose would be enjoying heaven now.*

"Anyway, we grew up, it was good there for a few years. Then my mom came down with it. And she passed away."

*One morning Grandma Kate tripped in the kitchen and began to shake. Scalding coffee went everywhere and when the sun was fully up on her face Joe and Virgil, Ivory and Fred could see a familiar tinge in her skin.*

*They tried even harder this time, as if they could somehow save both of them. They traveled farther to distant cities, tried older treatments and newly invented treatments. Nothing worked. They wrote more letters, called on more experts and witch doctors, prayed day and night with candles lit in a ferocious display of faith. They buried Kate next to Rose determined not to weaken or feel the pain.*

"Then there for a while it was Ivory and I, my dad and my brother, there at the main house. Then she graduated and then she got married. She was so happy."

*Ivory took over making breakfast for Joe and Virgil and her granddad Fred with a determined sense of humor. It seemed that overnight she had found an eagerness to live her life to the fullest. She wore a red dress to her graduation ceremony and laughed like she had something to prove to life itself. Fred and Virgil and Joe sat stiffly in the rows of chairs at the high school graduation ceremony dressed in their finest hats and vests and stiffest new boots, never waning.*

*They sat almost exactly the same way in the front row of the church when she exchanged vows with Don Donahue. This was the church that Grandma Kate and Rose had dedicated every Sunday to. This was the church that had meant everything to them as women. The three men had never been there before. Ivory carried a bouquet of red roses. She clearly adored Don the bronc rider and mechanic. Fred tried not to disapprove too much. He knew it likely wouldn't matter too much in the end anyway, he had made that mistake with Rose. Ivory's father never returned from Europe. Fred wouldn't have had to have been so hard on them. So Fred did his best to ignore Don.*

*They missed Ivory terribly in the mornings when the sun rose in the main house kitchen but they knew she was not far away. Probably singing and carrying on, just making a different breakfast in her own house there on the south part of the ranch. She was exuberant about taking care of her own house and yard and the three men were happy for her to have that, each in their own way. They saw her almost every day.*

*Then the shadow of fate started to make all of them nervous as it crept closer. Fred's personality turned inward and hardened as the seasons went by. Virgil remained single. And finally when the illness came for Ivory, Joe had cut and run and taken a cowpuncher's job down south.*

"My dad and Virgil are just carrying on, waiting for her to die. I couldn't do that anymore. Rose, my mom, and now Ivory that is too much. Ivory deserves to have a happy life, to have a family of her own. I wanted that for her."

Joe's voice turned emotional as he spoke about the waiting. Otto knew now what Joe from Nebraska was running from.

"I keep thinking I can find a way to save her, somehow."

Otto let one tear fall as he sat his horse in the evening light and listened. He could do that for his friend. Joe didn't notice as he kept talking.

"That doesn't make sense but it feels true. I would do it, whatever it takes."

"They won't be seeing any more doctors you said?"

Joe put his hand over his left front shirt pocket and tilted his head back to the sky.

"They made one last trip to Denver, another round of quacks and fakes looking to take your money but having no answers. Ivory wants to go in peace."

Otto thought he could understand that. Then Joe spoke as though answering himself.

"She really does love that house."

Then he spurred his horse, it was time to start back.

# 58

# Joe Won't Go Home And Otto Watches A Rock

The Landin Ranch, NM
August of 1951

They rode back to the main place at an easy pace. Otto wondered if Joe was going to be leaving, to go home and see Ivory one more time. Joe answered before Otto got to ask.

"I don't know if I will go back."

Otto didn't reply to that but decided to change topics.

"How's that rock you picked up yesterday?"

Joe stopped his horse. He remembered how observant Otto was and how much more he knew than he ever let on. Otto noticed everything but it was easy to think of him only as the man who had everyone laughing all the time.

Joe took the rock out of his shirt pocket and held it up.

"There's something different about it. Here, what do you think?"

He handed it off to Otto and they rode on.

Otto could feel a heartbeat like rhythm coming from the round smooth rock in his palm, it was warm. Much warmer than it should have been. He held it up between his two fingers just as Joe had. It was a tan and brown color, just like most of the rocks in the region. Visually unremarkable in every way. How had Joe spotted it? Otto stopped his horse and considered his friend before asking his question.

"Why did you notice it?"

Joe shrugged.

"I don't know. Just caught my eye."

Otto turned his attention back to the rock in his hand.

"Well you are right. It's a different kind of rock."

"You think so?"

Joe's voice lifted slightly.

"It's alive. So, yes."

Otto said it calmly and with authority. Joe stared at Otto and then at the rock between Otto's thumb and finger.

"What do you mean it's alive?"

"I mean it is old and it is alive, it probably has a more complex life going on right now than either you or me."

Otto handed it back to Joe, who put it right back in his shirt pocket. They finished the ride home at a faster pace.

That night in the bunkhouse Otto pretended to read a paperback romance novel that he had already finished. Otto was an avid reader. Stacks of worn out yellow dime store novels sprawled under his bed. Joe was staring off into space not pretending to do anything. It was going to be hard to go to sleep tonight. Otto jumped when Joe started to talk.

"Ivory will be okay, she will be with her grandma, and her

mom. They will help her."

Otto couldn't think of a thing to say to that and went back to staring at the page he had yet to turn all evening. The silence in the bunkhouse that night was profound and they sat on in companionable silence, almost as if they were waiting for something.

They both looked up when they heard a sound in the windowsill. The rock was sliding slowly across the windowsill. It paused and then turned slightly, as if it was taking in the best light or the best view or turning to look at them. Joe looked at Otto sharply but Otto didn't take his eyes off the rock. Several long, heavy moments passed.

"There are some people I could ask, if you want to know more about this."

Otto's voice was quiet, low and slow as he kept his eyes locked on the rock.

Joe was looking at his rock again, his eyes getting bigger and bigger as a delayed reaction caught up with him.

Otto continued monotonously, he had not even blinked.

"But even if you don't want to know anymore, are you sure you want this? There might not be another chance to change your mind. You should think carefully my friend."

Otto's voice was low and slow, soft and measured without any of the usual humor. Joe stood up a little too fast, crossed the room to the windowsill and gingerly picked up the rock and held it at eye's level in the palm of his left hand. He seemed peaceful now and resolute.

"I'm sure."

Then he tenderly put the rock back in the windowsill exactly as it had been.

Joe went to sleep quickly after that and slept soundly but Otto stayed up all night in his boots and spurs and hat and watched the windowsill from behind his book.

# 59

# Mary And John Landin

The Landin Ranch, NM
August of 1951

Mary and John Landin were married in 1891. They felt the end of the American West. They were married for ten years when they saw the turn of the century. They were part of the dust bowl and the great war and then the second world war. They never had children. Their adventure along this lonely river was all there would ever be for them. Their ancestors had taken this land violently and held it violently. They had done the same.

John and Mary were not at all surprised when eminent domain took their neighbor's ranch from under them during the second war. They knew we would all come to what we deserved sooner or later. They felt whiplash from the careening decades behind them and a sort of vigor as they approached their end.

The bomb testing hadn't yet melted the atmosphere. They wouldn't be here when the nuclear arms race finally blew up the world. Mary supposed you had to leave something for the young people. They were both over eighty now and neither of them sat a horse anymore. Otto had been there for them ever since he came back from Europe. She was grateful for that, there was no one like Otto. Now with Joe from Nebraska there with them, the four of them felt more like a little family to her.

Since the letter had come to Joe, the mood had grown dark on the Landin ranch. Otto still made breakfast in the bunkhouse as the sun came up every morning. Hat, boots and spurs, spoon in hand he made an even bigger mess than before. The flowery apron was really coming in handy as he splattered and spilled. Otto was a tough and expressive soul. Grief was no stranger to him so he felt that he could carry his friend's grief. He had sisters and a brother and nieces and nephews galore. Carrying the suffering of another was something he could do.

Every morning Joe still cleaned the coffee off the counter and the grease off the stove and the egg off of the floor and the toast off of the table and more coffee off the counter as Otto went back for another round. They still rode out every day. Otto still went up to the main house porch for instructions. Mr. Landin still drove too fast for a man that couldn't see. Mrs. Landin still made a brittle cornbread. They still wore down a string of horses between them. They still slept hard in a hot, still bunkhouse as summer in New Mexico eased on.

Chloe thought Joe's face was getting harder and leaner. Mrs. Landin thought he was losing weight. Joe told Otto he was not going to go home now and he was not going to go home for the funeral. He had seen enough and had enough. His temper was running thin and as the summer started to age Joe was turning into a harder man and a harder cowboy.

One morning on the main house porch Mr. Landin asked Otto about Joe's family situation. There was no polite way to say, did the girl die yet?

"How is his family back home Otto?"

"No change that I know of."

They all stopped to watch Joe saddling horses in the distance. He was out of hearing range.

"The poor dear."

The boss's snowy haired wife paused for a long time. Then she spoke again suddenly.

"What is going on with him and that rock Otto?"

Otto inwardly nodded to her in appreciation of her observation, she had seen what the boss wouldn't be able to. Outwardly his emotions and expression did not change.

"Grief. Beyond that it is hard to say. Something very old. Something new."

Otto waved dismissively in the direction of the McAllister Federal Testing Range.

Mary's eyebrows frowned. The world was changing again. John was a walking fossil and she was a mean old spirit from the frontier and Otto was shell shocked, but Joe. She watched him place the rock back in his shirt pocket. The desert had already come for Joe.

Otto nodded his head in the slightest gesture of respect and took off for the day.

The truth was the rock situation had spiraled out of Otto's ability to navigate. He would have liked to say that a grieving man was obsessed with caring for a rock. He would have liked to have said that the man was delusional and thought the rock could talk to him but it was wasn't that simple. Forces were at work all around Otto and all he could do was grasp at the wind.

The rock moved of its own accord and had its own sort of heart beat. Otto was sure the rock was having its own life experiences and on some sort of trajectory. The rock had become friends with Joe and it rode around in his front shirt pocket every day. Joe spent every evening in a rocking chair holding the rock loosely in his left hand. Otto saw them as two living beings that had come together at a critical time.

Otto wasn't afraid of the rock, only extremely cautious, but for his friend Joe, he was afraid.

# 60

# Paul

New Mexico
August of 1951

Campfire light flickered over Otto's face as he listened. Joe's rock was resting on a larger rock near the fire. He had taken it from the windowsill with a gloved hand and placed it in a leather pouch in his saddle bag, after Joe had fallen asleep. He had half expected Joe to wake up or to follow him but Joe had slept on. The younger man was under a lot of strain and slept very deep and strange nights these days. No one followed Otto, no one knew where he had gone.

Now Otto was seated in the desert across from his friend Paul. Paul declined to touch the little rock. Otto had been relieved when Paul recognized the living rock immediately. He said they were as old as the desert, as old as time.

"They take on what is around them. They carry burdens, sometimes they have carried burdens from human beings. They usually appear to people in pairs."

Here Paul stopped talking to steal a glance at the rock in question.

"And that pair might stay with a family for many generations, protecting them, healing them, sharing their burdens."

"A burden like grief?"

"Sure. But they work in partnerships. Your friend must have something that this entity is looking for."

The moon moved across the sky far overhead of the two men. The wind and living beings stirred in the desert all around them. Not far away, underneath the sagebrush the agendas of a mighty bureaucracy hummed away.

Otto changed the subject and spoke haltingly.

"I'm nervous about the, latest developments, under the old McAllister ground."

"Who isn't?"

Paul leaned in closer and spoke again.

"What have you seen Otto? What do you think is going on?"

Paul clearly had his own insight, he just wanted to know Otto's take.

"More power. More uranium, more plutonium, higher grades, maybe something else entirely. Much more power. The dirt is humming with the strain of it all. They are pushing much farther this time around."

"Then there's your answer. These are living beings too."

Paul gestured casually to the rock. He had the gift of existing in an untroubled state of mind. He continued on, visiting with Otto was always a pleasure. Paul would be returning to the university on the coast in September. He would be teaching a full course load.

The teacher in Paul spoke as he explained his thinking to Otto.

"By laws of nature they take on and equalize the forces around them. Suppose they have been taking on the ever increasing radiation, placing them under more and more strain and pressure. You say there has been a marked increase lately-"

Here Paul paused with a nod of respect to the little rock that lay listening.

"Possibly this living being sought out your friend because it needs something, something to do with the increasing radioactive activity. They have protected people but it is possible they need protection in return."

Otto could see his answers coming together in front of him, so clearly he could almost touch them.

"Joe is from up north, Nebraska. He is running away but he needs to go home to his family, it would be the right thing."

Paul smiled with eyes in satisfaction and threw a bit of sagebrush into the fire.

"It needs a ride out of here. That's something your friend Joe can give them."

# 61

# The Mate

The Landin Ranch, NM
August of 1951

Otto was up making breakfast. He opened the bunkhouse door to throw out yesterday's scraps to the dog and there on the step in the sunrise light was another rock. Otto stood perfectly still and stared at it for a long time. He never wondered if it was the same rock, the initial impression was of an entirely different personality. But it looked just like Joe's rock. There it sat, perfectly still, square in front of the bunkhouse door, waiting.

Otto's eyes prodded the dust and the dew in the dim light and found exactly what he had expected, a little traveling trail behind the rock. It had scooted smoothly and slowly across the open dirt as though pulled by a magnet underneath the ground, leaving a little trail behind it. Otto could not recreate in his mind's eye what had happened when it got to the step. But then the trail resumed in the dirt on the cement and that is what brought this rock to where it was, right in front of him. How far had it come from exactly? The dog never did get his scraps.

"Joe!"

Otto barked, his voice harsh with nervous energy.

"Joe! Get out here."

Almost no one had ever heard Otto speak so loudly.

Joe held his rock loosely in his left hand, fully dressed but with his eyes still full of sleep. Those eyes were starting to take on a dead inside look as the heaviness of grief compounded inside his soul. He stopped short and stared in wonder for a while. Then he moved impulsively to quickly scoop up the new rock and Otto threw out an arm and stopped his friend.

"In the name of all things holy friend, what is going on here?"

Otto wanted to grab Joe's shoulders and shake him and stare deeply into those eyes and find some explanations but he didn't because his dark eyes were locked on the new rock.

"They are a couple."

Joe stammered.

"That's the female."

Otto's eyes flitted toward Joe for a half a second. So what Paul had said was true.

"When I picked this one up, I separated them. I didn't know."

Otto stared even more intently at the rock on the step, as though determined to suss out if this was the truth. The rock didn't move.

"So she came to find her mate?"

Otto spoke slowly.

Joe picked up the newcomer lady rock and nodded.

The two friends ate their breakfast slowly that day and drank an extra pot of coffee. Joe placed the two rocks side by side out on the table next to the plate of toast. Otto thought they looked happy. Sun was streaming into the bunkhouse, it was time to go soon.

Joe spoke slowly.

"I think they are happy."

Then he looked to his friend to see how much Otto was going to tolerate and Otto dropped his shoulders.

"I think they are too."

His voice was not unkind.

That day Joe took the second rock in his shirt pocket and left the first one in the windowsill but he was careful to set them both side by side in the windowsill as soon as he got home that night. Otto ignored the whole business because he was deep in thought.

The next morning Otto woke up first and he lay still and stiff until the sun was up enough to see outside. Something was wrong. What was going on around here? He decided to get up and face it. But he lay still another little while, staring up at the ceiling. Then he put on his boots and his hat and went straight to the bunkhouse door and opened it. Two more rocks on the front step. Little trails in the dust behind them. Otto squinted meanly at the two of them, stepped backwards inside and shut the door.

Then he went to the windowsill, the original two rocks were

gone. Otto spotted them perched on poor old Joe's chest, his calloused hand clenching them loosely and falling up and down as he snored on.

When Joe woke up Otto was drinking coffee at the breakfast table staring at the wall pensively. The two new rocks were sitting perched on a scrap of leather next to the plate of eggs. Joe still had the first two rocks clenched in his left hand. His eyes looked worse than ever but he was dressed and ready for the day. Otto turned his head as if he had just now seen Joe.

"Two more rocks this morning. What is going on?"

Otto leaned across the table conversationally, a coffee cup nestled between his two strong hands. He wanted Joe to square with him.

"Why are they here?"

Joe sat down heavily, he was so miserable he could barely blink.

"I don't know why these rocks are coming to me."

Otto changed topics.

"I think you should go home and see Ivory before she passes away. It will be a terrible thing but hiding out down here is not going to make it any easier."

"I have to help her. Somehow. I can't go back because I have nothing."

Joe started to cough. Otto couldn't understand. There was no way Otto could understand. They had already seen this disease devastate his sister and turn her laughter into a wheezing whisper for help and he had not been able to help her.

"No one could help her."

They had already seen this disease kill his mother. The three of them had stood there helpless, hats in hand, again. He would do anything to save Ivory, he would do anything to help her.

"I would do anything to save her. I just don't know what to do."

Anger started to heat up inside him because time was running out. He couldn't stand beside Ivory's bed and look down at her skeletal living remains and have her look up at him. He could see her eyes begging for help, for him to throw her some kind of a lifeline and for him to have nothing. And he had nothing.

Otto waited quietly for Joe to go on.

"I would have done anything to save my sister. We did everything and more. And we took all that experience and we tried even harder to save my mom. We all knew it would come for Ivory someday. I've had years and years and still, I have nothing. No way to save her, no way to help her."

The morning sun shone and shifted on the breakfast table and the two new rocks. Joe looked at Otto and Joe was wrong. Otto understood far more than he was letting on.

"I can't go back because I can't help her."

"I understand that friend, but I think she would want you by her side. Even though you can't help her, just to be there for her."

Otto started to say.

"Dying is a very hard thing."

But caught himself in time and said instead.

"You don't want her to have to do this alone."

Joe jumped up from his chair.

"She's not alone! She has Don."

Joe had a short temper these days.

"And Virgil. And my dad. She's not alone."

Joe threw open the door to leave. There were two more rocks on the front step and Joe swept them up in his empty hand. Then he spun on his boot heel and grabbed the other two off the table for good measure and stormed out to get the work day started. Today was going to get hotter than he had thought.

Otto sat very still and his eyes fell on the small crucifix on the wall next to the kitchen clock. His little sister had given him that too. They were up to six rocks now.

Otto could hear his life changing forever. He forgot about the cattle, the horses, the outfit, the Landin's and all of his responsibilities. Otto stayed still and listened to the dirt and the ground outside the bunkhouse. Everything was accelerating. Mankind was forging new ways into the future over there. All over the world nuclear arms testing was racing unchallenged and changing the compositions of the world.

The coming generations would never know how different they were from their ancestors. They would never know how different their world was from what it had been. They would never fully feel how much their planet's place among the stars had changed. So many things could not be helped. Otto still lived in the war. The United States had better be developing arms over there and they had better be the most powerful in the world. What they did beneath the desert across that barbed wire fence was none of his business. He wanted no part of it.

Otto fixed his eyes on the small crucifix again and started to pray. He had left most of himself in Europe. He would always be a military man. The price had been high. Thank God he had been able to help pay it. What the government did under the ground was none of his business but these little rocks above it, a kid named Joe and somewhere up north a young woman named Ivory, they were.

# 62

# The Testing Date

MFTR, New Mexico
August of 1951

Agent X stood in the main office of MFTR-7 and contemplated all the paper in front of him. He couldn't concentrate. Everything was on track, things were going well, he had plenty of work to do yet today.

He shook his head as if something was bothering his ears, he couldn't get past it. The colonel watched him cautiously as the wiry man became more and more agitated. Finally the agent folded up his paperwork in frustration and strode from the room.

He would have to look for what was bothering him. This was one of the most critical secrets in the world right now. This sort of thing was exactly why he was here.

He didn't find what he was looking for in the main underground corridors. He didn't find it in the warehouse cover. Finally in a jeep out on the road across the complex, driving toward the main gates, Agent X found his answer.

High on a ridge, far across the flat, on the private property side of the fence, a man on a horse sat relaxed but straight in the saddle. Agent X could just make out his figure. He recognized the man from the cattle drive on the flat that day. That had been the day he had driven here.

He would have to push back the testing date.

# 63

# Ivory And Rose

The Heart Seven Ranch- South Place
August of 1951

The congregation was too quiet without Ivory. The church had become a sleepy place without her powerhouse will to make things happen. The front left pew was empty. The sermons dragged on. The kitchen in the basement was a little dirty for the first time. The stained glass window failed to dazzle and even the lilac bushes wilted. The air inside the building was stuffy and still. The sheriff shifted restlessly in the boredom. He had a guilty conscious. He should have taken issue directly with Fred Hart. Or even the mighty Virgil Hart, he had been wrong to let Ivory rile him. Aggravation that she was, he should have been a better man. So his thoughts continued as the preacher droned on.

Doris turned her attention to new complaints as her mind churned away and her children squirmed beside her. She was seeing Dismal with a new set of eyes. The cemetery outside their building flourished in an odd sort of way even as the church building felt more and more dead. The sun glinted off the glittering white headstones that read Rose and Katherine. Doris thought it was all enough to make one say their prayers.

At the Heart Seven south place, Ivory was sleeping in the sunshine in the corner bedroom. Don watched her sleep from the rocking chair. Gregory had told him he wouldn't be needed on Sundays for a while. Don was too tired to ask questions.

"Please don't go..."

Ivory whimpered in her sleep. Then she let out a wail and tried to thrash restlessly. She was still asleep, having nightmares. Don had never seen her have a nightmare before. She was crying in her sleep, painful fearful crying. Rattled he jumped across the room, his heart was breaking. That was when the bedroom door moved and his blood ran cold.

He stood very still, barely daring to inhale. Ivory was calming down. Her brows relaxed. Her head falling heavy on the pillow again.

Don watched the coverlet, the mattress, Ivory's face trying to see evidence of what was scaring him. She was sleeping quietly now. Then she spoke.

"I love you too Mom."

Don stepped rapidly but quietly out the front door in his socked feet to look up at the tree branches above him and figure out what to do now. After a time he sat down on the front stoop in his socks.

That Sunday afternoon Ivory asked him a question.

"You know how when someone is dying, the moment the people by the bedside leave, that's when they pass?"

Don nodded.

"I think I need you to let me go."

Her voice was tender, apologetic.

"I'm so sorry Don. You are going to have a great life."

He started to cry but she was having none of it.

"No. We both know this is true. We had a good run. It's over now. Let me go."

Don's face was looking better. The look on her face was a shadow of the beaming pride she used to turn toward him but he would take it.

"This is the best thing you can do for me now. The bravest thing for us is to stop dragging this out. Leave me behind. Like we were never more than friends."

He understood then what he needed to do. She smiled at him with satisfied confidence.

"I'm ready to go. You get ready to leave too."

Don wiped his face with his shirt sleeve.

"Do you want me to say goodbye too?"

Ivory snuggled her face into the pillow sleepily. She seemed at peace.

"Nah, it might not be right now. I just want you to try it. Let's just say, see you later my friend."

Don leaned down to kiss her forehead.

"See you later my friend."

Don was putting bridles and halters into a canvas bag when he heard the piano music, a classical piece played with precision and energy. Surely Ivory couldn't play like that. He eased the canvas bag down, this was all getting to be a bit more haunting than he was prepared for. He thought carefully for a while.

That was the first time he ever looked in the tall, narrow bedroom windows from the outside. Ivory kept them uncovered because she said she wanted to feel the hills around her, see the leaves above them. The piano music churned on softly inside the house. Ivory slept on in the bed they used to share.

# V

# Part Five

# 64

# Barb Remembers The Hayfield

Barb was praying when Allan showed up. She was praying for Ashley's life. She missed her mom and her dad.

Barb let a few tears escape and let herself miss them. She missed the place where she grew up, the missed the hills and the valleys, the long highways. She missed the cattle and horses, the winter feeding. The gate she had stood in when her mom sorted the heavy cows in the spring. She missed her Uncle Virgil and how they had pushed the calves up together in the back of the herd, horseback in the early summer and again in the fall. He had been a great cowboy, a great cattleman. They had made a good team sorting pairs and grabbing calves. She had known with him that she was one of the best cowgirls in the west, because he taught her. Barb started to really cry when she thought of her dad and the little tractor she had raked hay on all growing up. In her mind's eye she was waiting on the seat for his go ahead to flip the switch and throttle it up. She remembered the way the hayfield felt, the smell of the drying grass in the heat, the sky. The way her dad would smile, he had loved to put up hay. Barb wanted to go back there. She desperately wanted to go back. He had been so happy in the summertime, filled with joy.

That's the thing about when you sell the farm, Barb thought to herself, you can never go back. Well it hadn't been a farm. Barb had sold the mighty Heart Seven. How could she have done that? She was crying like a baby when Allan sat down beside her. She saw how she must look and then she wiped her face and started to cry harder. She hadn't solved anything. She had just tried to save herself. And now Ashley was going to pay. They were all going to pay.

"Oh Barb! What is going on?"

Allan stood up again and pulled her on her feet to hold her close. He knew Barb too well to think that she was breaking down over a gallery or a car.

"I'm so scared for Ashley."

Allan was surprised as he stroked Barb's white hair gently. He hadn't known Ashley was struggling.

"What is going on with Ashley?"

"I think she is going to end up paying for my mistakes," Barb looked up into Allan's eyes.

"I thought that if my parents would just sell the property, they could move on and all the trouble would stay behind them. Now I see that maybe they knew better. Maybe I was the one that was wrong."

Then Barb started to breakdown in earnest and Allan looked to the left and right nervously. He wasn't sure the local power grid would be able to handle a full on Barb meltdown. The lights flickered crazily around them so he offered a solution.

"Why don't we go for a drive? Let's get some coffee and get on the road."

# 65

# Don In East River

Don had never been to the airport in East River. He got out when Emmy and Phoebe did and waited for the plane to arrive with them. This was the most beautiful, clearest spring morning. He sat with them and smoked, trying to control his own excitement. Don had spent most of a century on the ranch. He had never seen an airplane up close. He wanted to walk around and look at everything. Instead he stared pensively out at the sky where the airplanes were.

When Ashley came into sight in the dark doorway and walked down the ramp he felt he was seeing Clyde again, all over. He fancied he saw a little of himself in her too, though he knew that wasn't really possible. At any rate, this was a woman out for revenge. The two of them would understand each other beautifully.

She was afraid of the man and the woman that got off the plane behind her. Don had been standing next to Emmy and Phoebe, ready to greet Barb's younger daughter. Now he moved forward with great energy. These were probably the people that were threatening Barb. He set his hat back farther on his forehead, a man and a woman, professionals from the urban world. He could tell already that they were seasoned and that they had sold their souls a long time ago. But Don wasn't worried. They had never met anything like him before.

# 66

# Ashley Arrives

When Ashley stepped off the little plane onto the tarmac Phoebe knew she had been experimenting in substances. She was wrapped in a hoodie and sweatpants as if she was cold and had a backpack casually thrown over her shoulder. The skin had gone all tight under her eyes.

Ashley's eyes wandered over each of the people around them. Phoebe tried not to turn her head and look with her. Something was wrong here, cold feelings were creeping up on Phoebe.

There were only five people getting off the incoming flight. That seemed normal, two couples and Ashley. One was a couple heading to a pickup with a local license plate. Phoebe suddenly wished she had a local plate. It was the other two, they were good at looking at ease but odds were they had never seen this particular remote little piece of ground before.

Emmy was caught in limbo. Ashley wouldn't want to be

touched. So Emmy wrapped her own arms tight across her own body to help keep herself under control. Her little sister was dying. Emmy could see her long, slow death all around her and in her as she stepped off the plane. Everything, absolutely everything was wrong with this time and place.

Emmy looked to Phoebe and Phoebe nodded slightly. They were stuffing Ashley in the back of Phoebe's car and then they would make tracks. They were bigger than her and Phoebe was a fast driver.

Ashley smiled tightly at Emmy and reached out for her hand. Heart soaring Emmy grabbed it. None of them looked back as they took big measured steps across the pavement to the white sports car. Phoebe eased the clutch on the powerful engine as she pivoted the car tightly and then quietly, easily leapt forward and away.

# 67

# The Man In The Cowboy Hat

Another agent was waiting in the parking lot to pick them up in a four door pickup with local plates. If they wanted to follow the white car, they were going to have to hurry up. She leaned over the steering wheel to try to catch their eye.

They were talking to a young man in a cowboy hat. She hadn't seen him there earlier.

He was wiry and athletic, he leaned in as he spoke to them.

"Did you bring any luggage on this flight?"

He was standing aggressively close to the pair of agents. The pilot, the flight attendant, the other couple and the airport ground person had all stopped to stare. The last thing they needed was to attract a lot of attention. The woman spoke.

"No, we have everything, thank you."

She made to step around him but he side stepped with a big grin. He reached his hand out to the man as he walked backwards with a jump in his step and a smile.

"I think you are mistaken, you see when this plane was

coming in I saw some baggage falling out, landed in that field over there around those bales."

He pointed. The agents were becoming irate. Their connection would have to leave without them to follow the target if they didn't get out of here quickly.

He wasn't intimidated by them at all. Then as he continued to chat he saw that moment when their understanding of him changed.

"Looked like some bodies if you ask me, sordid assignments, wasted lives. And lots of cash, just cash falling everywhere over there."

Don moved to grab the man's upper right arm. The ghost had a grip that was solid and stronger than a man's. The sunlight fell strangely on his face, his shirt was a little old fashioned, his hat brim a little shorter. His face was smooth and his eyes bright and sparkling with humor.

"None of that sits very well with me."

Don pointed to the pilot and the flight attendant without breaking eye contact with the woman agent.

"You could get back on this plane you know. Those two could take you back to Denver. Besides, your friend over there needs to get moving."

The two women were slamming the car doors on the aging sports car.

The people on the tarmac at the East River airport all turned their heads. They could hear something. Wind, the wind was going to pick up, wind was coming. The ground crew moved quickly, their thoughts on the plane. A freak wind storm, a tornado, they didn't know but they would need to make some decisions quickly. They could hear a wall of wind coming as the sky darkened around them.

The man in front of Don had finally had enough.

"Get out of our way."

He made to shake off Don's grasp but couldn't and Don leaned in closer with a smile, this was so much more fun than he remembered. The white car was out of sight now.

"I'm going to walk away. Don't forget that luggage."

The wall of wind fell across the airport hard and then let up just as suddenly. No one saw where the young man in the short brimmed felt hat went. It had all happened so fast.

The pair of agents ran to the pickup and the driver accelerated toward where they had seen Phoebe go. Don lit up a smoke from his seat behind the driver and sat back to laugh to himself obnoxiously. This was going to be so much fun.

# 68

# Coming To Dismal

Mr. Hammond sat on a horse in a muddy lot, waiting for a cow and calf to pair up when Emmy called him. He knew he was old. He wondered how many years he would still be horseback. Or how many years his family would tolerate him going horseback alone, even just around the place. He was older than anyone knew. Today he really felt that. Then the phone in the front inside pocket of his overcoat buzzed.

"Hello?"

"Hey it's Emmy."

Mr. James Hammond knew that tone of voice, no matter who it came from. He kept his eyes on the sky and sat the horse still.

"It's good to hear from you. How are you and Miss Phoebe?"

"Well we are almost home. We went to East River to get my sister Ashley at the airport."

Mr. Hammond nudged his horse back toward the house, the pairs would have to wait. Nora could run out here on her four wheeler and shut this gate. Trouble was coming to Dismal.

"And we've got some kind of trouble. Someone burned down my mom's art gallery in Santa Fe and someone burned up her car too. Anyway two people came with Ashley from Dallas to Denver and to East River, she doesn't know who they are."

"You said you are almost back to the place?"

"Yes, Phoebe is making good time."

The unsaid question hung on the air between the two of them. Emmy wondered if this was what having a grandfather would have been like or a dad. She was probably wrong to put the business man and neighbor in that position.

"Why don't you come on over here, you don't need to stop at the house for anything?"

"No, we'll come directly over. Thank you."

"Emmy, where is your mom?"

"Her friend Allan went to pick her up, I don't know if they will go back to Dallas or somewhere else."

"She will go back to Dallas."

Mr. Hammond spoke with careless confidence as he put the spurs to his horse and they leapt back toward the house with surprising ease.

"Do you know her?"

"We went to school together. Has Phoebe seen anyone in that rear view mirror of hers?"

Phoebe shook her head no.

"No, she hasn't."

"All right then, see you soon."

"Mr. Hammond, one more thing," Emmy looked in the rear view mirror at Ashley in the backseat, hopefully she was sleeping and not passed out.

"It's Ashley, I think she might need an emergency room."

Mr. Hammond didn't break pace, his mind was on dialing this cell phone to call his sons.

"Bring her here."

Then Mr. Hammond was gone.

# 69

# Mechanical Difficulties

The woman driving the pickup found that even when she floored the accelerator, the pickup wouldn't go any faster than fifty miles an hour. Don listened to their drama bemusedly. This hadn't been a problem earlier today. They were losing their target, they had lost their target. They finally pulled over to the let the man drive. They knew where their target was going. They would catch up with her.

Now their top speed was only forty miles an hour. They were angry. Careers were being lost as the accelerator refused to give. Don listened from the backseat. There was nothing wrong with the vehicle, she had driven it over from the base. She hadn't even shut it off at the airport. Their angry voices spurred Don's curiosity. He was learning quite a lot from watching them.

These people were not to let Ashley out of their sight. That was their entire job. They reported to someone, these were just a few members of a bigger team. They wanted to know everything she did, everyone she talked to or saw, everything she picked up or dropped off. There were to be no lapses. Don smiled wickedly from the backseat, well they had a lapse now, wasn't that just too bad.

Don frowned as he turned his attention back to listening. He needed to take the time to learn what was going on here. He could do a better job if he understood, he chided himself to think this through.

They weren't to let Ashley out of their sight. Don tried to listen carefully. The agents were speaking to remote agents and discussing live footage. There were teams analyzing the audio and video surveillance right now. Ashley was very valuable to them. That much he could tell. They were in some ways a security detail. Don scratched his forehead underneath his hat. But mostly they wanted to observe what she did. That's why they were so upset right now that they couldn't see her. All these people were reporting to someone. Questions kept coming up, there were things that someone wanted to know.

Don wondered why Ashley was so incredibly important to them. What could she do for these people that made them so much money? Don could tell these were money people. All of this outfit ran on huge amounts of money and it all centered around Ashley. Phoebe had a terrific head start thanks to him. If they all wanted to see something, wanted to hear something, wanted to know so much. He could give them that, good thing he had all day.

The radio in the pickup cab blared on, playing some pop driven country hit. The driver turned it off angrily. The radio came back on. The agents exchange glances silent in that moment.

The pickup sped up. The windshield wipers came on.

The agents far away and the agents beside him spoke back and forth. The driver gripped the steering wheel, fearful as the acceleration careened between fast and slow. He couldn't feel any resistance in the brakes. He couldn't force the ignition. There were no other vehicles on this highway. Next the steering wheel forced out of his grip and slowly swerved along one ditch and then the other as the speed picked up. Agents in offices were forming hypothesis. The agents in the pickup were afraid. Don laughed and they heard him.

These people that needed to see everything. What they really needed to see, was that Ashley was protected by another entity besides themselves. What they needed to hear was that she was part of a much bigger story. They needed to know that the Heartless Ranch was haunted. The driver couldn't open the door to bail out.

They needed to know that Dismal was Ashley's home. The pickup stopped dead in the highway and the three agents leapt out and dropped for cover in the ditch. Don sat back comfortably and titled his hat sideways to keep the sun out of his eyes. He waited patiently. They would have to get back in and try again, their superiors far away would tell them to.

# 70

# Surveillance

Don could her Emmy's voice. A recording of a phone call between her and James Hammond. Don leaned in to listen carefully.

"And we've got some kind of trouble. Someone burned down my mom's art gallery in Santa Fe and someone burned up her car too. Anyway two people came with Ashley from Dallas to Denver and to East River, she doesn't know who they are."

"You said you are almost back to the place?"

"Yes, Phoebe is making good time."

"Why don't you come on over here, you don't need to stop at the house for anything?"

"No, we'll come directly over. Thank you."

"Emmy, where is your mom?"

"Her friend Allan went to pick her up, I don't know if they will go back to Dallas or somewhere else."

"She will go back to Dallas."

"Do you know her?"

"We went to school together. Has Phoebe seen anyone in

that rear view mirror of hers?"

"No, she hasn't."

"All right then, see you soon."

"Mr. Hammond, one more thing, it's Ashley, I think she might need an emergency room."

"Bring her here."

Don thought for a moment. These two had been trailing Ashley since Dallas. Phoebe would be almost to the Hammond's place by now. Barb was with someone named Allan and probably headed back to Dallas and Emmy thought Ashley needed urgent medical attention. Don was lost in thought while the agents discussed.

"If she's going to be staying here for a while..."

The other agent interrupted rudely. Then a third voice spoke from a speaker device.

"Do not engage directly with the neighbors. Repeat, do not engage target directly at this time."

Don listened to the drama in the chain of command.

"Her sister's house or the neighbor's house."

"We can get surveillance set up at the sister's place while she is hiding out at the neighbors. Then we can get the neighbor's place next."

Don smiled, suddenly the pickup could reach seventy miles an hour and handle normally again.

The original pickup driving agent let the man and woman off along the highway, the house was within sight. They could walk in without leaving tracks. She continued on and then pulled off into a pasture, she drove past the no trespassing sign over the knoll so that she couldn't be seen from the highway and settled in to wait. They shouldn't be long at all.

Sometimes Ashley was able to detect and get rid of the surveillance devices and they had to go in and reinstall. They had gotten in the habit of using several sets so as to space the visits out longer and make sure they got accurate surveillance. Sometimes they got lucky and she didn't bother to look for them. From what the agent could see this would be the perfect setup, stuff everywhere, there were hundreds or even thousands of placement choices.

The man and the woman walked through the tall grass up the driveway, instead of on the dirt track. The highway was as empty as it ever was, no one happened to pass by and see them. Don wanted to walk beside them, talk to them, scare them away. This was really important though so he needed to think it through. He could watch them do whatever they were going to do and they would think they had done it.

Then he could take their devices back down. That would be more helpful. If they came back he could always run them off then.

# 71

# Mr. Hammond And Ashley

As they sped along in the back of the Mustang, Ashley replaced Emmy and Phoebe's phones with newer, more secure versions. Then she set herself up a new one and put the three old ones in a bag. Then she did a series of scans. There were a few trackers she would need to lift off the car when they got out.

When they parked in the yard, Ashley was impressed. What she had seen in the video chat with Emmy on Emmy's first night at the ranch was still stuck in Ashley's mind. To some degree she had expected more of the same.

This was clearly a working place but orderly. The house was a sophisticated mid century modern. There were no lawn ornaments or wind chimes or other clutter. It all just seemed very, under control. When she met Mr. Hammond and Nora she thought that their home matched them perfectly.

"Good to meet you."

Mr. Hammond thought she looked like Clyde. Ashley

thought he looked like a western magazine cover. Nora thought the girl looked like she might need a hospital.

A pair of men much younger than Mr. Hammond waved to them from where they stood in the corrals in the distance then turned back to their discussion.

"Two of our sons, Brian and August, they might be in here in a bit, come in."

Nora gestured toward Ashley and Emmy and Phoebe. Ashley excused herself with a gesture and nonchalantly removed five trackers from the Mustang and put them in a special bag. They all watched her silently. Next she rifled her backpack and her clothes for a moment and opened the bag again. Then she took a zippered case out of her backpack and stuffed the bag into it and pulled the strained zipper shut. Her audience watched until she joined Emmy and Phoebe back on the sidewalk as if there had been no interruption.

"What do you have that case lined with?"

Mr. Hammond's voice sounded gruffer than he meant for it to.

"Lead, copper, a few other things."

He nodded, silently impressed. Ashley hadn't made it this far by being a punk.

Phoebe stopped to look around and back up the road behind her and then made eye contact with James as she looked. He spoke first.

"Do you have the keys? We will park it in that steel building over behind the barn."

Phoebe hesitated only fractionally.

"Don't worry, I'll leave the garage door open and the keys

in it. You will be able to get to it if you need to."

Phoebe handed him the keys and followed Emmy up the sidewalk protectively.

"So how's your mom?"

Nora had never known Barb well but the business they had done with her had changed the course of Nora's life dramatically.

All three women looked worried, a little sick and in Ashley's case more than a little guilty. No one had talked to Barb since before Ashley landed. Nora waited to ask more questions until James got there.

They didn't have to wait long. Emmy was surprised by how gruff he sounded when he spoke.

"Brian is going to stay here, August is going over on the hill to have a look. We should know if your company is at your house here shortly."

Phoebe followed Nora and James' eyes to a large radio terminal sitting on a saddle blanket on a desk in the kitchen. Ashley spoke quickly.

"Tell him not to approach them, it's not worth it."

Ashley's hair and skin looked funny, even her nail beds and eyeballs were off. Nora looked at her husband. She was thinking maybe their next drive should be back down to East River to the hospital.

"So Ashley, I've known your mom my whole life. I'm a little older than her, in school she was in the same grade as my younger sisters. Well one older and one younger. We all went to school together. Barb was born right over there at Emmy's house. I imagine you have figured out that she could power all of Dallas, if she wanted to?"

Ashley nodded.

"And you all know that she is cagey. She's never been caught, never been cornered. She runs it high and tight."

The four women nodded with eyes wide.

"So my question to you young lady, is, when did all of this start?"

Mr. Hammond had not meant to frame the question that way. Ashley had not planned to let anyone help her but now that she was here she spoke simply and shrugged.

"I was in college. There was a professor."

Ashley knew that Mr. Hammond didn't have a lot of space right now for formalities. She didn't either.

Nora knew what to say. Phoebe and Emmy nodded in agreement as Nora spoke.

"College girls are stupid. Easy victims."

Mr. Hammond made the next guess with surprising ease and accuracy.

"So this outfit, whoever they are, have been calling your shots ever since."

Ashley had been hoping for relief in that moment when the truth finally hit the air. There was no relief. Mr. Hammond seemed satisfied.

"Okay. Well then, we will get you doctored up while we wait for August to radio."

Ashley felt very afraid. What if this family was harmed too? They needed to know what they were getting into. They needed to know how careful they needed to be. She put three folded pieces of paper in front of James and Nora.

Phoebe and Emmy looked terrified. Nora unfolded the first one and held it out while James adjusted a pair of reading glasses.

"A gallery in Santa Fe burned down."

Nora summarized for James. He felt the paper between his fingers.

"This is on printer paper, with no date and no specifics."

Ashley's voice was truly miserable.

"It's a mock up, prepared ahead of time."

Nora narrowed her eyes, James nodded slowly in affirmation. The gallery had indeed been burned down. He picked up the second piece of paper. The older couple didn't say anything at first. Then James handed the piece of paper to Emmy and Phoebe.

Nora spoke for James too while Emmy and Phoebe read.

"You were right to come here. We aren't going to screw around with these pieces of shit."

Ashley looked at Emmy.

"I am so sorry."

Emmy was trying to think of some kind of joke. Some sort of jab at her own weepy nature through the years. but as she saw her own name next to the words suicide she just held her silence. Ashley would do anything to take care of her, clearly she had been.

Nora and James were looking at the last piece of paper and

then handed it to Phoebe too. Emmy looked over Phoebe's shoulder and inhaled a little quickly. This was a missing person report. Were they planning to kidnap Ashley? Phoebe spoke quietly.

"So you would have just disappeared one day?"

"Nora, we need two lemons cut in half please. Four pieces please."

Mr. Hammond disappeared into the back of the house and returned shortly. He set a small rock on the kitchen counter. Then he lifted the radio.

"Brian, would you go out in the shop and bring me that small roll of fine gauge copper wire?"

Emmy and Phoebe were looking at the rock. It looked like an ordinary small to medium sized stone. Mr. Hammond perched on a kitchen stool at the island with his reading glasses still in place.

"This won't work anywhere else but it will work here, in this place, for me in this scenario."

He gestured in Ashley's direction.

Ashley understood exactly what he was talking about.

The man named Brian strode in onto the linoleum in boots and hat and set the wire and a pair of fence pliers to his dad's right hand before leaving again without a second glance.

"Put this in your left hand. Put this in your right hand. And now hold this wire please."

James ran a length of the copper wire around Ashley's back, into her right hand and across her front and back into her left hand. He looked at Emmy for comprehension and she volunteered as she looked at the big, loose wire circle.

"A complete circuit, of sorts."

"Correct. And now we set this rock."

He set the wire that ran in front of Ashley on the kitchen island and then held it in place with the rock.

"Now we wait for a little while."

Phoebe spoke first.

"What's the lemon for?"

Mr. Hammond smiled as he replied.

"Oh. For drinking. Strong lemon water to balance your acidity level."

Emmy asked the next question.

"What's the rock for?"

"It's a balancing rock. It takes into itself whatever excess exists in the world around it. In this case, all the extra electricity that is going to be running in this circle very shortly."

"What happens to the rock?"

Phoebe was curious.

"I have a fence post up in the hills where I leave it for a couple months, all the wind and the rain, that sort of thing, it will calibrate itself."

Nora asked the next question.

"You just set it on top of the post?"

"No, I have one of those mesh bags you use. Then I hang it on a nail."

Ashley was starting to look a little better. She had the next question.

"Where did you get this rock?"

"My mother."

Nora was incredulous. She had been married to James a long time and had seen a few things in this family. But Grandma Doris?

"Grandma Doris? Had this rock? I guess I saw her as too straight laced for this sort of thing."

The radio static filled the kitchen. Then August's voice crackled in.

"They are over here all right. Their pickup is parked on the road up to the north windmill road. Looks like two of them walked in, I can see them in the yard now."

Nora picked up the radio with the cord.

"Thank you. Stay far away. These are the kind of people that kill and kidnap people."

Nora saying it out loud cleared the air.

"Will do. I think they will be taking off here soon."

Mr. Hammond could see that Ashley was feeling much better.

"So I have a few guesses about what kind of work you do for these people but would you care to elaborate?"

Nora wanted to hear the story, so she spoke to encourage her.

"We are going to need to wait for a while."

Ashley didn't mean to sidetrack but she had things on her mind.

"Well, sometimes I wonder if they are bluffing me. Maybe I have gotten a little paranoid. But that professor, I went to her funeral."

Emmy started to cry as Ashley continued.

"But I don't even know if that body was for sure dead, that all may have been a front too."

Mr. Hammond was taking his boots off gingerly.

"That's very astute of you. I agree. They are bluffing a little. Or you would have been gone a long time ago."

Nora handed him a granola bar as he continued.

"However that doesn't mean you are paranoid. I think your assessment of their capabilities and intentions is right on the money."

Nora was making sure everyone had lemon water and granola bars. Who knew what was going to happen next. Mr. Hammond's voice took on a philosophical tone.

"Dangerous people that are taking on too much are very dangerous. Like a wild animal that feels cornered."

"I feel like I'm the cornered wild animal."

"Ah."

Mr. Hammond waved his hand dismissively.

"There's a coward at work in here somewhere."

"What do you mean?"

Nora and Phoebe and Emmy listened carefully to Ashley and James visiting.

"A whole team terrorizing one lone woman? Getting you to keep these kinds of threats a secret, for years. Somewhere there is a son of a bitch that feels just pretty smug. So yes, I would say there's a coward at work here somewhere."

Mr. Hammond pulled his boots back on slowly.

"I bet you've been giving them a run for their money."

Ashley smiled for the first time in a long time.

"Actually I took it all."

Mr. Hammond laughed generously.

"I knew it. You are a brave piece of work."

"What's going to happen next?"

"Well, I think this horse shit has gone on long enough. I wouldn't worry about it too much more."

Nora spoke to clarify.

"He doesn't mean to be dismissive."

"Well whoever these power hungry little pieces of scum are, they have never been to Dismal. There's more going on here than they can imagine."

Mr. James Hammond smiled at Emmy and Phoebe and then at Ashley.

"Are you ready to go see your family home? I think you will like it."

# 72

# Bad People

Ashley's first impression was of sitting down at a campfire after a long and scary day. The heat of it all reached to her bones and comforted her.

What she saw was a ramshackle house with dead weeds and new weeds growing up all around it and a kitten on the doorstep. A metal windmill was clanging in the wind, the tail and fan spinning around wildly. The three women stepped cautiously out into the brisk air. Nora and James went ahead of them in their pickup and August and Brian would be coming up the driveway any moment behind them. Emmy was grateful for their support.

"Do you think they should go home?"

Nora had asked with concern.

"Why not? These people got what they wanted today or they wouldn't have left. The doors lock. We can be there real quick if they need us. And they will be safer in their family home then anywhere we can house them."

Phoebe thought he had a point.

Now they all approached the front of the house slowly. There were three rusted coffee cans on the cement step.

Mr. Hammond laughed aloud.

"Brian come look at this!! So much for their surveillance efforts!"

He picked up a small piece of plastic from the can and then tossed it back down in contempt.

The coffee cans were filled with all the tiny cameras and listening devices the agents had planted.

"They shouldn't have wasted their time, Don is a persistent little cuss."

Brian and August exchanged glances.

Phoebe tapped Nora on the shoulder and pointed at the door. There was writing scrawled in the grime.

You Had Visitors

Ashley didn't know what to think.

"Mom always said the place she grew up was haunted, is this what she meant?"

The question broke the eerie reverie as the wind moved in the dead branches overhead and behind the house.

August handed two of the coffee cans to his brother and made to open the door and let everyone inside. It was time to be getting in for the night before the evening really settled.

"Can we put those inside please? I have some tricks I can do with them."

August nodded and set them inside the door on the kitchen floor for Ashley.

"Thank you."

When Nora declared that she was satisfied with all the doors and all the windows she turned to Emmy.

"I think you should have the phone company reconnect your landline. I'll get you the number tomorrow. Just one more backup."

Then she turned to Ashley.

"How are you feeling?"

They needed to get going into Dismal. She had texted Zoe to stay at the school until they came to pick her up, there were some bad people around.

# 73

# One Client

Barb felt as if her shell had been damaged. She would need to retreat for the winter to nurse her wounds and recuperate but instead this was spring time. She had never been so glad to be with Allan.

Barb hadn't known what to do about the distinct possibility she was bugged. In the end she shut their phones off and stuck them in her bag under Allan's spare jacket in the trunk of his car. That was the best she could do. The car was old enough that it was manufactured before satellite connection. She was scared to talk at all but she reasoned that maybe it didn't matter that much if what she had to say was overheard a little. Allan looked at her in expectation as they got back on the road.

"Ashley is an independent tech contractor."

Allan nodded.

"She's been contracting with the same government group so far in her career."

Allan paused and nodded. In the later part of his career he himself had been an independent contractor. He was an engineer with a reputation for creative problem solving, someone they called when things had not gone to plan.

"Just the one client?"

"I know."

Barb wrapped her hands around her steaming coffee cup.

"And I think, I know, that she has developed something that she shouldn't have."

Allan looked at her sternly over his glasses as his heart leapt a little with nervous energy. Barb was a strange and powerful woman with a strange history. He looked as far down the highway as he could see and then at Barb.

"Where is she now?"

"At the ranch with Emmy and Phoebe and James and Nora, the neighbors. They couldn't be anywhere safer actually."

Barb looked pensive for a moment.

"We grew up being neighbors. I sold my ranch to James when I inherited it. He was the obvious choice."

Allan waited until she was ready again before asking his next question.

"How do you know that she has developed something?"

It was an astute question that Barb didn't want to answer.

"Because she did it in our apartment and there was an accident."

Allan tried not to whistle but he sat back to think even while driving. He was impressed they weren't both in prison by now. Barb had lived an interesting life sure, back in the day, but Ashley was still very young.

"And you are sure her client in the federal government?

"Actually I am."

Barb nodded confidently. Allan echoed her confidence.

"That would explain the one client thing."

"So what is the conflict point?"

Barb looked at him confused.

"Hmmm?"

"There is a conflict or there would be no coercion."

That's when Barb put to words what she had known all along.

"So these people think they will use me to manipulate Ashley."

"It's terrible but I think it sounds likely."

"Well I hope she hasn't given them an inch."

# 74

# It's All Gone

The apartment felt like a wasteland when Barb opened the newly repaired door.

Barren, fenced off and avoided, why would anyone come here anymore? Emotion choked in her throat a little, her little family was all grown up. Their family home irrelevant. Allan gripped her hand tightly.

"I know that you, don't need protection."

He eyed her stacks of amulets and talismans and started over.

"You don't need radiation protection. But I probably do."

Barb pulled her mouth to the side a little as she thought. Radiation protection gear wasn't just lying around to purchase anywhere. Surely Ashley had some in her lab? But putting gear from the damaged lab on Allan wouldn't make anything better. She turned back to him protectively, even standing here in the door probably wasn't the safest thing for him. Allan spoke before she could.

"I'm staying right here, you go in and take a look and report back. Then you get what you need and we are getting out of here."

Barb felt all the years coming up to strangle her. Where had she gone wrong? The open concept living space had never felt so enormous to cross as it did now. She could still see Allan from where she stood outside Emmy's old bedroom door. She grasped the door knob and let the door swing open. She knew what to expect. Contrary to what she pretended, she was not the kind of woman who let anything go on in her domain without checking on it once in a while. She had been pleased with the insulating layers, her daughter had done a good job. Ashley knew her stuff.

Now she was surprised to see the meltdown with fresh eyes and new emotions.

"Tell me what you see?"

Barb called out an answer across the echoing apartment.

"It looks like it got too hot. It's all melted and used up and emitting. She got in over her head on a project, her power source melted all her equipment."

"What kind of equipment?"

"She had low pressure chambers and high pressure chambers and a holding unit and her power units..."

"You'd been in there before?"

"What kind of an idiot do you think I am?"

"Fair enough. It's all gone?"

"Um, yes. There's a lot of destroyed tech. Then it looks like she threw things everywhere, took the good stuff in a hurry."

"And the power units?"

Allan didn't say her controlled substance stockpile.

"Nothing here. I don't think she would leave them here."

Something was making Barb's skin prick. She shut the door firmly.

"Allan, something's not right in here."

"Then come back out here!"

He kept his tone under control but he was very afraid for her.

"Walk. One step, two step. Come on girl. Move it!"

Something about the unusual wording made Barb move.

"I want to go pack some of my things."

"I don't think so. What if there's someone in there? I'm not calling the police or the doorman and I'm not armed. Don't make me come in there after you, you crazy lady."

In the end he did because she didn't listen and disappeared into her master suite. He found her with her hand to her mouth in the doorway of her closet. She was deteriorating in front of him. Velvet jewelry trays were on the floor, vault doors stood open, there was broken glass. The place had been torn apart.

"It's all gone."

With that Allan picked her up and carried her out of there before he got too sick to be able to.

# 75

# A Family

"My turquoise! All of my stones. The collection!"

Grief was tearing at Barb in waves of pain.

Allan pulled the apartment door shut with a slam and punched the elevator button.

"Pull yourself together. It's just stuff."

Barb responded instantly with an impressive calm. Allan understood her so well. He pulled her into the elevator and pushed the lobby button.

"We are not coming back here."

As the doors slid shut he wished they would have taken the stairs, that was no good either, it would just take longer.

"What are we going to do?"

Barb wanted to chew on him for carrying her like a sack of grain. He didn't look that strong.

"I wasn't done in there you know."

"No. You really were. And what do you mean what are we going to do? We are going to go find Ashley."

Allan doubted there was any place in the world where they could hide. But he needed to know what Ashley had invented, stumbling around in ignorance wasn't going to help anybody. He had waited a lifetime for Barb to say to him the words he wanted to hear. These are your daughters, this is our family. Or maybe later for Emmy or Ashley to say, I would like us to be a family instead of acquaintances. He had thought it was appropriate to be invited into these sorts of relationships.

Now he no longer cared. He had been wrong. Ashley was just like him and she was going to need his help. Enough stupidity was enough. Now he turned to Barb as they strode hand in hand across the lobby, Barb hurrying to keep up with his longer stride.

"I need to know exactly what happened to you."

# 76

# At Home

Ashley was looking at Emmy's new old sewing machine when she saw something outside. Phoebe was blowing up the air mattress she had found at the dollar store. Emmy was making microwave popcorn. No one would be sleeping very easily until the wee hours of the morning.

"It's really cool huh?"

Emmy meant the sewing machine.

Ashley didn't say a word about what she saw. Emmy would freak out. Still, she felt a little nervous. Everyone had seemed to accept that a ghost had supposedly gathered all the cameras and listening devices much more easily than she had.

She had no trouble believing in that level of paranormal activity. This place was loaded. She imagined ten of her homemade power units hidden under a metal frame bed. This place was like trying to get comfortable on top of hundreds of them. They might as well just have a sleepover in a compromised nuclear power plant without any safety barriers or containment design. Just for fun.

She didn't need to break a Geiger counter to know that the level was off the charts. That could easily explain an increased level of paranormal activity. And yet it all felt just so, right.

"This place feels so weird, so comfortable."

"I know, it's the strangest thing. Everything your eyes see tells you that you should just leave, drive away. But it feels right, like home. Even to Phoebe."

Phoebe nodded, she was putting pillowcases on some brand new pillows. Thank goodness they had made that dollar store run before heading on to the airport.

Ashley's mind was back on the ghost gathering up all the surveillance tech. Why would a ghost do that? Who was the ghost? Did anyone know? She wasn't going to ask, everyone was on edge anyway. And didn't ghosts exist because of unfinished business or lack of acknowledgment? Where was the body buried? With that last thought Ashley finally spooked herself. Emmy handed her a bag of microwave popcorn and plopped down in the corner of the horrible love seat. The room wasn't large, the air mattress was crowded up against the disgusting upholstery.

Emmy and Phoebe didn't mind at all. Ashley looked skeptically at the threadbare brown carpet. It would have been cleaner just to go lay down in a street. Why hadn't they cleaned anything?

Emmy waved around casually.

"I'm sort of waiting."

She almost said to remodel but stopped herself in time. She didn't want to cause upset.

"It's important to be respectful."

Ashley gripped her brand new pillow and her popcorn.

"How do you two do this?"

Phoebe laughed.

"Well I've always been kind of into this sort of thing. And I don't think this is a bad place, like I don't pick up on that at all."

Her expression soured as she remembered the lightning strikes. She would need to tell Ashley about that but not tonight. Emmy was talking.

"So I really think the ghost, whoever they are, is probably on our side. So it is creepy and all that. I am the biggest wimp, you know that. But to me, this is just where I need to be right now."

Phoebe was contemplating Ashley being afraid of a ghost instead of being abducted by the fricking FBI or CIA or something. Emmy was not far behind her.

"How do you, sleep at night? I mean..."

Emmy was still processing all the missing puzzle pieces about her sister's life. Now it was Ashley's turn to show confidence.

"Target practice."

She pulled her backpack closer to her.

"I carry. I practice. I can afford to put in the rounds. And it doesn't technically make much logical sense but it still helps me sleep at night."

Emmy and Phoebe were both feeling a bit better as they

looked from Ashley to her backpack and back again. She was right. It didn't actually hold up very well under too much analysis but it was better than nothing.

Ashley was remembering the writing on the screen door, no one had even bothered to wipe it off, they had just walked right in. So she spoke again.

"But the intangible, the things that don't have to obey the laws of the physical. The unpredictable and malicious, that scares me."

Phoebe nodded understandingly.

"Correct me if I'm wrong but you deal in unstable isotopes, that's why they release the energy, because they are trying to stabilize?"

Ashley nodded and Emmy piled on.

"And you pioneer new technology, powerful and dangerous stuff if I understand correctly. So don't you technically deal in the intangible and things that operate outside the rules constantly?"

Ashley nodded as she objected.

"Everything obeys some set of rules. We just can't always see or sometimes we don't know, what those rules are, yet."

"Well try to think of this place..."

Phoebe didn't say the word ghost.

"Think of it like that. It's just something you haven't figured out yet."

Emmy smiled proudly at Phoebe.

Ashley was asleep within minutes.

# 77

# Nora Waits Up

Down at the end of the driveway next to the broken mailbox August and his mother Nora sat in the dark in a crew cab pickup. Nora was bundled against the cold. Nothing was going to happen, the best way to make sure of that was to headed it off before it got started. And so she would sit here silently in the blackness.

August spoke softly.

"Do you think Dad and Barb were close back in the day?"

Nora was glad to have something to talk about. She knew that the question was about a romantic relationship. Her children did not know very much about their dad's first wife. There just wasn't much to discuss.

Nora knew that the two of them had been in love, she had had a lot of problems, she had left him and later divorced him. Later on Nora had come along.

Privately Nora thought having a failed practice run might

have done James quite a lot of good in the big picture but she would never say that. Nora had even met her husband's ex-wife. And she agreed with everything she had heard, lots of problems.

That part of the past just didn't come up because there wasn't anything interesting to say. But she knew, that from her children's perspective, the things that don't get talked about sometimes accumulate mystery. Many things that don't get talked about are very important. They are just mixed in with a whole bunch of stuff that really isn't. So Nora spoke softly.

"I don't think so, he was a little older than her and she left right after graduation."

She paused to choose her next words.

"She was not your dad's first wife, not by a long shot. I have only met Barb in person maybe once but I don't think she is the type to put up with any man for very long."

"That wasn't what I meant."

August spoke tenderly. His mom remembered that he had been such a tender little soul as a kid. The broken off engagement had really left a scar. He probably thought he would always feel broken.

Nora thought that he had very nearly missed marrying a bitchy little brat that would have divorced him in the end anyway. She would never ever say that to him.

"I know. I think your dad knows all the things he knows, just from being around the family. His mom and Barb's mom were very close, being neighbors all through the years."

That seemed to answer the question.

## 78

# Don Waits Up Too

Don stood in the doorway between the kitchen and the living room, casting subtle fragmented shadows. The girls usually left some lights on, tonight they had turned on every light in the house. Emmy and Phoebe were having a frantic whispered discussion on the love seat. Ashley was sacked out on the air mattress on the floor.

So Ashley was on the wrong side of the law. Ivory would have loved her.

Don remembered that the old couple had journeyed to Dallas twice. Once to attend Emmy's high school graduation. Then years later to attend Ashley's. He supposed they had gone once or twice when the girls were still small but he didn't remember the specifics. Barb had certainly never brought her kids here to see their grandparents.

It was odd to Don to think that Emmy had never known Clyde or Gladys, or the woman that Gladys had been when she had still gone by the name Ivory. It was crazy that Ashley had not known them at all, when everything she was had to do with who they had been.

# 79

# Zoe's Questions

Zoe crept out of her bedroom over on the neighboring Hammond ranch. No one told her much of anything and then they told her not to say a word to anyone in town or at school.

Emmy and Phoebe were still living in the haunted house and Emmy's sister Ashley had flown in from Dallas today. Phoebe and Emmy had driven down to pick her up. Then somewhere in there bad trouble had come up. Her mom had said there were some dangerous people around. And Zoe had waited at the school for her parents to come pick her up. So Zoe took careful steps out to the kitchen, her mom left one light on above the stove at night.

Zoe gave up with a heave of tense shoulders, her dad was sitting up in his recliner in the den. The TV was on low, throwing it's weird lights all over the scene.

"What's up?"

He muttered gruffly, he was feeling very tired and old.

"Where's mom?"

"She went with August to go watch over at Clyde's old place for a while."

Zoe looked afraid and he softened his tone.

"Nothing to worry about too much. That's what you do with nights like these. Spend two or three hours doing something like that, watching. Then you spend a couple hours doing something else. Pretty soon morning is on the way and you've done it."

"What are the two of them going to do?"

"Probably nothing, she just wouldn't have been able to sleep."

"What happened today? Who are these people?"

Zoe perched in another recliner. James debated.

"You remember hearing about Barb?"

"We bought the Hart pastures from her."

"That's correct, she lives in Dallas. She had an art gallery in Santa Fe get burned down. Whoever it was also destroyed her car."

Zoe was thinking hard.

"Why would they do that? What could they gain?"

"Exactly."

The night stretched on around them.

"So Ashley, that's her name right? She is coming to stay with her sister because of that?"

"More or less."

An owl hooted.

"That doesn't actually tell me what is going on."

"I know."

"I'm pretty grown up you know. Keeping stuff a secret doesn't help keep people safe, it just creates a bunch of confusion."

"Ashley was followed from Dallas to Denver and from Denver to East River, by two people. And she was afraid."

Zoe didn't say anything.

"So they came over here, the three of them. August went up on the hill and sure enough, they went over to Clyde's old place."

"How'd they get there?"

"A third person picked up them up in a pickup at the airport."

"Why did they go there, if she was over here?"

James snorted in amusement.

"They set up surveillance cameras, microphones that sort of thing."

Zoe was shocked.

"Why?"

"Why do you think? To watch and to listen."

"Why is that funny?"

James had started to laugh to himself as the scenarios in his mind got funnier and funnier.

"Why is that even remotely funny?"

"Oh because it didn't work."

James was drying his eyes with a tissue.

"Don sure can be an annoying little shit when he wants to be."

"The ghost?"

"Yeah, the ghost over there."

Zoe thought this was the most interesting story she had ever heard, ever.

"Why didn't it work?"

"He went around behind them and put all their little cameras and such in a coffee can."

Zoe stared at her dad, she didn't know what to think at all. Maybe August would be able to tell her more.

# 80

# The Surveillance Footage

David did something he didn't usually do and went to the desks of his reporting operatives. They were waiting on him for staffing decisions. Constant surveillance in a place like Dismal would be much harder to pull off without attracting attention than it had been in Dallas. The existing sweep had gotten a room at the old motel in Dismal but if they were going to stay they would need a convincing cover next time they spoke to a local. And yet none of that was on David's mind and there were many, much more interesting, things being discussed by the active teams.

"So none of them ever established a feed."

"No. They did establish a connection. Then there is say twenty to thirty seconds of footage before it goes dark."

David heard what they were saying.

"Show me."

A face crossed the screen at close range. A young man wearing a cowboy hat. David formulated the rest of the scene in his mind. This person had squatted down and looked at this video device before detaching it. The landscaped blurred across the monitor and then went dark. This person had followed along behind his agents and collected the devices as they went, there were many so David visualized a bag. That's when the scene went dark.

"Back it up and pause."

They all stared at the face for a while, seasoned and beginners alike. There was a lot to know just from that one shot. David questioned the team rookie first, he wanted a fresh perspective.

"What do you think?"

"A little younger than our target. We've never seen him before. Maybe a local?"

"You're saying maybe no connection other than proximity?"

"I think it's possible. We thought the place the sister moved into was abandoned but this is a small community. I think probably a local."

David pushed.

"You think he lives there?"

"Well it doesn't make sense but maybe. Without foreknowledge about Ashley or any connection to her, it makes sense than he would counter our surveillance just for his own privacy or out of spite. He looks like he thinks this is funny."

David turned to the group as a whole.

"What else?"

A woman spoke up quickly.

"He looks funny, there's something about the skin and the

eyes."

The woman at the desk zoomed the still shot in more closely. Another operative spoke up in response.

"He didn't buy that hat or that shirt recently. It's not a big difference, but those are vintage."

There was something off about the eyes under the hat. He looked very young. And like he was having the time of his life. He was having the last laugh at them even now.

David wondered if the locals knew him, if he got along with the locals. He tended to agree with the first opinion, this was a local that just happened to be there. But now David also thought that this wasn't a well known person in the Dismal community. No one had brought up the big question at hand, they were waiting for their boss' timing.

"So I'm told that our operatives never saw anybody."

The room stayed quiet.

"But according to this footage, these devices were in place what less than thirty seconds before he followed along behind and removed them."

The team was listening carefully.

"That house is not very big, and the spaces outside it are open. How can it be that they never saw this individual even once?"

Everyone was left to their own thoughts. Ashley was a strange woman, an interesting character. David was the only one that approached her directly. She was one of the assets he managed personally. They were all just supporting surveillance. Still, they heard everything she said and read all her texts and tallied every purchase she made and every person she acknowledged on the street. She was a solitary cat and astoundingly capable, self controlled and patient. She tolerated their presence in her life, one agent smiled to themselves, just about the way a cat would.

"She would have left the devices where they were, even after she knew about them."

Another agent offered a banter, almost forgetting his boss' presence.

"Yes, well when she takes them down we have to go put a new set up and it's just easier for everyone that way."

The comment got a few barks of laughter, it was true. She was a cooperative surveillance target, thoughtful, considerate even. In many ways she had depended on their being there. David could not afford to have her be intercepted by any foreign operatives, cartels or representatives of powerful people. She usually had devices on her with enough illicit information to start a world war. Beyond that there was everything she would know. They would not have let anything happen to her. The only thing she had to be nervous about was losing her freedom to David's decision making. Thus the cooperation.

Actually, the entire thing had been an enormous risk, letting her walk around in Dallas like that, letting her travel. By all common sense measures, her work should take place in a highly secure facility. But no one said that.

No one said, what now boss? Are we done here? If you bring her in, you won't need this support team anymore.

David had to agree with his team. This youth did not know Ashley. She had stumbled into something that already existed in Dismal. They could not leave her there if they could not guarantee security there. There was an empty component of a facility in New Mexico that would be the perfect fit. He had already ordered renovations.

# 81

# Barb's Story

"So where did this all start, for you?"

Allan was driving, not speeding, not aggressively but driving much more intensely than was normal for him. Barb crossed her arms in front of her chest.

"I was born this way."

Allan looked at her sideways. He wasn't in the mood for evasive humor.

"That doesn't tell me anything."

"I was!"

Allan looked at the road ahead as he gripped the steering wheel, they had time. This would probably be one of those tasks that would benefit from doing it correctly the first time around.

"Well then, tell me about your childhood."

"I am not going to do that."

"Tell me about Ashley's childhood."

Barb got quiet.

"Fine."

"Well, my mom was, sad. She was a very sad person. A very broken person. My dad was, different. A very strong person but quiet. They were very, cautious. Formal."

"Tell me more about your mom."

"She lost her mom when she was young. She was raised by her grandparents. Then she lost her grandma when she was a teenager. She never talked about it. Doris told me."

Barb looked at Allan.

"Doris was the next door neighbor, she was close with my mom."

Allan nodded understandingly, this was going to be quite the story whether Barb realized it or not.

"That must have been really hard for her. I'm sure she was very sad."

"But you know that wasn't all of it? She was very sad about the town, about Dismal, about the ranch. Just about the whole world really."

"Why?"

"I think she felt like she had responsibilities that she could never quite fulfill. She felt she needed to make everything okay, make everything be a certain way. That made her sad. And she was sad because she wasn't always well received in the community. And even later, when she probably would have been or could have been, she didn't think that she was. She kind of hated everybody."

Allan empathized.

"She must have felt very alone."

"Oh she did. But she had a fabulous imagination. You know our house was red on the inside? In a world full of light greens and yellow and the occasional light blue. She had a lot of style, a lot of vision. I think that helped her feel strong."

"So other than the neighbor Doris, was there anyone else she was close to?"

Allan was imagining a small child version of Barb, alone with her sad mother. Who was also alone, in a red house.

"Her uncle Virgil, she was very close to him. They were the last two family members of the original Heart Seven ranch."

Barb's voice had turned proud and a little smug. She continued before Allan could ask. He was still driving along but both of them were lost in the story.

"It was a very big ranch, a dynasty. They ruled Dismal like a monarchy. They put thousands of cattle on that train, thousands upon thousands through the years."

Barb was lost in looking at the scenery as she talked.

"Virgil never got married. And he was the last one in his generation, his siblings had both passed away. His sister, my mom's mom, you know passed away when my mom was young. So my mom was his only living relative."

Allan wondered where this was all going.

"But they were much closer than just business, he was still at home when my mom went to live with her grandparents, his parents. So they knew each other very well, like siblings. They were family. So yes there was Doris and Uncle Virgil around when I was a kid."

Allan looked at how ramrod straight Barb sat in the passenger seat as she looked out the window, at her impeccable outfit and her sharp features.

"Why wasn't your mom well liked in the community?"

Allan knew immediately that he had touched a nerve.

"Well there had been deaths."

Barb brushed it off angrily as if it wasn't important.

"But I think it went back much further than that."

She paused to gather her thoughts.

"I think all of that had much more to do with who she was in the Hart family. You know the Heart Seven ranch being so dominant in the community. That was where her problems came from more than who she was as a person. She was actually a very soft soul."

Allan did not think that Barb could ever be described as a soft soul but perhaps her mom had been. Allan pictured a woman as harsh as Barb on the outside but softer on the inside. Where had Barb's personality come from?

"Who died?"

"I don't want to talk about it."

Allan let the conversation drop. He fumbled with a water bottle while he drove. So far he didn't have any clues as to how Barb, and Ashley, had become so powerfully strange. But this was already far more than he had even hoped to learn. They had time.

"My dad was strange. He loved the weather and he loved haying and he loved big horses. But there was something about him, he just never really was at peace."

"Where did your dad grow up?"

"I don't know."

Allan looked at Barb, this was a promising lead.

"When you asked, they never would say?"

"Well, no. A lot of things about all of that were complicated."

"And you were an only child?"

Allan knew that but it seemed worth re-establishing.

"Yes. I think that they had not been together very long at all when they had me. As I think back, even when I was starting school age, they were still getting to know each other. They were a bit, removed."

"So you were very much alone?"

Allan thought that this all painted a very bleak picture that made a lot of sense.

"Oh I don't know, I was and I wasn't."

"Doris must have meant a lot to you."

"Oh yes. And her girls, well all of her kids really. I think to some extent she made them be friends with me. But underneath that and after that, they liked me for me. School was not easy for me. But they were always my friends, I think they really, understood me. Appreciated my strengths."

Allan circled the conversation back.

"And he would have been your great uncle, Virgil?"

"Yes, but I adored him. And he was very fond of me too."

"One Christmas he brought me a horse. I named her Angel. She was quite old I believe."

Barb smiled and laughed aloud a little.

"She was gentle, sleepy to a fault. A big light colored thing. Actually now that I think about it she may have been part draft. Virgil knew my dad had a soft spot for the drafts. That sounds about right."

Allan was glad to hear Barb relay a happy memory when the conversation took what he found to be a strange turn.

"I always hoped she would come back after she died. I missed her."

Allan knew they had hit a chord of truth there for a moment but he didn't press it.

"The land has really changed so much."

Barb was looking out the window.

"When was the last time you took this drive?"

Barb laughed out loud.

"Never. I have never come back."

Allan looked at her a little sadly but she didn't notice.

"My dad would have loved all of this."

Barb waved her hand generally at the scenery. Allan agreed gently.

"It is beautiful."

"Oh he would have loved it for it's industry. He would have talked about irrigation and production potential and crops and herd numbers. And he would have loved to see these tractors."

When Allan looked at Barb he saw a glimpse of a happy little girl.

"He loved tractors so much. I mean he loved the teams and the hayfields but he loved tractors too. I remember when I was old enough to start driving the rake tractor."

Allan didn't understand a whole lot more of the story that Barb told. But he understood the joy and the connection, the love of a family and a shared love between family members. His own father had been an engineer and his mother an architect.

As he listened Allan would have called what she was talking

about a love of the land. He was sure Barb would have harshly rebuked such a suggestion. She was not by nature very sentimental.

"So why were you so upset with your parents?"

Barb looked shocked. She wanted to ask him why he thought that she was. But he was not wrong and probably the never coming back was a dead giveaway. Allan pressed on.

"We need to understand Ashley's situation and I get the feeling it is an extension of your situation. I don't think giving an explanation would really hurt you that much."

Actually Allan believed it would probably hurt her quite a lot.

"I thought they needed to leave Clara County, leave Dismal, leave Nebraska even. The world is so much bigger than that little bubble."

"Any reason in particular? It sounds like they loved the ranch, loved the land."

Barb bristled.

"They did. It was wonderful. But it wasn't very healthy. They clung onto some things that they could have gotten rid of. They could have made a new start for our family. Or even later, they could have a made a new start for each other. Or even just for themselves. There was no reason for them to have to stay."

"What did they hang on to?"

Barb exhaled loudly.

"I am not ready to discuss that. I might not ever be ready to discuss that. But I wasn't the only party in that fight. They knew how I felt about it all. Then when Virgil died..."

Barb shut her own thoughts off mid sentence but Allan didn't let it go.

"What happened when Virgil passed away?"

"He left half of the historic Heart Seven ranch to me."

Allan stared through the windshield, waiting.

"My mom was probably the rightful heir to the whole thing. She grew up there. That ranch was her entire existence, her entire identity. She sacrificed everything to that entity. So many people worked their whole lives to build that stability for future generations. She couldn't believe that he would break up that long of a legacy by dividing it in half."

Allan thought he started to see the problem.

"I was so frustrated with them at the time. There are so many wonderful places in the world, I was living in Dallas. They wouldn't even consider moving. They wouldn't even come visit me. I told them all the things that I thought. About how it was all bad living, not a good way to live. They said they had responsibilities. I told them to walk away."

Barb thought that Allan looked sympathetic and genuinely disturbed. So she continued with her story.

"So it all escalated. We fought all the time. They would call me and I would end up yelling at them, hanging up. They meant everything to me."

"Virgil knew all about the fighting. He knew how I felt about the place. He got a kick out of how much I loved it in Texas. I think he split the ranch because he didn't want me to have to wait."

Barb looked at Allan to make sure he was following along.

"By all rights he should have left the entire ranch to my mom and then when she passed it would have come to me. But he didn't want me to have to wait. I think he wanted to give me a good life. He would have given my mom a good life, when she was younger, if he possibly could have. In me, I think he saw a chance to do that."

Allan was afraid to hear what was going to happen next.

"So I sold my half of the Heart Seven ranch."

The car felt like all the oxygen had been sucked out instantaneously as they rolled along the highway in front of them.

Allan thought for a while before he spoke and in the end Barb beat him to it.

"I sold it to Doris' son. Well, really to the whole Hammond family. James Hammond was a little older than me. I knew him well enough to call him up. I trusted him. I thought the Hammond family deserved to have it, if anyone did."

Stress tears were falling from Barb's eyes and she did her best to hide them.

"I thought they would make a new start out of the ashes of something very old. And they have."

Allan thought about pulling over to try and hold the love of his life but he kept the car on the road. Barb appreciated the gesture and the decision. She pulled herself together and her voice changed abruptly as she continued and put some tissues back in her leather handbag and closed it.

"And they have."

"You know James is a grandpa now? He has a bunch of kids and a bunch of grandchildren. They expanded their cow-calf numbers and they even put in a feedlot. They have bought some other land too. They have really built a big operation from the sounds of it."

Allan felt a little lost at all the industry talk and shot her a half glance.

"They deserved to. The Hammonds were just a little homestead place. You know milk cows, hogs, big gardens, a little bit of cow calf. They wanted to make it. They wanted to make it so badly. And now they have."

"But you and your mom?"

"She never spoke to me again."

"And you?"

Barb beamed at him from the passenger seat.

"Well you know the rest of the story. I built a wonderful life. Two beautiful daughters, a little family of my own, a business and a career, a home, friends and community. All the healthy things and it has been good."

When Barb said the word family, a connection between them was almost made but they both shied away at the last moment.

"You know me very well. It was all unfortunate, painful but it's in the past."

As Barb said it the irony struck her as they raced up the highway headed back to Nebraska. Allan thought it was all he could see in the future but he decided to leave that for the moment.

"What about your dad?"

"Well he was very upset with me also. He was a loyal person. And he was angry about how much I hurt my mom. He thought there could have been a lot of ways I could have gone about that. That I could have done a lot better somehow."

Allan felt the pain rise up in his own throat.

"But in the end, people were the most important thing to him. He wasn't from around there. It wasn't his ranch that I threw away. So in the end he wanted us to have a good relationship."

Allan was thinking.

"So you sold half of the big ranch to the neighbors and your mom inherited the other half, instead of the whole thing."

"Yes, that's it exactly. She and my dad expanded their herd. She had always run cattle, worked the Heart Seven. But until then it had just been Virgil's name on the titles. She hated the Hammonds for buying it from me. But with Virgil gone she still expanded quite a lot. And they did that until she died. She loved to ranch."

"And you never saw her again?"

"No, I did. They came down for the girl's high school graduations."

Allan thought that sounded like a totally depressing empty gesture.

"The girls were pleased, my dad was pleased."

"But she never spoke to you again?"

"Yes that's pretty much it. Then after she passed away, it's very ironic actually, my dad, he leased the rest of the land to the Hammonds."

Allan looked at her sharply.

"He had a good working relationship with them. Mom would have been furious. But he was very practical that way. Now that I think about it he was probably just laying the ground work for his next move. He was a very loyal person."

"What was his next move?"

"He left the second half of the Heart Seven ranch to Emmy. Instead of to me."

Allan stared at Barb.

"So he repeated the pattern in a way?"

Barb nodded.

"And now here we are."

Allan had a few more clues than he did when he had started the conversation but not many. Barb's dad was definitely a shadowy figure, there could certainly be something more to find out there.

What were her parents responsible for? Why wouldn't they ever leave the ranch? It sounded like something more than love of the land, especially with Barb's bitterness around the topic. That was probably part of the picture of their current problems, whatever that was. And the business about the horse named Angel coming back after she died, that was worth noting. Allan kept his mental tally running. And who had died? Barb's mom had been involved in something shady as well. That merited more digging too.

The Hammond family, particularly the ones that had grown up with Barb, would be the best sources of information. Other than that it didn't sound like there was much of anyone left to ask. Barb herself was probably the only one that really knew what he needed to know.

# 82

# A Pattern

Barb took over driving after they stopped to eat. This gave Allan more time to think and ask questions.

"So, there was a riff between you and your mom over land. And there has been a riff between you and Emmy. That's a pattern."

Barb could have murdered him with the look she shot across the car.

"Emmy is easily confused and sentimental to a fault."

"Barb."

"No, you're right that's not entirely fair."

Barb adjusted her sunglasses as she drove and kept talking.

"But you have to agree that we wouldn't be in this mess right now if Emmy had listened to me and sold the ranch when she inherited it."

Allan didn't know why he would have to agree with that at all.

"Why would Ashley getting involved with the wrong people have happened differently if the ranch had been sold?"

He paused then asked a different question.

"Would your health or abilities shall we say, be different if the ranch was sold?"

Barb didn't answer. He pressed on.

"Would Ashley's?"

"No."

Barb admitted his point heavily. "I think that ship sailed a long time ago."

"So if the ranch was sold, you and Ashley would still be packing a current and Ashley would still be in trouble with some bad people. The only difference would be that Emmy wouldn't have a ranch and wouldn't be there right now."

Barb was slow to speak.

"I guess you're right. I have just had this idea in my head for a long time that we could ditch the problem."

Barb paused another long while before she continued.

"You know what? You are right. At this point it would make no difference at all. Even when Emmy inherited it would not have made a difference."

They didn't talk for a long time.

"So I was saying there is a pattern."

"What?"

"A pattern."

Allen replied patiently.

"Why would that matter?"

"Because in problem solving patterns matter. Patterns are clues. Especially in science."

Barb was not convinced and she spoke irritably.

"Okay."

"Patterns in stories matter. So I was observing a repetition.

An echo."

Barb was really cranky now.

"Okay I get it, sure."

Barb drove and Allan took a little nap. He was surprised that he could but it was a way to give Barb some privacy to think. When he woke up she was ready with a question.

"You think I should make up with Emmy?"

Allan wasn't sure he was ready to visit again.

"I think we should stop for coffee again."

"You think I am doing to her what my mom did to me?"

"I think she would be very happy to hear that you aren't mad at her anymore."

"Who said I wasn't mad at her anymore?"

Barb was getting more irate by the minute. Allan looked down the highway uneasily.

"You said you understood that even if she had listened to you and sold the ranch, we would still be in this situation with Ashley."

"I do understand that! You are making this sound like it is all my fault!"

That's when Allan finally let his frustration get the better of him.

"Is it all your fault Barb? Because you can be pretty damn selfish."

He hadn't meant to raise his voice. Barb started to cry.

"I'm sorry."

They both said it at the same time. Just then Barb saw a gas station.

"You're right. We should stop."

When they got out they were each surprised by how badly they needed to hug the other and then by how tightly they found themselves being held.

# 83

# Matt Sends A Text

Matt typed out his text to Emmy one more time.

"How are you? I am planning a trip to the islands. Any chance you would want to go with me?"

He did not include any emojis. He was stretched out on top of the covers. Megan was hot. The dates had gone well. She was good in bed and having her there at the office all the time was the best. He could easily take Megan on this trip. He had bought her another orchid for the front desk. He shook his head as if trying to clear it and then sent the text. He was looking forward to his morning run.

Emmy's face had an imprint from the love seat upholstery on the side of it. Her phone buzzed and woke her up. Phoebe and Ashley were still asleep. Emmy looked around at the morning sun in their living room before she looked at her phone.

"How are you? I am planning a trip to the islands. Any chance you would want to go with me?"

A text from Matt, the first one in a long time, what seemed like years actually. She looked at Ashley's face, even asleep she didn't look very healthy or peaceful. They had secret agent surveillance, trouble, as the Hammond's would put it. They certainly had ghost trouble and probably more kinds of trouble on the way. What would the day bring?

She laid the phone back down. There wasn't really anything to reply. A world where you could plan and go on trips sounded surreal and odd. Her mom's gallery had burned down and her car had been destroyed. Ashley had been followed here by secret agents. Her own life had been threatened. Their house had been bugged and then debugged. And here they were waking up on the same old sofa.

Emmy thought about the baby calves that could be seen from the road now. They were everywhere. Beth was still taking college classes, Zoe was still in high school. But what would happen to Ashley? Emmy looked at her baby sister again. What would happen to her mom? Would they ever talk again? What could she possibly do about any of it?

Her phone buzzed again. Emmy picked it up in aggravation, just an advertisement email. But Matt had always persisted, she should probably just send a reply and get that over with and forget about it.

"I'm good. No thank you. Have a nice time."

She didn't include any emojis.

Then she put her head back down and tried to go back to sleep. She would have rolled over but Phoebe was in the way. And she couldn't get up without disturbing Ashley. So she looked at the wood paneling on the wall and the dusty flat screen

TV in front of the dusty box TV and the crocheted orange owl wall decoration above her. She watched specks of dust float around in the light.

# 84

# A New Arrangement

David had made a decision. He would talk to Ashley in person. If she wanted to remain at the ranch, instead of accepting a new laboratory position in an underground base, she would have to accept surveillance. That would cut down on the drama. She needed to get back to work.

"Why aren't you going to bring her in? That doesn't even make sense."

"Because I know Ashley. And I want her to flourish. She has an entire lifetime of critical work in front of her. But she's selfish and stubborn. If I pressure her she will shoot herself."

"All the more reason to set up a more professional arrangement."

David glared at the agent.

"I want her to develop the breakthroughs that she is capable of. And I want her to do it from the depth of genius and her love of the outdoors. Not from a position of giving me the minimum that she can in order to get by. Getting those advancements is worth whatever risk we might incur keeping her on an isolated ranch instead of in a base."

The woman thought she started to see what he meant.

"So we will not be putting any new information in her hands to extract. Given a little time, what she knows right now will become less relevant. She will become less of a security risk. Our position will change to making sure that no one else gets the new tools that she will be developing."

"What about the unidentified individual?"

"We set up a perimeter, a facility, the locals won't bother Ashley if they know she does tech work for the nation's defense."

"You think it will resolve itself?

"Yes I do."

# 85

# In Reserve

Nora heard the aircraft while she was standing in her kitchen. She looked toward the ceiling with her hands in dishwater. Then she shut the water off and ran for the door. James would have already heard it. She was going to be the last one to arrive over at Clyde's old place.

She ran by her four wheeler that she kept parked at the end of the sidewalk at her yard gate this time of year. She took the time to lift a garage door because she wanted one of the newer pickups with a full tank of gas. She cussed that she didn't have her wallet as she threw the automatic transmission in reverse. She would go back for it. She was already going to be the last one there, she had better be the one that brought some money. God knew where the end of this day was going to find them.

Brian Hammond didn't hear the incoming chopper echoing across the vast and empty landscape because he was shredding a bale of hay in the processor. Instead he saw the shadow pass over him.

He thought of his kids and his wife back at the house. He thought of the baby they were expecting. He thought of his dad, probably already at Clyde's house. He thought of his mom and brother sitting up all night to watch out for their land lady. He had plenty of time to think as he ran across the pens. He could make it to a vehicle faster on foot then by trying to navigate the tractor through the cattle but he had a little ways to go. Whatever was happening would be well underway before he could get there.

No one would have heard the helicopter in Dismal.

James heard the incoming aircraft from a pickup where he was unrolling a bale to some still heavy cows. For the second time in two days he wondered if he was in danger of another heart incident. Then he dropped the bale with the hydraulic arms and floored the accelerator with a jarring roar that made the lumbering pickup lift up out of the bumps clumsily. They were still a little ways out. He could probably beat them to Clyde's house. He gunned the poor worn out engine as he careened down the pasture trail.

James stumbled a little as he fell out the pickup door.

"Emmy! Emmy!"

He yelled as he ran the senior citizen's run up the sidewalk.

Emmy heard him and she could hear something else too.

"Phoebe! Phoebe wake up! What is that sound?"

Phoebe knew with a start of dread what that sound was as soon as she heard it. They were going to land practically on top of them.

Mr. Hammond stood just inside the kitchen door looking out into the yard at the helicopter that was landing behind his pickup.

"What do we do Mr. Hammond?"

Emmy was right behind him.

"We don't get anybody shot. We de-escalate every chance we get. And we make it easier for them to take all of us than to just take Ashley. And we make it easier than that yet for them to try again another day."

He said this as a man got out of the helicopter and strode up the walk toward them. The pilot shut the craft down and the silence fell suddenly on the ranch.

"Nora and Brian will be here any minute. We stall."

Mr. Hammond felt something very cold brush his shoulder and he looked to his left to see Don. Good old Don, eternally young, he was looking out the screen door in disinterested disbelief. James Hammond met Don's eyes. Then he put one finger to his lips in passing. Don smiled. James wanted him to wait in reserve. Well, they would just have to wait and see what these visitors wanted. He was making no promises.

Nora made one more executive decision as she careened through the sand and gravel.

"Sheriff, this is Nora Hammond."

"Good morning, what can I do for you?"

"I'm on my way over to Clyde's old place."

The sheriff set his coffee cup down in the cup holder. He knew that the granddaughter and her friend had been living there the last few weeks.

"Someone has been threatening Ashley and following her, they followed her to the ranch yesterday and put up surveillance cameras. Three people, August saw their pickup at the motel last night."

The sheriff signaled to turn onto the highway headed out of Dismal toward the old Heartless Ranch as he listened to Nora continue. He would call the motel in a moment.

Nora's voice was cutting in and out and she sounded a little frantic.

"Did you ever know Barb?"

"No, that was before me."

"Someone burned down her art gallery and her car a few days ago."

The sheriff was mildly impressed and he sped up a little.

"What's going on this morning?"

"That's what I'm telling you, there is a helicopter landing at Clyde's old place right now and James is already over there."

"A helicopter?"

Nora knew this was the sheriff's personal phone line but she wanted to cover her basis thoroughly.

"I'm almost there sheriff and I'm calling you because if these people hurt my family, I am going to shoot them."

Nora looked around the cab a little emptily. She was bluffing. There wasn't so much as a BB gun in this pickup. Still that ought to get everyone's attention and make sure he made good time. And no matter what did happen it might help keep some of the suspicion on herself.

# 86

# Play The Game

"Good morning."

Mr. Hammond spoke loudly as he stepped out onto the cement step back into the mid morning spring air. His mind, for a moment, back on a heavy cow he had planned to check on again by now. Things would just have to wait.

Emmy understood instantly what he meant by de-escalation. Friendly, almost pretending that we all knew each other and all of this was normal. David assessed the older man in the cowboy hat in front of him. This would be the neighbor that leased the agricultural ground, likely an old family friend.

"Good morning, is Ashley here?"

David started to say but the older gentleman interrupted him loudly before he could say the name Ashley clearly.

"Quite some bird you got there!"

James pointed with a long stick that Emmy had seen him holding, it was broom handle. He didn't seem to find holding a broom handle to be unusual behavior at all.

"Loud. Long range. Unmarked military maybe. Kind of new."

David played along and looked back at the aircraft and the pilot resting in the spring sunshine. Emmy waited a few moments and then stepped out of the house with her hand outstretched.

"Hi, I'm Emmy Donahue."

David shook her hand, this would be the sister. She was bolder, more aggressive in person than he had observed her to be through the years. She was still shaking his hand.

"I didn't catch your name?"

"David."

"Good to meet you. You hire Ashley for some of your tech work?"

Phoebe was watching and listening from the shadows inside the kitchen. She could see Ashley, still asleep on the air mattress in the living room to her left. Yesterday had really taken it out of her. And she could see Emmy's back as she talked to the man from the helicopter. She didn't like him at all, bad vibes. Should she get Ashley up and try to go out the back door or through a window? Should she take Ashley to hide somewhere?

She wasn't picking up that Mr. Hammond or Emmy expected such dramatic action. But they were nervous, afraid even. They were doing a great job. Phoebe jumped, Ashley was looking at her with wide eyes from her horizontal position. Phoebe put one finger to her lips and nodded.

"She has been one of our finest contractors, I'm sure she has an illustrious career ahead of her."

Just then another pickup careened up the driveway around the bend and into the yard behind the aircraft. It slowed for a moment and then drove recklessly around the helicopter and came to a stop in front of it nearer the house.

Nora jumped out to see the pilot and a man in a suit looking at her and Emmy and James looking at her.

"Emmy! Is everything okay? I heard the helicopter."

She gestured at it, the thing was much bigger up close than she had expected. James was proud, she was doing a beautiful job of normalizing a concerned neighbor.

"I think so! This is David. This is my sister's boss."

Emmy walked around David down the sidewalk in her slippered feet to meet Nora just to be doing something that stretched out the moments. Then Emmy moved slightly to the left into an offensive position.

"Her boss from Dallas. Your office is out of Dallas right?"

David was spared having to answer that by a white SUV with a police emblem on the door and lights on the top appearing and parking behind the helicopter. The officer assessed the group from a distance before offering a friendly wave of one hand. Emmy waved back.

The officer strode purposefully up toward the house, Emmy took that moment to reach inside the house door and grab some better shoes. She had them on when the officer walked by David and approached the step.

"Good morning, Emmy I don't think I've met you in person."

Emmy shook his hand while he continued.

"It's nice to meet you. We are all so pleased you've decided to live here and be a part of our little community out here. Welcome to Dismal."

Emmy shook his hand a little longer.

"Thank you. My friend Phoebe will want to meet you too, we really like it here so far."

"I'm not surprised, you remind me quite a lot of your granddad. I expect you might find yourself at home."

Then he turned to David with another hand shake.

"Good morning, you must have urgent business, to fly in without people expecting you."

David didn't miss a beat.

"I'm afraid I do. Ashley handles a great deal of sensitive information that involves our national security."

He let that sink in.

"And I have to be able to maintain her protective security. It's something we do, even when she travels."

Here David nodded kindly to Emmy.

"Or visits her sister."

David gestured broadly around him.

"In such a rural place, I must say this is some unusual geography."

David nodded respectfully to the officer and Mr. Hammond and Emmy between them.

"Her security is a priority and we need to make some arrangements. Is she here?"

He knew perfectly well that she was. Emmy didn't like him even one little bit. Nora thought his words sounded reasonable but that nothing she felt or saw matched what he was saying. Mr. Hammond thought he was a slick piece of shit for sure. This was their coward. However his mind was wandering back to that cow that was calving, they had done what they came to do. No one was getting abducted today. The sheriff thought they were far from done with this conversation but felt a little relieved. He didn't predict anyone getting shot this morning. Emmy spoke up.

"So that's why you showed up unannounced? To make security arrangements?"

"Possibly, if she plans to stay. And I really do need to discuss her current project with her and setup some secure communication. When she is ready."

Nora stepped onto the step with a word behind her.

"I'll go get Ashley and Phoebe up, they had a big day yesterday I'm sure they're still asleep, you probably have," here she cast a glance at the aircraft gleaming in the sun.

"Other things to do today."

Emmy hesitated and then followed her inside.

Another pickup parked beside the police cruiser and another man in a hat approached the group. Mr. Hammond turned to David.

"Speaking of security, you will want to know that Ashley was followed from Dallas to Denver to here, by two people. They were met by a third at the East River airport."

David didn't imagine for a moment that the old man didn't know that those were his agents. He did imagine that the officer had driven by their vehicle on his way here, still parked at the Dismal motel. He didn't know that August Hammond was helping them with the fuel pumps at the Dismal gas station right now.

"That is interesting. We entrust her with very critical work. She is often followed, usually by agents from many different entities."

David let that sink in for a while. Then he continued with a different tact.

"I can see she is very well cared for here but she has a responsibility."

"What do you want?"

Ashley emerged from the house looking like she partied too hard the night before and had no intention of slowing down. Her hair was askance and sweat glistened on bare skin. She was aging, turning from an overgrown kid into a delinquent young woman. She looked very pretty.

"You to stay where we can protect you. I know you are upset but you are a professional. We need to work out some security arrangements."

"Cameras weren't enough?"

She smiled coyly at David. Nora and Emmy, Brian and Mr. Hammond, even the Sheriff were caught a little off guard at her abrasiveness and casual tone. She seemed a little unhinged, impulsive. Like she was thinking of doing something incendiary.

Maybe they weren't all off the hook, surely she would calm down and make some arrangements and let them leave?

Don had been watching from a distance, trying out David's

seat in the helicopter. He had half a mind to arrange for them not to leave today at all, at least by air.

But he wasn't sure they needed the aircraft blocking up the driveway and yard or more people coming to try to fix it. Now that Ashley had entered the scene he was more interested in hearing what people were saying than in looking over the inside of the chopper. She looked more like Ivory than ever, she was about to do something terrible. She had war on her mind.

The people facing the helicopter were staring, David turned to see the young man from the surveillance walking toward the picket fence gate and the sidewalk.

"David!"

Ashley raised her voice as she said his name and he was surprised that he jumped with a start. Smashing sounds filled the air and set everyone in a panic. Ashley was dumping little pieces of tech out of a can onto the cement step and sidewalk around them all. Tiny devices hit and rolled everywhere, hundreds of them around the group of people's feet. Emmy gasped. James made to grab for Ashley's arm but he missed. She was faster than she looked. She laughed at all their reactions as she dumped the other two cans worth of tech on top of the first batch. The pilot watching from the distance thought she didn't look crazy anymore, just smart and very brave. She was changing their understanding of her, from now on they would be expecting something jarring and unusual.

"There's your security arrangements."

"There is no place in this world where you can walk away from what you are involved in."

David's cold professional voice was as easy for everyone to understand as if he was speaking directly to them. Mr. Hammond, Nora, Emmy, Brian, the sheriff, Phoebe in the kitchen and Don the ghost standing behind him, all understood him perfectly. They all seemed to have forgotten about the young man in the hat they had seen.

"Now we have some choices to make. You can do the work required of you in an underground facility with a custom laboratory and a team at your disposal. Or you can do the work in your own way, here in the fresh air."

David gestured around him as they all felt chills of their own personal nightmares running up their spines.

"But I have to be assured of your security."

Emmy wanted to step forward but she held herself back. Don was grinning mischievously but Mr. Hammond was holding him in a death stare. James noted that he seemed to be the only one that could see the ghost among them at that moment. In the end no one said a word so David continued.

"Obviously, you are well cared for here."

He smiled humorously as he looked at all of them. He was ready to play their own game and normalize the situation again.

"I want to place a team of three in Dismal, the personnel will rotate. And I want to place cameras. A minimal number of cameras. Provided you leave them alone. And I want you to get back to work."

David glanced briefly at the sheriff, at Brian and Mr. Hammond, then back at Ashley and then Nora and Emmy. Ashley crossed her arms in front of her and smiled smugly. She had one particular project in mind.

"I think I can do that. Are you going to show up here like this again?"

David didn't miss a beat.

"Only if I have to, it's been good to see you Ashley."

"Rot in hell David. Give my best to your wife."

With that parting salutation, the pilot whisked David away in the helicopter and left a hodge podge of highly stressed people standing awkwardly in Clyde's old yard.

# 87

# A New Start

Ashley looked around her at the landscape in the brilliant sunshine. So this was it, her mom's home, Emmy's home. And she was going to be staying for a while. The hair on her arms was standing up. This was the most unusual feeling place she had ever been. What was going on around here?

"Well, I'm going to go check that cow, see if she's calved yet."

James nodded to his son Brian and got in his pickup without so much as a backward glance. Nora spoke with Emmy for a moment, nodded to the sheriff and then walked with Brian back to her pickup. The two pickups left the yard one behind the other. Don sat down on the step for a smoke and Phoebe crept to the kitchen doorway to look out into the sunshine.

"I'm the Clara County Sheriff, Ben."

"Emmy Donahue and my sister, Ashley Donahue."

Emmy was a very good looking woman. He directed his question to Ashley.

"You work in national security?"

"I'm an independent contractor. I handle specialized data extraction, from damaged technology."

Ben didn't know what to think. He wanted to say, are the two of you going to be okay? However that wasn't within his line of duty. Instead he settled for giving them his professional and personal phone numbers and driving away.

Ashley turned to Emmy.

"So, I am going to be staying for a while, I think. Suddenly I am a national defense asset and my work is critical to our nation."

Ashley smiled playfully. She wished Emmy would laugh.

"Does that really solve anything?"

"No, probably not. But it buys me some time, I feel as I look around here that I have a lot to explore, to learn. I'm sorry, buys us some time."

"Thank you."

Phoebe eased out onto the step.

"You know it probably wouldn't hurt if you would become a bit more of a, public person. Public personality."

"Uhhhh."

Ashley groaned sarcastically but Phoebe persisted, her voice undulated persuasively to lighten the mood.

"Well you know, your sister hates social media planning but she is very good at it. I bet you two can work something out."

They were reaching for a new normal. Emmy was determined that they find it.

"So you are going to live here with us, and do your tech development work for David."

Emmy dropped his name with the tiniest hint of sarcasm.

"With some nuisance surveillance. And you are going to become a more public figure, I will help you with that. And you are going to do some exploring and growing as a person. And then when the next thing comes up, we will know more, have a better idea what to do."

Phoebe and Ashley nodded in slow agreement, leave it to Emmy to have a solid plan hidden underneath a whole lot of vague passivity. And to be the one that needed to articulate it. Phoebe was starting to smile. Ashley grinned.

"Yeah, yeah, yeah, do you want to show me around?"

Emmy grinned back.

"Well we have no shortage of things to explore."

In that moment with Emmy and Phoebe, Ashley felt that for now everything was going to be okay. Then Emmy spoke again.

"How do you think mom is getting along?"

# VI

# Part Six

# 88

# The Steel Mills

Kansas City, Missouri
August of 1951

The steel mills in those days, were their own world.

Clyde was a solitary man with impeccable clothes. The steel mill was his life back then. He spent his days prowling the walkway grids and watching men and machine closely with shuffles of paper gripped in his fist and a pencil behind his ear. His mind was always on the clock, on the calendar. After the war Clyde had taken work in the steel mill and now his position as foreman was all he had left for a soul.

He yelled so much over the din that he had no voice left in the evening and it didn't matter because he didn't see anyone in the evening. The steel they were producing was of the finest quality ever made. His contracts were fulfilled on time and profits were high. His hands and face had lost their sensitivity to heat. The flesh around his orbital bone had fallen and he was a hard faced clean shaven man. He had gone a little deaf in one ear. He fully expected to be running the mill in the next five years.

Clyde was a hard man with unyielding expectations. His workers respected that because he was harder on himself than anyone else. They all felt the pride that he felt. Their foreman never wavered, never blinked, never missed a beat and there was a sort of peace that came from knowing him well. Those that knew him best knew that he had no wife, no children, no parents or siblings that he ever spoke of and no past, future or existence outside of steel. Rails brought long trains of supply cars into the mill yards and loaded trains left the mill yard destined for every corner of America but for Clyde the world started and stopped at the edge of the yards.

Today he had already yelled himself hoarse. Mid morning he missed a step and tripped on the walkway between levels. There was a new worker on the south side of the main level that was making him nervous.

In his own mind Clyde called him bad memories and then bad eyes. Clyde thought the man had probably left his mind in the war. The first time that they had locked eyes Clyde had known that the new man wasn't seeing him. He was seeing something far away. Something only he could see. Clyde reminded him of someone or something else. Clyde tried not let that scare him.

Now Clyde could feel the man watching him when his back was turned. Clyde needed to get him out of the mill but cool reason meant that he couldn't fire him. Even if he had a reason to, bad eyes would be hard to fire and even harder to be rid of.

He didn't show it but Clyde the foreman was worried. Every day he felt more tension. The situation was building and his mind flitted from one scenario to the next. Bad eyes was a brute of a fighting man with a heavy forehead and a prominent bridge of a nose. His eyes were glassy like what was inside him was clouding his vision. The mill was a dangerous place on a good day. How could he move this worker along? What could he do to diffuse the situation? He lay awake on his bed that night, eyes roving the ceiling.

The next day bad eyes made a terrible mistake. Clyde had been waiting for it, hoping it wouldn't happen. Bad eyes wasn't always seeing what was in his hands or in front of him clearly. There wasn't any room for mistakes here and the accident had finally happened. Only one man was burned and the crisis was over quickly. Clyde had an opening.

"You are fired. Get out of here."

Clyde spoke firmly with a sense of calm. His speech was clipped as if he was holding his pencil and marking down an order. He didn't believe in letting men go publicly, it was a better practice not to make a fuss. He was the foreman.

He knew he shouldn't turn to walk away but he did it anyway. He was the foreman. The bigger man hit him so hard and so fast that he only came to a moment before bad eyes hit him again. Clyde found himself in a fight for his life. He wasn't unnerved until he had taken six hits without landing any. That was when he realized that this man meant to kill him.

A distant worker noticed the fight in progress and motioned to his partner. Men were stopping and turning to stare. Blood was running down Clyde's face and out of his mouth. He couldn't see straight and the hard years of experience started to bubble up in rage. He wouldn't be killed this easily.

In muscle memory he made a bid to save his own life. He struck an upward blow at the bottom of the nose and drove the momentum back into the man's skull. When the big man fell Clyde fell with him and drove the back of his skull into the cement girding with all his strength and momentum. Then he pulled the man's head back and smashed it into the girding again and again and then the man was dead.

Clyde ran. The railroad cars around him were blurring by, the sweat and blood were in his eyes. He stopped to double over in pain and then ran on. Everything was quiet, everything was moving in slow motion. He had plenty of time inside his own mind to look for exactly what he needed and he ran until he found it.

The outbound train that was already in motion and the closed car that needed repair with it. He fumbled for his pocket knife and then one last rush of adrenaline as the train started to move faster. Inside the car he slid the door shut again and collapsed in the semi darkness. He didn't know if they would follow him into the rail yards right away or if his men would follow him at all. By the time the authorities arrived they would have a hard time knowing which train he had left on, if they were sure he had left on a train. He could have slipped out of the rail yard and into the city just as easily, he was the foreman. Clyde started to black out. He had been the foreman. But now that was all gone.

# 89

# Otto Asks Questions

New Mexico
August of 1951

"Some kind of a test coming up. New people. New cargoes. They are working toward some upcoming date. They are uncertain about what the outcome will be."

Otto smiled at Chloe across the mahogany counter. There had been six rocks there at the bunkhouse with Joe. Then there had been fifty-six rocks. Now there were probably closer to five hundred and sixty.

"Thank you sweetheart."

She hadn't actually told him anything more than anyone in town could have. But sometimes she did. She had leaned in close to him across the counter, in the gesture of two people who shared far more than conversation. He could still smell her perfume. She was young for him but she had never let that sort of thing slow her down. Now she was touching up her lipstick. Otto hesitated to ask but then he gestured to her to lean in close one more time.

"There's a new man over there, in management. A leader of some sort. Would remind you a lot of me. Has he been in here? What do you know about him?"

"He does remind me of you! No, I know who you're talking about but he doesn't come in here."

Otto was only a little disappointed, he had known the answer anyway.

Chloe wasn't much of a spy, or even a gossip. The people here were proud of their top secret military base. Otto sought information from Chloe because her specific viewpoint sometimes subtly provided the pieces he was missing. Now he knew for sure what he had suspected, there was someone even more intuitive than himself on the other side of that fence.

He had hesitated to ask because in putting the words into the air he would give away his position. He had chosen to do so to test the air. Otto had been watching the base since he had returned from the war. From the moment the other man had driven across the flat he had been watching Otto watch.

Otto was as much a patriot as anyone on that base. They could look at his records of distinguished service and see that. He was not a foreign spy. Otto was worried about being cast as paranoid, having lost his mind. He thought about the moving rocks in the bunkhouse. He was not unstable at all and he knew it but he was on the edge of getting himself into trouble.

So he had tested the air.

# 90

# Paul Visits

The Landin Ranch, New Mexico
August of 1951

When Otto let Paul in the front door of the bunkhouse Paul let out a long low whistle. There were rocks on the kitchen table, the sideboard and the kitchen floor. Paul could see hundreds of rocks in the kitchen alone.

Paul declined to come in but Otto pulled him through so he could shut the door.

"I came to ask how things are going over here."

Otto answered with a long suffering glance. Paul peered into the next room where Joe was stretched out asleep on his cot, surrounded by the little buggers. There were even some rocks perched on top of him. The sun would be coming up soon.

"Coffee?"

"Sure."

Paul looked around the room curiously from where they sat at the kitchen table. Some of the rocks were moving but very slowly. He could feel it more than he could see it. Otto was watching Paul look.

"They're shy. You should see them when it's just Joe."

Paul could have whistled again.

Paul asked the question that was foremost on Otto's mind.

"What do you think is going to happen to him?"

Otto shook his head.

"Nothing good."

They sipped on as the rays started to ease in the kitchen window. Paul would be on his way soon.

"What are you going to do Otto?"

Otto leaned over to check on Joe in the next room as he replied.

"He wrote a letter to his brother. We are going to take them, all of them," Otto gestured broadly.

"To his brother. Out of range of the weapons test."

Paul nodded serenely.

Otto returned the nod as he sipped his coffee.

When Paul spoke again Otto jumped.

"You know, I would be prepared for some sort of explosion."

Otto's eyes widened.

"It's possible you know. These living beings take on excess. They have taken on the excess radioactivity around us, taken it into themselves."

Otto was hanging on every word as Paul continued.

"That's why all this, unusual behavior."

Paul gestured lazily around the bunkhouse.

"This is not their natural state or behavior."

Paul paused for emphasis before continuing.

"When they pull the trigger over there, I might expect a mirrored reaction."

Otto rested his temple on his fist over his coffee cup in angst but Paul didn't stop.

"I might expect it in your friend over there too. He's very deeply intertwined."

They leaned in their chairs to check on Joe, he was still dead to the world.

"What do I do?"

"About your friend, I don't know. About your rocks, lead. That's what you use to contain radioactivity. Take them far away, put them underground if you can, protect them with a lot of lead."

# 91

# A Letter Received

Dismal, Nebraska
August of 1951

The post mistress handed Virgil the letter postmarked in New Mexico with curiosity. She would have enjoyed starting the latest gossip about Joe Hart.

She was not disappointed because Virgil tore it open right there at the mail counter. He read the first few words and then moved his body to shield the letter from her. She had been watching his face and he was relieved to see that she was not looking at the letter he was holding. He looked up at her unwillingly.

"Could I bother you for an envelope and a pen?"

She met his eyes willingly, Virgil was a very handsome man. Also a very wealthy and lonely man but more important than that she was a lonely person herself. She handed him the pen. He tore off the bottom of the piece of paper he was holding and wrote one word on it.

"Yes."

She was already addressing a new envelope by looking at the discarded envelope from New Mexico upside down on the counter. Virgil put the scrap of paper in the new envelope and she licked it shut and put a stamp on it while he watched.

"Thank you."

"You're welcome."

He started to ask a question but she interrupted.

"It will go out with this evening's post. I'm the post mistress, it will go."

"Thank you."

He really was grateful.

When the evening post left Dismal the darkness was settling in for another long, hot August night.

Virgil put beans on two plates at the supper table in the kitchen of the main house of the mighty Heart Seven ranch. He remembered eating here with his parents and Joe and Rose. He remembered Christmas here with Ivory and Joe and his parents. He looked at the empty chair where Joe usually sat and then the two meager place settings.

After his dad had eaten Virgil pulled the letter from his shirt pocket and unfolded it on the table in front of Fred.

*Virgil,*

*Would you please meet me this coming Thursday? You remember that place where Rose almost fell over when we were kids?*

*Best Regards,*

*Joe*

Fred looked up truly shaken. The handwriting was odd. Someone had filled it in in places, to make it more legible. The effect was unsettling.

What had Joe gotten himself into down there? Fred missed him terribly. Would they be able to bring him home?

"I already sent a reply."

Virgil was pouring himself a cup of coffee from the stove.

Fred stared out the window into the black night, a smaller and older man than he had ever been before.

# 92

# A Very Close Call

The Landin Ranch, New Mexico
August of 1951

Agent X left the base with a small attachment very early that morning, the two jeeps trailed out across the flat ominously. They were cleared through the gate and turned toward the Landin ranch. The test was behind schedule but he was not frustrated. Taking care of loose ends and annoyances was his work and he was good at his job.

Mrs. Landin saw them coming out her kitchen window, later she thanked God for that happenstance. Mr. Landin met them with a casually armed reception outside of her garden gate. She watched closely from behind long lace curtains inside. Very few days did they forget that they were ranching next to a top secret military base. Everything could change in one day, maybe today was that day.

She could see her husband conversing with the leader. They

were looking at the bunkhouse.

"Do you have a warrant?"
"In most cases, I don't need a warrant."

Joe was stacking rocks just as fast as his narrow frame could go. Otto had been assembling luggage, a steamer trunk, some suitcases, a carpet bag, even an old fashioned women's hat box and a large metal lunchbox. Joe slid the steamer trunk under his cot.

"Come back with the county sheriff."
"That won't be necessary."

Otto hopped out the opposite facing bunkhouse window with surprising agility, Joe shut the window behind him. Otto was rattled, he hadn't even felt them coming until they were in the yard. He barely remembered his hat. No one had ever gotten the drop on him quite like this.

He made it over the ridge out of sight, hanging low to the ground in the sagebrush he had run for his life. Now he grabbed a bit of halter rope from a gate post. Otto was a man that followed his whims. He had left that bit of rope there on a whim two days ago. He made his getaway on his boss's fastest horse that morning, streaking bareback down the gorge.

Agent X knew Otto was gone. He had known he might not catch him that day. He also knew he would have plenty of chances.

Joe stumbled out of the bunkhouse and ambled directly to Mr. Landin's side in a long legged sort of way with the his eyes still full of sleep and his shirt half buttoned. He was a soft spirited young man with haunted eyes and a health problem. The agent knew Joe was not the man he was looking for.

"Is there a problem here Mr. Landin?"

Mrs. Landin couldn't hear what Joe was saying but she thought he was very brave.

Agent X smiled with good humor at his optimism and met Mr. Landin's eyes before speaking. His voice was crisp and clear, unemotional.

"I don't think so. And I certainly hope there won't be."

# 93

# Open All The Gates

The Landin Ranch, New Mexico
August of 1951

"We need lead."

Otto and Joe were seated with Mr. Landin. Mrs. Landin was loading a hamper, she would be going to stay with her sister in Texas for a while. Both Landin's exchanged grim looks.

"Not for what you think. It doesn't matter what form it is in."

Otto finished by admitting.

"Lead insulates radioactivity."

Joe looked down guilty. Mr. Landin considered the room for a moment, his eyes fixed on the cattle in the ranges around them.

"If you open the gates between the south range and that upper west pasture, actually open all the gates Otto if you can. Everything can find their way to the river eventually."

Mr. Landin looked at his aging wife.

"I think I will take you over to Margaret's, maybe stay for a while. The ranch will still be here when I get back."

They all paused to wonder if even that was true. Ranching down here had been like this since before the war ended. Mr. Landin would have sold it all years ago but river ground was so hard to come by, his grandparents had been very lucky and the market would have dealt him a massive loss. So they kept on. August would be hot in Texas too.

"You can have everything I have in there, help yourself."

There just wasn't much else left to say. Mrs. Landin went back to packing.

Joe rode out to open gates under the imposingly open blue sky. Otto drove out in the Landin's new pickup with the stock rack in search of all the bullets that could be purchased by other people. Mr. and Mrs. Landin left in the car shortly afterwards. The ranch house and the bunkhouse sat quiet and empty.

From his office under the same sky Agent X gave the go ahead by telephone.

"We are going ahead with the test."

# 94

# An Impromptu Ceremony

The Landin Ranch, New Mexico
August of 1951

The letter they sent had specified Thursday. Otto paced the bunkhouse relentlessly. He hesitated to start out with no one to meet them. Joe was asleep again like an overgrown teenager.

Otto continued to ruminate. One of Paul's eccentric friends had brought them ammunition marked as belonging to the United States government. On top of that there were crates and sacks marked that way as well. Otto pressed both his hands to his forehead. He hadn't seen that in time and now it was all mixed into the rocks and he didn't time to sort it out. If they were caught, Otto knew he could not afford to be caught.

Someone was coming. Otto could see the headlights. He held still in his socked feet to listen to the air and his body. Nothing to be worried about. Joe woke up and stood beside him looking out the window in his sock feet. Chloe the girl behind the counter eased gingerly from behind the wheel, she left the car running and the headlights blazing. Virgil opened the door before she could knock.

"They moved the test up."

She looked curiously inside the bunkhouse but there was nothing to see, the luggage was all tucked away. She looked Joe up and down in appraisal.

"Paul told me you would want to know."

Otto reached for his boots and his hat. Joe pulled a steamer trunk out from under his cot, to her it looked disproportionately heavy.

"Did Paul say anything else?"

"Yes. He called it an impromptu ceremony. There will be an impromptu ceremony over there tonight. A loud one."

Otto would have to thank Paul someday, between the drums and the dancers the atmosphere would be disturbed enough that he just might be able to get out without the agent being able to pick up his trail.

Chloe watched the two men pulling luggage of all sorts from all around the bunkhouse. She didn't ask or wonder what was inside. Otto could feel the far away drums warming up the air. He walked Chloe to her car and gave her a parting kiss. Then he handed her a sealed envelope.

"If you think, for some reason, that Joe and I might need

more time. Deliver this to the guard house at the gate of the testing range. Tell the guard to open it. Inside there is another envelope addressed to Agent X. If you think we are in the clear, just burn it."

Chloe narrowed her made up eyes speculatively and pulled the car door shut.

# 95

# The Heart Seven

Heart Seven Ranch Headquarters, Nebraska
August of 1951

That August night was very quiet and still on the Heart Seven. Virgil slept restlessly upstairs. Fred sat alone in his study. He intended to sit up all night. Then something outside the house changed, the most subtle of shifts. Maybe the wind picked up, shifted directions. Maybe a pack of coyotes were venturing into the yard. Fred wondered what else it could be.

Upstairs Virgil's eyes popped open. He lay still for a moment before swinging out of bed and rushing down the stairs carrying his boots. He wasn't surprised to see his dad in his lawyer's chair in the den but he didn't slow down to visit. He grabbed a jacket and paused at the gun safe in the back of the hall.

Fred followed him to the front door and watched him rush down the front steps and out into the night. He stood still and watched through the doorway as Virgil ran across the ranch yard. Fred heard the car start and saw the headlights sweep across him and the main house as Virgil accelerated out of the shed in a wide circle and out toward the road. This was not Thursday but Fred could feel it too. Now was the time.

Virgil put the hammer down toward the Colorado mountains. Short of hitting a deer he didn't expect problems of any kind. There was no one out tonight. He felt that fate was with him, he would not hit a deer. So he pushed the heavy church car faster into the dark of the night. Back home Fred sat back down to wait it out. These were the prayer vigils he had kept throughout his life. He wished Katherine was there to sit with him.

# 96

# Where Rose Almost Fell

Colorado
August, 1951

The air was cold up here, he had known it would be. The night was still dark. Virgil stood alone on the high mountain pass on a narrow scenic overlook where the highway widened. The drive had been long and he had driven fast. For a moment Virgil wondered if his impulse to come tonight had been wrong. He was getting nervy, irrational. He took off his glasses. The worry and smile lines around his eyes were getting deeper. He prayed silently with his eyes open, lost in thought. Eventually he felt something in the night, maybe he heard the very faintest echo of a far off engine and his heart leapt with a thrill. He had not been wrong.

Otto had the pickup unwound as they climbed the hairpin turns and snaked their way up high into the mountains. The headlights flitted over the pine trees and empty highway. This was a very dark night. They had made it out of New Mexico.

He had felt the agent looking for him a time or two but Otto was confident the cover of the drums had been enough. They had gotten away clean. He would rather die than go to prison. He would rather die than be taken into that base. Scenarios flitted through his mind. Being a part of the Landin outfit after the war had been a good place for him. His life had been good. They would never take him alive. How had he gotten wrapped up in all of this? Joe coughed in his sleep.

Joe, and his dying niece Ivory. Otto thought of the crucifix at home on the bunkhouse wall. Joe had run away to the desert in his desperation to save a family member's life. Joe was a pure and powerful soul.

Maybe God was here tonight. Joe was a pure and powerful soul, the living rocks had come to him for help. Only a few individuals in a century ever set eyes on even one set of them. Otto's eyes kept flitting to his mirrors. The luggage in the back was starting to glow. There were hundreds of pairs of rocks back there. This was the most dangerous thing Otto had ever seen. He started to laugh to himself to lighten the mood, if they got out of this alive and free what a story they would have to tell.

Otto misjudged the angle on the next hairpin curve and the heavy truck wobbled alarmingly. Otto realized he had sweat through his shirt and now he was cold and clammy. How Joe had fallen asleep again was beyond Otto. The kid never stirred as Otto hammered the truck up every incline and barreled through tunnel after tunnel.

In Joe's mind, the thing was taken care of and so he slept on.

Joe was awake when they rounded the last blind curve onto the opening on the peak with the scenic overlook. This was where Rose had almost fallen over as a child. Joe smiled at the memory. Was she here with them tonight, his sister, the angel? His heart thumped when he saw his mom's church car and Virgil stepping out into the night. Were there two angels here with them?

Otto watched the two brothers shake hands in his headlights. Joe was gesturing to the stock rack. How would he explain the cargo to his older brother? Otto judged Virgil to be older than himself, a seasoned business man and a good cowboy. He could easily imagine him as the boss of a major operation. What would he make of all of this? The brothers strode around to the driver's side door and Otto jumped out with startling agility to shake Virgil's hand.

Virgil was alarmed at the change in his younger brother, how he had aged. He listened carefully with his head inclined slightly to the left, his body stance mimicking Joe's.

"Living rocks... mate for life... run in couples... very old... live in the desert down there... taking on radiation from the nuclear government facility... become radioactive themselves... don't touch them."

Otto reached for his gloves as he overheard that last part. Joe had been touching them. Maybe it was too late for him and Joe. Virgil was still hung up on the mate for life part. He made eye contact with Otto for confirmation. Otto nodded his head a fraction of an inch wearily.

Virgil stopped listening and walked to the back of the truck, carefully lifting the burlap with two wary fingers he saw and felt the eerie glow. He also saw the crate labeled property of the United States government. He dropped the burlap quickly and sized up the entire cargo. They had been through a strange time for humanity in the last thirty years, Virgil knew the real deal when he saw it. His brother had gotten wrapped up in some strange experimental government research down south. Now he needed help getting free of it all.

Joe was talking again.

"They take on the characteristics of what they are in relation with, like me for example."

Otto turned his head so sharply he hurt his neck.

"We are connected."

Virgil didn't fully grasp that one, he was looking at the weight load on the axle of the pickup truck. The rocks must be disproportionately heavy.

"They became nuclear because they took on that quality from the stockpile the government has hidden down there. They bonded to some of the materials being used."

Virgil was feeling a strange weight around the back of his ears. What were they going to do with all of this? He tried to keep listening. Joe was still talking.

"When the next bomb goes off, it will be underground, the chain of events will be mirrored in these rocks."

Otto inhaled sharply, Paul had been right. Otto hadn't known that Joe was cognizant of all the things he was revealing now. Otto was relieved that Joe was more with it than one might have thought.

Virgil's voice startled Joe and Otto.

"They are going to blow up?"

His voice was quiet and deathly serious, he had seen recordings of nuclear tests. Surely the wide open desert would have been a better place for that.

"In a manner of speaking yes, and they will die."

Joe was still speaking brusquely. Virgil squinted his eyes and blinked a few times.

Joe continued without waiting.

"They could survive this but they need to be insulated."

Joe kept going in his detached and high pressure voice.

"That's why they came to me."

Virgil and Otto continued to listen hard and patiently high on the mountain peak. Joe was in over his head.

"They need distance. You have got to take them home to the ranch. Put them in the cellar, that one over at the south place is big and deep. Line the cellar with all this ammunition."

Virgil raised his eyebrows in blank incredulity.

"Ammunition?"

"Lead. You need lead to insulate radiation."

Joe replied rationally.

Virgil looked over at Otto harshly, Otto closed his eyes painfully. Joe's demanding but patient voice brought Virgil back.

"Line the cellar with the ammunition, stack the rocks in

the center, shut the cellar up. That should be enough distance and enough insulation, when the government does their test the rocks will mimic it. But they should survive."

Visions of nuclear bomb tests were playing in Virgil's mind as he looked at the loaded truck.

"How much time do we have?"

Joe was moving to unload the first crate of bullets.

"Go directly there, go as fast as you can."

# 97

# Goodbye

Colorado
August of 1951

Kate's church car squatted alarmingly low on the road. Everything had been moved over.

Virgil didn't doubt that they would make it. This was a sure thing now, he was just along for the ride. There was a sense of power around the cargo, a sense of momentum. The cargo was imparting some of it's strength into the car already, into him already. They would never be the same.

Otto felt relieved to see the contraband gone. They needed to get back down to the Landin ranch under Agent X's nose. Paul's distraction would be coming to an end. Otto didn't intend to get arrested but he also wouldn't let Agent X start thinking about Nebraska.

Virgil pulled his hat down in the cold wind as he looked out over the high mountain pass. Otto was harassing Joe about something. Virgil turned his attention back to them. Joe unbuttoned his left front shirt pocket. He made to hand two of the small rocks over to Otto but at the last minute Otto refused to hold out his hand.

Joe walked over to his older brother instead, to hand him the last two rocks of the cargo. The first two rocks that had come to him. Virgil debated internally for only a moment. Then he held out his outstretched hand to take the burden from him. He put the two rocks in his own front vest pocket without looking at them closely. The glow shown through the fabric. Joe was suddenly very tired, looking very sleepy. He spoke with a sense of relief.

"We need to take this truck back to the owner. I'll make my apologies to the boss and then I'll come home."

Virgil didn't like the sound of that at all.

"You will come with me now."

Even as he said it he saw there was no room in the car. Virgil spoke again.

"Bring the truck behind me. We'll return it when this is all over."

Even as Virgil insisted he could tell it was no good. A sense of purpose and adrenaline was racing through his own veins. The rocks in his vest pocket were already starting to impact his thinking, his attention was turning to the task at hand. Joe spoke softly.

"I don't think that's a good idea. I'll see you soon."

Joe turned gently and got back in the truck.

Only Otto felt the pain of that moment, this was a goodbye. Virgil was overpowered by the sense of duty and chaos, he wouldn't feel that goodbye until later. Joe was going to sleep, finally at peace after a long hard run to a mysterious finish line. Maybe he would never feel the pain of that goodbye between brothers.

# 98

# The Cellar

The Heart Seven Ranch- South Place
August of 1951

Don had not yet left for work at the filling station that morning. Ivory was resting fitfully in bed. Torn between dedication and fear of piano music and ghosts Don had spent the night sitting on the step.

Don woke up when he heard a vehicle in the yard. Virgil was there in the church car, he had it loaded down with something. The front seat and the back seat were loaded to the roof, the tires were squashed way down. Virgil looked like he had been up all night but his eyes were very sharp and alert. He strode right up to Don.

"I've got something here I need to put in the cellar. Will you help me?"

His tone was hushed and powerful. The war had not been that long ago, Don had been too young to serve but he had grown up with those that did. Don didn't ask any questions now. When he stepped back inside silently to grab his boots, he looked in on Ivory. Her eyes were still closed and she was still breathing.

Both men sweated through their clothes that August morning as they packed and carried the burlap bags and stacks of ammunition down into the cellar. Don never asked any questions or looked very closely. He didn't want to know. He had never known his older brother in law or his father in law to be involved in anything, anything at all. They ran a straight forward ranch and were as well respected as an outfit could be. But Don knew that hard times and strange things happened to everyone, sooner or later. He would keep their secrets. He wasn't going to be staying around here anyway.

Virgil took a long time arranging everything very particularly. Don averted his gaze and waited outside as much as he could. He did watch carefully as Virgil shut the cellar door. He could tell the older man wished he had a padlock or something. Don left and came back shortly with a small length of wire. Better than nothing. Virgil knotted it through the latch and hook. He made exhausted eye contact with the haunted Don.

"Don't ever open this door."

Virgil didn't want to have to continue.

"Don't let anyone ever open this door. Don't look in here ever again."

Virgil didn't need to say any of it. Don was thinking about ghosts again anyway.

# 99

# Home In New Mexico

The Landin Ranch, New Mexico
August of 1951

"We came back."

Otto stood on the front porch of the main house, speaking with Mr. and Mrs. Landin. He inclined his head to listen, much as he did on a regular basis.

"She was worried about you two. Felt like we should be here."

Mr. Landin's eyes twinkled a little as if to say, we are old anyway and we wanted to know what's going to happen.

"How did it go up there?"

Mr. Landin had never asked for specifics.

"We got it taken care of. Joe wanted to come back here. But he'll be going home to his family soon. They need him up there."

They could see Joe shutting the bunkhouse door behind him across the yard. He looked like a peaceful shell of a person, happy and at ease. He had finally found the peace that he had been looking for.

Then Otto felt something happen in his bones and in the ground under his feet. He had been expecting to feel it or perhaps he wouldn't have noticed, it was a very subtle perception. He looked to the older couple in front of him to see if they had felt anything. But they were looking over his shoulder, across the yard.

Otto turned just in time to see Joe fall. There was an expression of stunned pain on his face as his life was snuffed out totally and suddenly. Otto later thought he might have reached for his opposite shoulder but it was all over too fast. Joe's body fell hard, face down in the New Mexico dust. He was dead before he hit the ground.

# 100

# The Wave Before The Storm

Dismal, Nebraska
August of 1951

In natural phenomenon like lightning, wild fires, floods, and storms of all kinds a sort of raw potential energy is released into our plane of being. Some people would call that God. Some people also experience the powerful forces in this world that are man made. What the people experienced that day in Clara County was both.

The actual test conducted underground in New Mexico was secondary to the reaction it set off in the living rocks, buried in the cellar, there in Clara County. They had stored up a force inside their own capacities that they were not compatible with. And when they were triggered, they let it out in a giant wave of heat and pressure. The grass around the ranch yard flattened in a giant circle as a wall of wind pushed outwards. The wind accelerated as it went, pushing out in a hard wave across the landscape.

The people could hear it coming far away and they did not know what it was. Then they started to suspicion and started to walk toward cover and then they started to run. When the wall of wind arrived it hit with a force that knocked down horses and damaged trees and buildings. The air was very, very hot. After the initial blunt blow came a steady harsh wind. After that first wave came a second wave, not quite as powerful. Then a third. The pressure in the atmosphere above the cellar dropped suddenly and severely. This was not a God made storm. Hundreds of miles away cold air fronts were drawn toward Clara County at a man made pace. The initial pulses of heat left a silence and a stillness behind them and an uneasy anticipation.

People could feel the storm system coming.

They could feel the drop in atmospheric pressure and the unnerving way it signaled to their basest instincts, impending disaster. The individuals that felt atmospheric pressure in their arthritis and headaches would have been floored in agony but they were spared. Because something else was happening in the land and the people around the Heart Seven South Place and the Heart Seven headquarters and the Hammond place and the track town of Lena and the little town of Dismal.

The living rocks pushed out the nuclear charge that they had been holding and then they were left in a pressure low point that called new relationships in, to them. They took on the sadness and the sickness of the people. They took on the unseen illnesses that hadn't developed yet. They formed a bond with the grasslands and the aquifers and the cottonwood trees and the rays of moonlight as they fell on Clara County. The living rocks formed a bond with the depths of the earth beneath them and with the forces of gravity and time.

The people that were alive that day would never ever speak of it because they moved forward from that moment changed, each in their own way. Many of them found themselves unburdened and some of them developed an extra keen sense of hearing. Each individual alive that day in that place, lived to an extraordinarily old age, many of them lied about it. Mr. James Hammond included.

# 101

# James Hammond

The Hammond Ranch, Nebraska
August of 1951

James Hammond was just a kid on that very strange day in Clara County in 1951. The air smelled funny, kind of like expected rain but different than that. The whole world felt tense with anticipation.

His mother Doris and his father Lowell were arguing and he was watching the clouds, watching the sky. There were no storm clouds to see, yet. No one had said anything but everyone knew that a storm would show up that evening, this was just how those sorts of days felt.

The fight stood out vividly to him. His parents were usually at odds and there was terrific tension between them. But they rarely fought. His mom was usually angry but his dad never engaged with that. He rarely said anything at all. Lowell pretty much accepted Doris and her suppressed layers of rage as she was and tried to love her exactly as she was, kind of like a very dangerous porcupine. His children had learned to try to do the same.

James would remember his dad as a quiet and dignified figure. The sort of hard working man who was above all of that, a stoic. What few people knew was that Lowell was a broken and thoughtful man that rarely spoke because he had a speech impediment.

So James watched the sky and pushed their angry voices to the back of his hearing, so that they were blurred and muffled. He didn't want to know what they were saying. He didn't want to hear his dad struggle painfully and he didn't want to hear how embarrassing he would sound. He didn't want to hear his mom capitalize on that. Doris and Lowell had reached the lowest point of a very low marital journey.

# 102

# Virgil Receives The Call

Heart Seven Ranch Headquarters, Nebraska
August of 1951

Virgil was asleep when the phone rang. He tried to let it go but the ringing went on and on. Finally he shuffled down the stairs to the library off the hall. His dad was staring at the phone. He watched as his oldest son lifted the receiver with a heavy hand.

"Virgil Hart? This is Mrs. Landin, in New Mexico."

"Yes ma'am."

"I'm afraid I have terrible news for you."

The receiver was loud. Virgil could see that Fred could hear what Mrs. Landin was going to say.

"Joe has passed away. The authorities are here now. I am so very sorry."

For Virgil the horses all over the ranch stood still. For Fred all the horses in the world ran together in a blur. Fred could only hear the conversation through some strange sounds that were disorienting him.

"Yes, they think maybe a heart attack or a stroke. Right here in the yard. We were all here to see it. He was happy, peaceful, it was so fast Mr. Hart. I don't think he ever even knew."

Virgil swallowed hard. In a moment he replied.

"That's all any of us could hope for. He was happy down there with you folks."

"He meant the world to us. I'm so glad we got to know him."

Virgil frowned painfully.

"Thank you for calling Mrs. Landin. I'll be in touch about the, arrangements."

Virgil put the receiver back the cradle. His dad had gone.

# 103

# Not Heaven After All

The Heart Seven Ranch- South Place
August of 1951

Ivory thought she had died. It was finally all over. No pain. She must have died in her sleep, a bit of luck after all.

She stretched her new found muscles as she lay in her bed. She could hear more distinctly now and her vision was sharper. She looked around the corner bedroom as if she had never seen it before. She was feeling giddy with the thrill of it all.

She hadn't expected heaven to be like this, in this same old place. She put her hand to her stomach, no pain. Then she moved her hand to her forehead. She felt powerful and strong, full of vitality. If this was heaven, who cared what it looked like? She didn't.

Ivory looked around the bedroom more carefully. This must be heaven. These were her things, this was her place. This had been her mother's bedroom when she was a small child. Yet, she felt nothing. The textures and details interested her. Ivory felt free. The rest of this heaven world might be just like this, familiar but free. She had heard of that sort of thing before.

Ivory stopped to whisper a quick thank you to God. That was when she had her first glimmer that maybe this wasn't heaven after all. Where was God? Where was Jesus? Maybe she wasn't dead. Ivory took her left hand in her right one and used her thumb to flex the muscles in the inside of her opposite palm in a motion of confidence and wonder. This was her body.

When she opened the bedroom door she saw Don standing in the kitchen. He was holding his left palm in his right hand. His gaze shifted around the room warily, he was standing up very straight. Their eyes locked on one another. Ivory spoke first.

"I'm not dead."

Don replied.

"There you are, I don't know what is going on."

Don looked at her in amazement, this person he knew so well. He felt differently about her. Kind, warm familiarity but somehow removed and detached. She looked radiant and full of life. She looked healthier than he had ever seen her.

"Are you feeling... well? Are you..."

"I think I am cured. I thought I was dead. But now I think I am all better. This feels like a, a new body. Very strange."

Ivory flexed her fingers and arms a little more.

The temperature was dropping suddenly outside. The sudden storm surprised Don and Ivory. A high force gale struck the house violently and the little single story structure under the cottonwood tree shuddered.  Ivory looked to Don in amazement and curiosity. This must be some kind of freak storm.

# 104

# Clyde In The Hayfield

The Heart Seven Ranch- South Place
August of 1951

A man named Clyde rolled off of a train east of Lena that morning. There was a good piece of land there to do that. Hungry, dirty, soul sick and tired he hoped he could blend in with the track people and bums. Maybe no one would ask any questions in this part of the world. This was the first time he had been a fugitive and it left a bad taste in his mouth. He didn't even have a hat.

Maybe he could have blended in there but he couldn't bring himself to stay so he struck out walking across the grasslands. Sooner or later someone would notice him but he would know what to do by then. The wide expanses of nature called to him. This was a very different sort of place than any he had known. His heart had beat for the industrial power of the nation. Now he encountered a new kind of heartbeat, pastoral and mysterious. He wished he had the kind of hat that would blend in around here.

He walked through empty expansive hay fields filled with stacks. The size and girth of the giants appealed to him. He had never fed animals in his life. The hay sleds, the rough lumber scaffolding of the stacking rigs sat empty for him to encounter. This was work done by teams of men and teams of horses. Clyde reached out to touch this world.

When the first outward heat wave hit Clyde fell down in the barren stubble of the hay field ground. He had served in Europe and for a while his mind flitted back there as he pressed his body into the soft damp ground. He stayed put for the next wave that he guessed was coming. This was a very strange place for explosion repercussions. What could possibly have caused them? When it was over he got back up carefully with eyes to all the horizons.

The pressure was dropping, he could feel it. High force winds beat down on him. There was no place in sight one could take shelter. No buildings, no trees, no canyons or cliffs, just soft ground and grass exposed to the sky. The skeletal haying machinery hemmed violently in the wind. Clyde had a bad feeling that this was just the start of the storm that was upon him. How could he survive a tornado in a wide open place like this? There was no place to take shelter.

# 105

# Ivory And Don Run For It

The Heart Seven Ranch- South Place
August of 1951

When the first wave of the freak thunderstorm wind hit the house Virgil knew it would take all the glass in the windows and it did. He wondered frantically where his dad had gone. Virgil had never experienced anything like what fell over his world in those moments. The pictures on the walls rose spookily up the walls and then smashed to the floor violently. The timbers in the base of the house moved eerily. This was the mirrored explosion Joe had told him about. There had been a delay of sorts.

Virgil felt that hell was raining down on Dismal. Guilt thundered all around him. What had he done? When the last wave passed he knew he had to let his dad fend for himself. He had to get over to Ivory's. What kind of explosion had come from the cellar? What had they all done?

Ivory felt the wind around the house picking up. Darkness was falling all around them outside even though it was still early. Ivory could actually feel a little lift in the floor beneath her feet, for the first time that evening she was afraid. She looked to Don.

"Should we be in the cellar?"

He grabbed her hand like a brave school friend.

"Yeah, we should."

When Don opened the front door the wind slammed it back against the siding. Lightning lit up the sky all around them in one continuous terrifying blur. The thunder claps were so close together that there was almost no separation between booms. Bending and crouching low Don grabbed Ivory's hand and they worked their way sideways across the yard from the house toward the shed with the cellar under it. The entire world was going to blow away.

When Virgil put the old church car on the road to Ivory's house, it moved faster than before. The car sat heavily and clung to the gravel as the wind hurled debris around him. Virgil was sure he would die in that car when he saw first one bolt of lightening connect with the ground in the distance. And then another and another. There would be fires to fight everywhere unless the rain came soon. When he rounded the bend with the trees the headlights fell in a swoop across the yard on the two figures struggling to reach the cellar. They showed no sign that they saw the headlights or knew he was there. The thunder and wind were deafening.

They were almost there. The windmill fan and tail overhead spun alarmingly. It was grotesquely bent and hung lopsided, pivoting this way and that. Water was curtaining across the full tank as the windmill churned on and on. A heavy tree limb had fallen on the edge of the stock tank and water was overflowing onto the ground. A little water path had started and water was moving down the cellar steps in a little mini waterfall and pooling at the bottom landing. Don had his hand on the doorknob, the damn wire would take time to work loose.

He turned to pull Ivory along with him and saw that she had stopped to pick up Mittens. She made eye contact with Don at the top of the stairs, holding the cat with both hands she started to take those steps. She felt the lightning come up from the ground underneath them.

"Don!!!"

Virgil saw and felt Don get hit by lightning. The transformer on the power pole exploded, Virgil thought and felt that everything exploded. He never decided what saved Ivory. He would say in later years that the tires on the car were the only thing that saved him. But Don had been standing in the water.

# 106

# Doris And Lowell

The Heart Seven Ranch- South Place
August of 1951

Doris Hammond looked out the window above the kitchen sink and she saw the headlights coming through the storm. It was Virgil in Kate's church car. She hurried to the door to let him in but Lowell was already there, listening. James and his sisters peered out from around the bedroom door jam like small raccoons in the dark.

Lowell gestured to Doris to join him. James watched as her face turned whiter and whiter. The rest of his life he would remember that as the moment his mom changed. Doris put on her coat and her boots and grabbed another coat and then she came back to the bedroom doorway and shooed his sisters back to bed. They peered out from under the covers, eyes wide.

"James, there's been an accident over at the neighbors. Don

Donahue has been struck by lightening and killed. You know the electricity is out? And the phone line is out? Your dad and I are going over there to try and help. I want you to stay here and watch out for your sisters, don't let anything happen to them. Just wait here until your dad and I come back. Do you understand?"

When Doris saw Ivory waiting in the back of the car she crawled in and held her like a younger sister that she had thought she was never going to see again. Ivory opened her eyes a little as Doris stroked her hair.

"I'm so sorry. I'm so sorry."

"Joe's gone too Doris. Joe died. Don is gone. And Joe died too."

"Oh honey. Oh honey I'm so sorry."

Ivory had walked against the wind with Virgil through the storm to the car. She was conscious after the lightning strike. But she wanted to hold very still. Virgil's voice had come to her through the storm and darkness and plunged her with his words into a place she would never escape from.

"Joe is gone too. I got the call from New Mexico. Stroke or heart attack."

A small figure in the doorway, James listened to the men as they talked. Virgil would take Doris and Lowell's car on to town to get the sheriff. Lowell would drive Doris and Ivory back over the Heart Seven south place.

Lowell didn't lose any time. When he shut off the car he left Doris and Ivory in the backseat and went to look by the windmill. Rain was starting to pour down on the car and the yard and the landscape. Doris was surprised when she saw her husband motion for her urgently.

When Doris saw the body laying in the water in the cramped space she noticed that the cellar door was open.

She made her way carefully down the steps to stand next to her husband. Then she stepped over poor Don's body and pushed the door open. She could feel Lowell leaning to look over her shoulder.

The underground room was glowing with green light. Doris took it all in. The gunny sacks and shattered crates, the shredded and torn suitcase, steamer trunk and pieces of carpet bag, the hundreds of rocks and bullets thrown all over and lying in heaps on the floor where they had fallen after they had hit the wall and roof. She could see it all in the glow. She narrowed her eyes and stepped carefully in her boots into the rubble. She heard Lowell inhale sharply behind her.

Doris made her way into the cellar, taking it all in. Then she took a handkerchief out of her pocket, squatted down and used the fabric to protect her hand and come close to one of the rocks. She wanted to know if they were hot.

Lowell pointed to a printed piece of wooden crate, it said property of the United States government on it. Their eyes met in the eerie glow. Her mind came back to Don's body laying outside the door, the water everywhere. Virgil in town and Ivory in the car, Joe dead in New Mexico. Ivory in the car.

The authorities were on their way.

When Doris came back to the doorway she could see Ivory standing at the top of the stairs in the rain, arms wrapped around her torso, holding herself in a hug. Doris pulled the cellar door shut with a firm click of the door knob. Then she looped the tie wire back through the latch. Lowell was watching her closely.

"We need to move him. Quickly!"

Doris whispered urgently and Lowell never hesitated.

Together Lowell and Doris carried Don Donahue's deceased body up the cellar stairs and laid him a few steps away, near the windmill. Ivory trailed along behind. Doris looked for their tracks. But the rain was still pouring, no one could even tell. Ivory was watching all of this from behind curtained eyes. Her arms were still crossed in front of her protectively.

"We need a padlock."

Ivory didn't respond. Doris had been hoping she would know where one was.

"We need a padlock Lowell."

Doris was more urgent, they were running out of time. When he came back panting Doris grabbed the lock he had taken off of the gas barrel and hurried down the steps. Doris moved the wire and forcing the padlock through, clicked it shut. The rain poured over her hands as she did and she did not shake or hesitate.

When she rejoined Ivory and Lowell standing over Don's body in the rain it felt as if this was really where he had been hit.

And the cellar, with the door that had always been padlocked, had absolutely no significance to the scene at hand. And that was how it was when the authorities arrived.

They took Don's body away in the undertaker's car.

Virgil remembered his dad and he was afraid. He could feel more loss on the air. He thought about taking Ivory back to their house with him. She was shaking in Doris' embrace and Doris was stroking her hair. Maybe leaving her here with another woman was the best thing. Who knew what he would find over at the main place? He looked to Lowell and then continued his gaze to Ivory and Doris.

"You will look after her?"

Lowell nodded.

Virgil drove off into the night.

When the sheriff spoke his voice grated along Ivory's nerves.

"Theodore tells me he got a call before all this storm hit. A lady down in New Mexico wanting him to come get the body of a Joe Hart."

Doris held Ivory tightly in her arms and glared at the sheriff.

"They said he had a stroke. And Don here, you say he was hit by lightening."

He put the emphasis on the word say. Then he bent down to look more close at Ivory's face, the last time he had seen her she had looked deathly ill. Then Ivory slapped him so hard they all jumped in shock. Retreating back a few steps he stopped to take it all in, his gaze roving over the ranch yard around them.

Lowell and Doris and Ivory all stared at him as he looked past them, his eyes lingering first on the windmill and then the ground and then the cellar.

"Well, you have had quite a shock."

When his car rounded the bend Lowell and Doris took Ivory back to the house.

She didn't want to lie down in her room so Doris coaxed her into the spare bedroom while she found a kettle and made some tea. The kitchen was such a wreck with shattered glass everywhere that Doris couldn't help but tidy up a little and Lowell collapsed heavily in a chair at the table.

Doris was reveling in how young she felt. She felt like an all new person, like all the burdens she had been carrying for years were gone. Then she remembered something.

"Lowell, the way you talk. Say something?"

Lowell had the kindest saddest eyes.

"I'm glad neither of you are hurt. Ivory, I am so very sorry about Don. And Joe."

Lowell spoke clearly in a tenor voice, his speech impediment was gone.

Doris remembered the glowing rocks in the cellar across the yard and the waves of wind and the strange lightening storm. They were all changed, they were different, the air outside felt different and the hills that rose around them too. Dismal had changed.

"I'm ready to be at home by myself now. Thank you for all your help."

Ivory spoke concisely. They hadn't heard her coming and they jumped violently. Doris looked to Lowell quickly. Lowell was looking at Ivory steadily then he nodded to Doris.

"Are you sure? You could come home with us?"

Doris asked her pleadingly.

Ivory was sure. She wasn't dying anymore and she was very hungry.

"I know it's a lot but I'm hungry. I want to cook and eat and take a bath and be in my own home."

"We should stay with you, I could stay with you tonight."

"Thank you for everything."

She left the emphasis on everything.

"But I want you to leave now. I just need to be alone."

She thought the emotions would come later but for now, she felt nothing. Except hungry. She was sure.

Doris was not sure, they had told Virgil they would take care of her.

As she looked out across the hills and adjusted her shoulders in her new feeling body she suddenly wondered about her kids. God knew what was going on anywhere tonight. So Lowell and Doris left Ivory alone.

# 107

# Ivory And Clyde

The Heart Seven Ranch- South Place
August of 1951

Clyde survived the lightening storm in a drainage culvert in the deepest part of the field.

The empty hay sleds he had passed in the valley were thrown high in the sky. The lumber of the great stacking rigs creaked and contorted eerily. Eventually the pieces came apart at the joints and flew heavenward.

He saw lightening strike the ground again and again, the wind howled and the thunder boomed in one long painful sound. The storm was so ferocious that he thought God had come to place judgment on him, personally.

When the storm shifted to rain he moved away from the muddy culvert and walked through a pasture in the torrent, loosely following a fence line to where one valley opened into the next. The massive hills around him stood silently judging him in the downpour. He saw and heard the sand wash down in flooding waves as gullies were cut in the faces of the enormous hills.

Clyde could see a group of buildings and trees up ahead. He would be able to take shelter there and get some sleep. Every muscle in his body hurt but he had survived the storm.

From the barn Clyde watched first an undertaker's car leave and then a sheriff. Someone had died then. Just very recently, probably in this storm. Three figures went in the house. Clyde was getting so tired. Then two of the people left in the last car. There was only one person at home now. The phone lines and electricity had to be out, half the country had been blown away. Clyde could smell bacon. He really wanted a change of clothes and a hat.

He froze in his steps when he heard the door open. He couldn't see the woman's face.

"I'm glad you're home."

The woman called out to him, warm and friendly.

"Supper is almost ready. How many sandwiches do you want?"

Soon Clyde was seated at the table in the kitchen, eating bacon, tomato and egg sandwiches across from a woman he had never met before. She seemed to be living alone. She ate like she was very hungry.

"So how was your day? I feel like I haven't talked to you in forever."

Clyde didn't say anything to that but watched her warily as he ate as fast as he could.

She seemed to be at war with herself about something, he watched her facial expressions change as she tried to decide what to do. He eyed the other sandwiches on the plate, and the hats he had seen by the door. He had never been good with women.

"I know you're not my husband."

Clyde swallowed coffee quickly that burned his throat. The coffee was wonderful.

"My husband was just killed, just now. He was hit by lightening. The sheriff came and they took his body away."

Clyde forgot about the coffee and the sandwiches and the door.

Tears were falling down her face. She wrapped her hands around the cup of coffee in front of her.

"I'd like to pretend that I've lost my mind and that I think you are my husband. I think it would help my situation. But I can't do it. You are someone else, someone else important to me. Who are you and why are you here?"

Clyde studied her face intently. He was a good judge of character and he was impressed by her honesty with herself. That was something rarely seen in women. He thought about the hayfield and the horses and the hats by the door.

"I'm on the run."

Ivory regarded him seriously as he continued eating. He was older than Joe had been and younger than Virgil. She could tell he had been a service man. His face was hard and fallen under the stubble.

"What did you do?"

She was staring at him so seriously that he felt compelled to answer.

"I killed a man."

Ivory set her chin on her palm sadly and waited for the rest.

"I was a foreman at the steel mills in Kansas City. There was a fight and I killed him. And now I don't know what I will do next."

Ivory crossed her arms in front of her where she sat.

"My husband's name was Don. Don Donahue. I don't know how I can continue on here, living in this place the way that I want to, without him. I think I might be in very bad trouble."

Clyde knew how she felt. He crossed his arms too then he uncrossed them and reached for more coffee. Ivory spoke again.

"What is your name?"

"Clyde."

"It's nice to meet you Clyde, my name is Ivory."

# 108

# Virgil Meets Clyde

The Heart Seven Ranch- South Place
August of 1951

Virgil found Fred asleep in the big upstairs bedroom at the main house. The floors were scattered with glass from the windows and the broken framed photographs from the walls. He found his mom's portrait in the shattered silver frame in the bed cover next to his dad. For now his dad would be okay.

The next morning Virgil drove to the south place full of foreboding. For him the windows were still shattering all around. He was right to be nervous.

When Clyde saw Virgil he knew that this was the moment that would make or break the deal. He had spent the night on a rug on the floor and now Ivory was making him breakfast and bringing him some shirts to try on. Virgil made to knock but then came directly in. Ivory saw him coming over her shoulder from the stove.

"I'm glad you're here."

Virgil approached the stranger aggressively across the kitchen table.

"Who are you?"

Clyde was at a loss for words.

Ivory put her hands on her hips.

"This is Don."

Virgil stopped and locked eyes with the stranger. He was a hard, athletic man, he had probably served in the war. He had clear eyes and a level presence. Virgil could tell that this stranger didn't know what to think. He shifted his weight back and waited. Virgil took the time to watch Ivory for a moment. She spoke first.

"We need to make some arrangements for Joe's funeral. I was just getting Don some shirts out. All the laundry in this house is dirty. I want to get some clothes done up for us to wear to the funeral."

Ivory rested her hand on the stranger's shoulder from behind the kitchen chair. The man was very deeply uncomfortable with that. Virgil looked at the pair of them. He didn't think Ivory looked crazy. Then he thought actually she did. Insane with fear like a trapped wild animal, crazy smart like a trapped cat. He remembered Otto and Joe high in the mountains. His mind flitted to the cellar across the yard, glass was still shattering around him. They might not be out of the storm yet.

Virgil looked at the two of them and raised his eyebrows.

"I think Don's nice felt will fit him, we could stretch it a little."

Ivory spoke over her shoulder as she went to fetch it from the bedroom.

"Of course it will, it fit last time he wore it."

# VII

# Part Seven

# 109

# Mr. Hammond Sees Clyde

Something caught Mr. Hammond's eye behind the television screen in the den. The Hammond house was a mid century modern with two steps down to this living room and a wall of windows behind the TV stand. He was surprised because the bright light usually gamed a person's eyes to where they couldn't see anything out in the dark expanse. Nora and Zoe were still in town this evening. The house was very quiet.

He got up stiffly in his sock feet and shuffled to the window with a different set of glasses. Maybe he should go turn on the yard light, the switch was by the laundry room door. Then he stopped. If there would have been a doorway to shift his body behind he would have done it. A figure on horseback was coming casually across the ranch yard. This was a dark night and James could make it out because there was a shimmer, even a faint glow, to the horse's hide.

By God that looked like Clyde back in the day. Mr. Hammond remembered hearing that you would smell burned toast before you had a stroke, he wondered if that was true.

The figure threw him a casual wave and dismounted in front of the gas barrels. He was carrying a small metal gas can with a screw on lid. Clyde the ghost was borrowing some gas. It didn't take long to fill the little can. Clyde swung back up with unnatural ease. That even looked like Midnight. That was the ghost of Midnight the horse out there. Mr. Hammond wondered if he should tell Nora about this. Then he realized he would have to, there was only one reason Clyde the ghost would need gas. Mr. Hammond exhaled in defeat, he was going to have to tell Ben the sheriff too. Clyde had loved to drive that car.

The cowboy on the horse stopped to look at him, silhouetted in the floor to ceiling house window by the ambient TV light. Then he tipped his hat graciously, amused. Then he turned the gelding toward home at a walk. The living Clyde would have been sure to make the gas right with them somehow. Mr. Hammond thought the ghost Clyde could just have it.

# 110

# Clyde Comes Home

Don the ghost was smoking a cigarette on the front step in the pitch darkness of a moonless Nebraska night. The old horse pasture below the house waited empty and still.

Emmy and Phoebe were asleep inside on their collapsing love seat with Ashley on the floor in front of them.

They had been watching sitcom reruns on a tiny phone screen before they went to sleep. Don had enjoyed listening in. He really missed watching TV with Clyde and Ivory. Those had been good years for him, good decades in their old age. He hadn't thought so at the time. But now he had had time to miss the comfort of family and routine.

Don smoked on. It had been really good to have Emmy and Phoebe here. Now it was going to get even better, now that it looked like Ashley was going to be living here too. The owls in the barn watched Don with careful eyes. He was lost in nostalgia. He didn't know that reckoning was finally riding up on him in his ghostly home.

Don saw something move in the distance, an eerie shift in the darkness down by the highway. Don felt he was the first one to see something spectacular. He forgot that he was the only one seeing it. He jumped up in excitement and tipped his hat back, cigarette forgotten. By God it was Clyde! Clyde was finally home!

Don started a hurried walk across the yard toward the dirt path driveway down to the highway. And by God that was Midnight. Clyde had loved that horse when he had been alive. Clyde had come back with his own ghost horse. Don hurried up his walk, some guys had all the luck. Don waved as his voice rang out.

"Clyde! Clyde! It's good to see you!"

Don hadn't seen another ghost in his entire haunting career. He was smiling from ear to ear. Don couldn't wait for it to be like old times.

Midnight came to a pause to look around and Clyde swung down slowly to shake Don's ghost hand solemnly. Don was so happy.

"Welcome home old man! Look at you..."

Don would eternally be stuck at the age he had been when he had been killed. He had died as a very young man. Clyde had died as a very old man suffering from lung cancer in a rural nursing home. And he had come back as a seasoned man in his prime, hardened and wise but still limber. His favorite denim jacket was still dark and crisp. His light blue shirt with the pearl snaps strangely modern and energetic. Clyde's hands flexed restlessly, he almost felt alive again. Clyde spoke for the first time as he shook Don's hand.

"It's good to meet you Don."

Confusion flashed across the younger spirit's face.

"Clyde I knew you almost your whole life."

Clyde answered Don stoically.

"It's good to finally meet you as an equal Don."

Clyde had first met Don as the spirit that was haunting the Heart Seven south place. Don had been the ghost that lived in his home with his wife and child. There had only ever been so much Clyde could do about Don. And in that moment, for the first time, Don saw things as they might have been from Clyde's perspective. Sudden doubt chased his joy away but Don didn't say anything.

So Clyde continued.

"Ashley's in a terrible bind down in Dallas. Things are about to get very exciting around here again."

Don smiled broadly and shook Clyde's hand again slowly. He sounded a little proud as he spoke happily and generously.

"Old man a helicopter landed here yesterday. She's here! She's been here. They're all fine. Asleep right now."

With that Clyde clapped Don's upper arm in vigorous grasp and the two ghosts and Midnight the ghost horse strolled back up the road toward home. They would have a lot to talk about but really, they had work to do.

# 111

# Clyde Was Flying

Clyde was flying.

The Plymouth Fury III careened down the flat stretch of highway between the hills where one valley curved gently into another. He played the clutch a little with his boot on a curve. That was a vicious curve.

Then he opened the engine up again on the straightest flat in this part of the Sandhills. This was one of his favorite stretches to speed. The world around him slid by in a surreal blur. Clyde laughed, it was good to be back.

It was so good to be back home.

# 112

# The Car On The Highway

Emmy was driving into the sun and she heard the car before she saw it.

Cruising at a top speed of fifty five miles an hour the Malibu was doing better than before. The shaking had even gotten less noticeable.

When she saw the curve of the green car coming up upon her, the lines against the landscape, she thought she had never seen anything so stunning, so beautiful. What a car. Wow that person was speeding.

She just caught a glimpse of a hat brim pulled low and single finger wave as her little Malibu trembled in the big heavy car's wake as they met. Emmy felt she had just seen something very important, what a car.

# Acknowledgments

This book was written using **Reedsy Studio**, an online writing app. Thank you Reedsy. You have built something super useful and Bunny loves you.

Another thank you to **Publish Drive**. You guys are the best.

All cover artwork and accompanying artworks were created by Bunny Hammond.

And thank you to the readers, you are without question the most important component in the life story of a novel.

# About the Author

Bunny Hammond is a pen name for the *This Is Dismal* series. The author lives in Nebraska with her husband and children. She enjoys fabric and textile design.

If you enjoyed this novel, please consider writing a review. Reviews are important in the book world and yours would make a difference.

If you would like to be notified when new novels in this series are released, please sign up for the newsletter using the link below or by visiting the Bunny Hammond website. Bunny dislikes email overload, so she has no plans to spam you.

You can explore the colors and patterns of the fictional Dismal world on the Bunny Hammond website, as well as on Spoonflower, where they appear as fabrics and wallpapers. Use the link below to visit.

You are also invited to follow the Dismal creative process

on social media. Check out the Instagram, Facebook and Pinterest links below for updates, art and glimpses behind the scenes.

**You can connect with me on:**

- http://www.bunnyhammond.com
- https://facebook.com/61571334758010
- https://www.pinterest.com/bunnyhammond
- https://www.instagram.com/bunnyhammond23
- https://www.spoonflower.com/profiles/bunnyhammond
- https://www.goodreads.com/book/show/242984729-this-is-dismal

**Subscribe to my newsletter:**

- https://www.bunnyhammond.com/newsletter

# Also by Bunny Hammond

*This Is Dismal* is the second novel in the *This Is Dismal* series. The first book in the series is *The Heartless Ranch Is Haunted.*

The second novel was written as a great entry point for your first *Dismal* read. The first novel, *The Heartless Ranch Is Haunted*, can be read as a prequel.

*The Heartless Ranch Is Haunted* is available to download as a free e-book. Although there are first and second editions, the contents are the same. Bunny intends to eventually add her illustrations to the first edition e-book, the one with the colorful cover.

THE
HEARTLESS
RANCH IS
HAUNTED

**The Heartless Ranch Is Haunted**

"Clyde was buried in the Dismal cemetery and his car abandoned and forgotten. So every night, just before dawn, Don visited the car."

When people said the Heartless Ranch was haunted, they were right. Don was haunting the Heartless Ranch when they were still putting the cattle on trains. Now the year is 2025 and Emmy will leave Dallas for a ranch in Nebraska to live in the house her mom grew up in. She doesn't know that her decision will impact the lives of everyone around her. Her best friend Phoebe, an artist who has never turned down a challenge, will soon be living in a haunted house too. Her mom Barb, a successful art dealer that emits nuclear radiation, will feel the past pushing in on her. Her sister Ashley, a young tech genius that specializes in recovering data from phones that have been destroyed, will be left alone in more danger than any of her loved ones realize.

The Heartless Ranch Is Haunted is the first novel in the This Is Dismal series.

Nothing is ever really gone.

www.ingramcontent.com/pod-product-compliance
Lightning Source LLC
Chambersburg PA
CBHW070902260626
47162CB00007B/2529